Advance praise:

"This is a nerve-jangling, urgent, brilli[...] [...] had
to. I had to know what was going to [...] [...] and
flair that went into its writing." - Rodc[...]

"Tender and harsh in equal measure, A Good Enough Mother - what an apt title
- is an absorbing story of women over generations suffering through and
somehow managing their various and variously intricate lives. And what a story it
is - 'epic', one might say, except that women are too sensible to conceive of life as
an epic venture. So, simply: a marvellous book." – John Banville

"'There is nothing that is ever made better by silence,' says one of the characters
in Catherine Dunne's new, complex and multi-layered novel, which sets about
revealing the secrets of several apparently unrelated characters across three time
periods. It comes as no surprise to anyone who knows her work that Dunne writes
with insight, empathy and skill in this exploration of the lives of women and girls
in Ireland, past and present. She reveals patterns established by a misogynistic
state and the ordinary families who comply – if not collude – with its diktats. But
this novel is not at all bleak. Its strength lies in the tremendous bonds established
between women who resist conventional definition and support each other
through trauma and grief as they create new lives for themselves.
Each separate strand of A Good Enough Mother is vivid and distinct until we
approach the end, when those strands are deftly drawn together to reveal how
interconnected the stories and characters are. In many ways their several
experiences are emblematic of women's lives more generally, not only in Ireland.
It will come as no surprise to Catherine Dunne's many loyal readers that the
women they will meet in the pages of this enjoyable novel are strong, capable
agents of positive change in their own lives and the lives of others. Crucially, theirs
are stories of survival, love, friendship and hope." – Lia Mills

"This is a novel of interlinked tales: some of which hark back to historical stories
known to us about female lives throughout the world, unique to each country
depending on its history. You may become most hooked on one of them. I did:
that of the horror created by the belligerence of one brother." – Evelyn Conlon

"'I kept thinking about this secret army of women. All of them – all of us – all over Ireland. Mothers of lost children': *A Good Enough Mother* stitches together the public and the private to devastating effect. Intimate, tender, terrifying, intricately patterned, and told with Catherine Dunne's characteristic empathy, this is an Irish novel for our times." – Neil Hegarty

"Nobody writes like Catherine Dunne. She is wise, clever, and profoundly compassionate. This is a compelling story exploring and comparing the lives of Irish girls and women over the past seventy years. It's deep, it's moving, and it's full of surprises." – Eilis Ni Dhuibhne

"This book is a complex patchwork quilt of women's voices telling the story of several girls – one as young as 14 – consigned by the church-state carceral complex to Mother and Baby Homes. It follows them through their subsequent lives embracing several generations, movingly demonstrating how the brutality of such institutions ramifies and amplifies through time. It is not, however, a story of suffering and no more; it is also an exploration of the redemptive power of love in all its expressions. In many ways this is a joyful book, revelling in the solidarity of sisterhood and crossing class and national divisions. Beautifully written and elegantly plotted, it weaves multiple stories and multiple voices in a way which is both intriguing and engaging. Socially engaged writing such as this can make an important contribution to how Ireland understands itself, its past and the legacy of the Mother and Baby Homes, while also providing hope for future generations.

I've never understood why Catherine Dunne is more famous in Italy – where she is literally a household name – than in Ireland. I hope this wonderful book will help to remedy that situation." – William Wall

"With characteristic deftness, courage and compassion, Catherine Dunne constructs an intricate patchwork of woven lives exploring motherhood – and its unspoken losses – in the shadow of sexual violence. Taut and reflective, this dark material leaves a lasting sensation of light, brilliance and hope." – Mia Gallagher

"Catherine Dunne has established herself as the voice of the world of women, their suffering and emotions, and the injustices they endure and overcome with courage. With Una Buona Madre, translated by Ada Arduini, Catherine Dunne weaves together, like in a mysterious noir, ill-fated and diverse lives. Switching back and forth between the lives of all her characters links a compelling present to a troubled past, shedding light on the very different ways of being a mother, together with the historic past of a Catholic country such as Ireland." – Eva Cantarella and Nadia Terranova, chairs for the Rapallo European Award

"It is a truly Irish novel in which the stories of women – Tess, Maeve, Eileen, Betty, Joanie – and their families unravel and intertwine within a timeframe that goes from the 1960s to the present at the time of the pandemic. Stories told in the first, second and third person from constantly changing points of view, with a coherent and compelling plot that never loses sight of anything despite the complexity of the constant shifts, even though sometimes the reader feels taken aback and must carefully put together the puzzle once again. Stories held together by a fine thread that keeps us hooked. It has been a long time since I couldn't literally stop reading at night. Every story is permeated with great humanity and depth, dealing with difficult and strong existential themes and realities with lucidity and without ever falling into honeyed sentimentality." – Laura Cimetta

A Good Enough Mother

Catherine Dunne

 BETIMES BOOKS

First published in the English language in Dublin, Ireland, in 2024
by Betimes Books CLG

www.betimesbooks.com

Copyright © Catherine Dunne, 2024

ISBN: 978-1-0686170-0-3

Cover design by Masa Radanic

For the survivors

Part One

Prologue

Summer 2019

I stumble on the second step as I try to board the bus. The driver glares at me. Blue shirt. Smell of aftershave. Spearmint gum and perspiration.

My stomach shifts and I turn my face away. He stops chewing for a moment.

Are you all right? he asks. His tone is sharp, accusing. You're not going to be sick, are you?

I shake my head. I look down; try to make my hair cover most of my face.

No, I say. I'm fine. I just tripped. Too much of a hurry.

I've already fallen once. My knees are stinging. I hide the palms of my hands, keep the grit and the grazes to myself.

He says nothing. I can imagine what he's thinking. So I make myself stand up straighter. I look him in the eye. I've become aware of the other passengers queueing up on the street behind me. They've begun to shift, impatiently. It's starting to rain.

I'm fine, I repeat, but I can see he's still suspicious.

Finally, he nods.

There's not enough on my Leap card, so I hand him a twenty euro note. He gives me the change, jerking his head in the direction of the seats behind him.

Sit close to the door, he says.

I sit in the second row. If he looks in the mirror, he'll be able to see just the top of my head. I can hide here. I take off my shoes, curl my legs under me, *make myself as small as possible. At the same time, I place my bag on the adjoining seat. I don't want anybody sitting beside me. I don't want Friday night chat-up lines. I don't want anyone to touch me.*

I look around, but there are few enough passengers. It's not yet midnight; way too early for the late-night party crowd.

I keep glancing out the window. Sudden beads of rain begin sliding down its surface. The windscreen wipers start to squeak; I keep watching the way they make clean, smooth semi-circles while the rest of the glass is dark and dusty. The sound they make feels oddly comforting. Ordinary. I feel a wash of relief.

The bus pulls away from the stop and begins to move slowly along the quays. The Liffey is on my right; glassy, yellow waves of streetlights ripple along its surface.

It's only then I begin to shake.

1

Tess, Summer 2019

Tess can't bear the sticky interior of the tram a minute longer. Air: she needs air. The doors slide to either side and she gets ready to step out onto the pavement. As she does so, a loose gathering of shrieking teenagers surges forward, making it impossible for anyone to move.

'Ex*cuse* me, please,' she says, her voice sharp with irritation. Why can't they learn to let people *off* the tram first? She ignores the face one of the girls pulls at her, pretends not to hear someone else mutter, 'Cranky old bitch.'

She turns quickly to her right, makes her way down the platform and waits at the Luas validator.

If only this low grumble of cloud would lift. It's kept the whole city prisoner for days now. Tess longs for thunder, rain, high winds, anything to disperse the steel-grey gloom. She presses her travel card to the screen and it beeps at her, a blunt, aggressive accusation. She tries again and is aware of a queue forming behind her.

On the third attempt, the machine grunts its assent and Tess marches away from St Stephen's Green, crosses to the pavement on the other side and begins to make her way down Grafton Street.

The walk to Connolly Station will do her good. She keeps her head up, lengthens her stride. She feels the beginnings of a gentle breeze on her skin, as it snakes its way up from the Liffey. She even starts to enjoy the swell of optimism that ripples along on its surface, that sense of leaving everything behind.

It's been one of those days. One of those weeks.

By the time she reaches the Spire, her annoyance has reduced to a murmur, a kind of background noise. All at once, the image floats again to the surface of her memory. She tries to push it under. But it resists, stubborn to the last.

Mike. That awful row at the weekend. What began as a quiet, companionable Saturday evening in the garden had ended up with his announcement and her fury. And now he's gone, off again for another four weeks, leaving her to hold the fort on her own.

'I don't have a choice, Tess – you know that.'

She remembers his face as he spoke. Sees the unmistakable double-blink of his blue eyes as he looked at her: a silent admission of guilt. She knows him so well.

'That's not true,' she'd flashed back at him. 'You put yourself forward for this – you've just admitted it. You could have opted to stay in Dublin this time.'

'Not the way things are going, I keep telling you.'

She'd watched the way Mike clasped the back of his neck with one hand, massaging the tightness out of the muscles there. It's what he does these days when he's stressed. It is like a tic; one she's beginning to see much too often.

'Everything is so volatile at the minute. You know that.' The mute appeal in his eyes almost made her weaken. 'I can't afford to rock the boat. Brexit is changing everything – we may even go under.'

'And what about Luke? What if he goes under?'

Mike shook his head at her. She could almost taste his exasperation. 'It's just teenage stuff. Bad-boy behaviour, pushing the boundaries. We've seen it all before.' He pauses, suddenly not looking at her.

'Mike – he's out of control. He rarely comes home. Won't answer his phone when I call. I don't even know where he is or if he's *safe.*'

Mike sighed. 'He's nineteen, Tess. I think you're overreacting. I really do.'

She doesn't want to remember the rest. The way she'd ignited, the way she said so many things she'd only thought over the years. The way Mike turned away from her that night, without even a hug. That hadn't happened in the longest time.

'Don't let the sun go down on your anger,' her mother used to say. It was trite then, and it's trite now, Tess thinks. Some things can't be resolved, or forgiven, or forgotten, with a goodnight kiss.

She reaches Connolly Station and makes her way through the crowds to the north-bound platform. Her train is just arriving and she hurries towards one of the opening doors. Packed, as usual. Not a chance of a seat. Everyone is absorbed by whatever is on their phones. She watches as people scroll down and across, down and across, over and over again and she thinks what a mindless activity it is.

Nobody looks up as a young, heavily-pregnant woman – just a girl, really – steps into the carriage as the doors are about to close. She looks exhausted. Her feet are swollen and there is a fine beading of perspiration across her upper lip. She looks around, sees there are no empty seats, and her whole body seems to sag.

Tess feels an instant tug of sympathy. She knows just how that young woman feels. You never forget, really. She glances at the nearest rows of seats to her right and spots a young man, early twenties, who reminds her of Aengus. He has headphones on, and his eyes are closed. He's nodding away to some inaudible concert inside his head. Tess steps forward and taps him on the shoulder. Startled, he opens his eyes and looks up at her.

She knows at once that she has chosen well. There is no hostility in his grey gaze, only surprise. He pulls the headphones off. 'Yeah?' he says.

She smiles at him and motions towards the girl standing behind her. 'I wonder would you be so kind as to give that young woman your seat?'

He jumps up at once. 'Yeah, yeah, 'course.' He gathers up his rucksack and a light summer jacket and stumbles, almost eagerly, out of the way. His headphones are now around his neck, and Tess can hear the scratchy sounds of something she thinks she recognises, a familiar bass beat she's heard so often at home, played at full volume.

The young woman smiles at both of them as she takes her seat. She doesn't speak, but her glance is grateful. She looks Eastern European, with that white-blond hair and large brown eyes. As she sits, one of the two youngish women opposite turns to her companion and says, in a voice that's meant to be heard, 'Didn't know pregnancy was an illness, did you?'

The other woman sniggers and both of them look down at their phones again.

Tess sees the blush that crawls across the pregnant girl's cheeks. Sees the way she glances back over one shoulder, her expression confused. She may not have understood the words, but it's clear she's got the message. Tess gives her what she hopes is a reassuring smile. She feels suddenly furious, and something else besides. Her eyes fill with tears and she turns away, looking out the window at the speeding city.

'Didn't know pregnancy was an illness.' The words keep repeating themselves, pushing each other around inside her head. That's like something Luke would say. It's something he *does* say. That, and so many other things that feel calculated to provoke.

She shakes the thought away. She holds onto the back of one of the seats, allowing the rocking motion of the train to soothe her.

*

As she walks around the corner into the park, Tess sees the usual summer sights. Kids kicking a ball on the green. Young teenagers sitting on the garden wall of Grumpy Murphy's house. The small boy from number nineteen trying to master his bike without the stabilisers. And there's his dad, running valiantly behind, one hand barely holding on to the saddle. She smiles as she remembers Mike, shouting encouragement to Aengus, running down the path of this same park. The street she has lived in all her life.

It's the smell of newly cut grass that does it: memory trails in its wake. The man from the council has been. He's just tended to the large, open green space in the centre of the clustering houses. She can still see the marks of the tractor-wheels across the flattened surface. Kids are hurling clumps of cut grass at each other, the sweet and scented remains that the tractor has failed to gather up.

It was always like this. Her brothers, Eoghan and Myles and Conor, used to do exactly the same thing as today's kids: chasing the neighbourhood girls around the green and throwing handfuls of grass at them. Their squeals and shrieks were familiar, uncomplicated notes, background music to Tess's early summers. Not for the first time, she wonders about all those childhoods made happy, or sad, or a resentful mixture of both, in this modest circle of North Dublin houses.

When Aengus was small, he used to watch out for the tractor's arrival every two weeks during summer. 'Tractor' was among his first words. Dan – long-haired, grey-bearded, bead-wearing, a hero among the local children – cheered from the tractor's cab on the day Aengus finally managed to ride his bike without stabilisers. It was the weekend of his sixth birthday, and Mike had completed circuit after circuit of the park until Aengus found his balance at last.

Tess cheered him on too, standing at the garden gate with three-year-old Luke in her arms. Luke had been so difficult, that weekend. She can still remember his tantrums, the way he – she stops.

Because right now she sees it. A Garda car, parked at the kerb. She tries to unpick the scene. Is the squad car outside her house? Or is it parked in front of her neighbour's?

There are two unfamiliar figures standing at the porch. Her porch. She begins to feel whatever fear has been lurking for weeks now in that troubled place beyond words. It makes her quicken her step.

Breathlessly, she reaches the door. She sees Aengus's face, white and strained. Just behind him, Luke's fair head. Aengus is agitated, almost shouting at her as she reaches the step.

'I tried calling you,' he says, 'at least three times. Where *were* you? Why didn't you answer?'

Guiltily, she remembers switching her mobile to silent as she was setting up the conference room for the directors' meeting at four o'clock. She must have forgotten to switch it back on again.

'I'm here now,' she says, evenly. Her voice has a calmness she doesn't feel. She turns to the two men standing there. 'Can I help you?'

The taller of the two nods, acknowledging her presence. 'Mrs McGrath?'

'Yes.' She takes a moment, makes a show of examining the man's identity badge, waits for her heart to stop thumping.

'I'm Detective Burke,' he says. 'And this is Sergeant Feeney.' He gestures in the direction of the shorter, stockier man who's standing to one side. Feeney doesn't speak, just dips his head once. It's an almost comical gesture. It reminds her of one of those dunking birds that Aengus used to love as a child. Feeney has a bald spot that he has tried, and failed, to hide. Out of nowhere, Tess thinks: *comb-over.* The man doesn't take his eyes off Luke and Aengus. An aura of alertness surrounds him. If it were a colour, it would be bright red.

Detective Burke is speaking again. His voice is soft. Everything about him is quiet, contained but authoritative. 'We need to have a word with Luke.'

'Why?' Tess glances towards her younger son, now standing beside his brother in the hallway. The sun hits the wallpaper to his right, making patterns of light and shadow that she doesn't remember seeing there before.

'We need him to help us with our enquiries,' he says. 'Just an informal chat.'

'That doesn't answer my question.' The sharpness of her tone surprises her. The man's studied calm, his impassive expression, have begun to make her angry. 'Why do you need to speak to him?'

The detective looks at her for a moment. Afterwards, she thought his gaze had been almost kind. 'We've had reports of an incident,' he says. 'Your son may be able to help us with our enquiries.'

'What kind of an incident?'

Luke pushes past Aengus and steps out of the hallway into the porch. For a moment, she is startled at his appearance. He has never looked so careless of himself. His hair is uncombed, unstyled. His trainers are undone. His eyes seem bluer than ever, the lashes darker, thicker.

'Luke?' she says. Something begins to tighten inside her, where her heart used to be.

He shrugs. 'It's okay, I'll go with them.'

'I'll come—' she begins, but he cuts her off.

'There's no point in you comin',' he says. 'I'm over eighteen. They won't let you in.' His tone is almost nonchalant.

Tess isn't able to untangle the thoughts inside her head. She reaches out one hand, but Luke flinches, pulls back from her. It is hardly a movement at all, but Burke notices it. It's as though she's just been granted another sense, one that is hyper-alert. She can see and hear and feel with a depth and clarity she's never known before.

'You're welcome to wait at the station, of course, Mrs McGrath.' The man's tone is courtesy itself. 'But we will need to speak to Luke on his own.'

Mrs McGrath. Tess lets it go, again. It's easier than arguing. She'd kept her own name after she married. But Doherty is your father's name, Luke had once pointed out to her. Another one women can't win, he'd said with a smirk.

Before she can reply, the detective makes his way down the path, with Feeney to his left. Somehow, Luke ends up between them. They are like mismatched men, the one tall, the other short. Luke is bobbing between the two of them, something vulnerable caught in their riptide. She watches, helpless, as Feeney places one large hand on her son's head and folds him into the back seat of the squad car.

For an instant, she imagines herself running after the two policemen, shouting abuse, lashing out at them with both fists, demanding that they give her back her son.

'Mum?' She's almost forgotten that Aengus is also here, at her side. 'Why didn't you answer your phone?'

'I had it on silent. That doesn't matter now.' She keeps her eye on the squad car, watching the way it reverses smoothly and pulls away from the kerb. She searches for Luke's face; sees the way he stares straight ahead. Not even one backward glance.

She becomes aware of a group of young people gathering outside her gate. Their faces curious, they glance in her direction, and then after the departing squad car.

'Let's go inside,' she says to Aengus. They step into the hallway, and she closes the door behind them. Now her legs begin to shake; they feel as though they might belong to someone else. She needs to sit down. But the need to find out what's happening is more urgent still.

She looks up into her son's anxious face. 'Do you know what's going on here?'

She hates even asking the question. 'Aengus the Responsible,' he'd once flung at her, 'that's me.' Aengus His Brother's Keeper. Aengus the Explainer. There were other names, too, hurled around the house over the years. But Tess doesn't want to remember them. This is not the time.

She follows him into the kitchen. He leans against the counter, his arms folded, waiting. She pulls out one of the kitchen chairs and sits, trying to drive away the hazy black spots that have begun to dance before her eyes.

'Well? Do you know anything about what's going on?'

Aengus runs one hand through his dark hair. It stands up, in the same endearing peaks as when he was a small boy. 'Luke asked me to meet him here this afternoon at five.' He shrugs. 'I'd no lectures so I said yeah.'

'Did he say why?'

Waiting for Aengus to answer, her anxiety rises. It's like a vice tightening: hard, relentless. She has the taste of cold metal in her mouth.

Aengus shakes his head. 'All he said was something happened last weekend. He said that the guards took a few of his mates in for questioning this morning. Now it's his turn.' He pauses, looks down at his feet. He pushes something invisible away with the toe of his trainer. 'Luke says they stitched him up.'

'What do you mean, "stitched him up"?' she asks, sharply. 'What mates was he talking about?'

'I don't know. That's all he told me. Really, that's all I know.'

Aengus's voice has begun to grow louder.

'It's okay,' she says, quickly. 'It's okay, I believe you.' She waits, giving him time to gather himself. His body finally starts to loosen, and she holds out one hand to him, speaking more gently this time.

'Sit down beside me for a minute. I'm not going to interrogate you, Aengus. I'm sorry for snapping.' She lets that settle between them. 'I just want to know what you *think* might be going on. That's all.'

But still he doesn't move. He remains standing and she sees the way his knuckles begin to whiten again. He looks over at her, and she watches, appalled, as his eyes fill.

'I think,' he says finally, 'I think that this time, Luke might have done something really bad.'

2

Maeve, 1979

The door creaked open, slowly at first. A blade of light across the darkness wrenched me out of a thin, edgy sleep. For a minute or two, I didn't know where I was.

I waited. I held my breath. I no longer trusted anybody, anything in that place. I watched as something pale drifted soundlessly out of the shadows, then back into the dark again.

'What's your wee baby's name?'

The words, when they came at last, were barely a whisper. I didn't recognise the voice at my elbow, not yet, but I began to breathe again. It was definitely one of us. None of the nuns would take up such small, silent spaces. And they wouldn't ask us that kind of question, either.

I looked up, trying to make out a face in the gloom. 'Who is it?' I pulled Belle closer, feeling her stir against me.

'It's me, Joanie, so it is. I've come to see how y'are doin'. And the wee babby.'

'I'm okay,' I whispered back. 'We're both doing okay. But you shouldn't be in here, Joanie. Go back to your own dormitory. You'll be in big trouble if they find out you're missing.'

I could sense, rather than see her shrug. Poor girl. Monaghan Joanie was even younger than the rest of us. I never found out who the father of her child was. We never spoke about things like that, any of us.

'They can't punish me worse nor they already have, so they can't,' Joanie said. She moved closer to the bed. 'Can I hold her? Just for a wee minute.'

I could feel her tremble. It was always cold in St Brigid's, cold enough to make anyone shiver, but that wasn't what was happening here. I didn't trust Joanie. I couldn't, once I'd seen the hunger in her eyes. I knew what she wanted.

'The baby's sleeping now,' I said. 'I don't want to disturb her. Maybe in the morning.' It felt cruel to make excuses. Joanie made me feel guilty and I wanted to offer her some small generosity of comfort that didn't cost me anything. 'Her name is Belle,' I said.

Joanie giggled. She tried to cover her mouth with one hand. In the other, I saw the small lemon-and-green-striped teddy bear that I'd knitted for her. We were allowed to use up scraps of wool and fabric in the evenings, once all our chores were done, and Joanie had begged me to make a teddy for her. Afterwards, she sewed on the little triangle of black to mark its nose, and the thin wavery line for its mouth. The eyes were two metal buttons.

I thought they made the bear's face look blank, sinister, but Joanie was thrilled. She gazed up at me that day in the sewing-room, her brilliant blue eyes shiny with tears. 'I'm goin' to keep this for my own wee babby, so I am,' she said.

So I am. So I will. So it is. So many of Joanie's sentences had these moments of quirky emphasis: as though without them, she was all shadow, no substance. It was as if she had to keep reminding herself, reminding us, that she was real. Some of the other girls teased her about it: 'Is this wee Joanie coming? It is, so it is,' but she never seemed to mind. Mostly, she saw kindness in us, even if it wasn't there. She was looking at me now, disbelief stitched into her expression.

'Belle?' she said. 'What kind of a name is that? Who calls a wee girl after a bell?' A pause as she took another step towards me. 'What were you thinkin'?'

'It means "beautiful" in French.' Even I could hear the pride in my voice, and I made a real effort to cover it up. I didn't want to set her off. 'It *is* different, isn't it? Do you like it?'

'Aye,' she said, having thought about it for a moment. 'I like the sound of it, so I do.' Then, realising what she'd just said, she began to giggle at her own joke.

Her round face emerged fully from the shadows. I could see the large freckles sprinkled across her cheeks, her ready smile. Her face still had its childish softness, all its openness and innocence. Her features were somehow indistinct, as though they didn't know what they'd be when they grew up.

Monaghan Joanie was barely fourteen. They had taken her baby from her while she slept. Sometime during the night, a couple of weeks earlier, they'd slipped into the nursery and taken him. One of the other girls, Grace, had awoken to the sound of their habits, shushing across the linoleum corridor. Terrified, she'd closed her eyes again, pretending it wasn't happening. She'd shifted quietly, turned her face to the wall.

'I didn't want to see,' she whispered to me afterwards. She hung her head as she spoke.

'Did you hear anything? What did they say?'

Rage unfurled inside me again as I looked at Grace: at her shamefaced glance, the way her eyes darted over one shoulder. There was always someone hovering around us, listening or about to listen. I knew Grace had her own son to care about. I knew where her terror came from. But still.

'No.' She shook her head. 'Nobody said a word. It was all over so quickly. I was even askin' meself if it had really happened.'

Of course it happened, I wanted to snap. I felt like slapping her. How many times does it need to happen before you believe it? We never knew when: maybe at two weeks, three weeks, six weeks. But it *would* happen, to one baby after the other. Furious, I turned away from her, from her gaping mouth, her fear-flickering eyes.

The following morning, there was no doubt. Joanie's howls filled the long corridor and ever since, she'd wandered about like a lost ghost, trapped somewhere between two worlds. The dreamworld where other people's babies lived, and the nightmare world without her own. I knew she didn't mean any harm; we all did. Nonetheless, when Joanie was around, we kept our babies close. Just in case.

'All right, so,' she said. 'I'll come back again in the mornin', so I will.' She turned to leave, and the sag of her shoulders made me want to cry. But I couldn't afford to weaken.

Joanie closed the door quietly behind her.

That was the fourteenth of February 1979, the day Belle was born. Valentine's Day. I didn't know it then, but that would be the last time Joanie and I would see one another for more than forty years.

3

Betty, Summer 2019

Ah, Jack.
I wish I was able to talk to you again face to face. I think that's
what I miss the most. Our conversations. I don't like the way the
house feels without you these days. It's just so silent and so . . . still.
I can't say it feels empty, because I have a sense that you're around
me somewhere, staying close. But everything around me is quiet, far
too quiet.

The other day I came across your reading glasses. I was dusting
the shelves behind your favourite chair – the chair that still has the
imprint of your head, after so many years of you sitting in the same
place, in the same way. Head tilted back, hands folded and resting on
your stomach, legs stretched out in front of you and crossed at the
ankle.

Something glinted at me as I was moving stuff around behind
you. I mean behind where you used to sit. It was strange – I'm sure
I've dusted there lots of times since you. But I'd never come across
your glasses before. And then the lenses caught a sudden shaft of
afternoon light and there they were. There *you* were.

That was one of the bad days. But I could hear your voice telling me things would be grand, wipe your face now like a good woman, and make us a cup of tea, why don't you?

So I did.

Then I put the glasses back in their case, went down the hall and into the bedroom and tucked them into the drawer on your side of the bed. They won't be able to surprise me like that again.

I've been thinking about the children a lot, recently. I'm always thinking about them, but you already know that. You did your own share of worrying about them, too, even if you wouldn't admit it. They'll be grand, you used to say: no matter what the calamity. Stop worrying, like a good woman.

These days, though, I think about them in a different way. Being on your own, Jack, means that memories and regrets and all the things you felt so keenly years ago, but thought you'd forgotten, make their way up into the light of day.

Must be the kitchen that does it. Any kitchen. It's really the only room in the house I feel at home in. I've spent most of my years in a kitchen, I suppose, one way or another. It's one of the things that used to make Tess so furious with me when she was a teenager. She did a calculation once where she added up all the hours I spent on a daily basis buttering bread, cooking dinners, making school lunches, ironing, washing up.

I can't remember the result of her sums, but I did my own recently. I used the calculator thingy on that fancy mobile phone that Aengus, bless him, gave me for my birthday. He put his own number in first, on something he called speedy dial, and it means I can always get in touch if I need him, with one miraculous touch of a button.

So I went ahead and did my own figures: adding up six kids, twenty-five years of childrearing, more or less, and three meals a day. That all came to about six thousand hours a year, every year, in the kitchen. But knowing that surprising figure was unsatisfying, so I didn't go any further. We both know that looking after a family is about more than the hours spent keeping its everyday wheels turning.

But Tess wasn't letting anything go, not that day. I can still see her face: 'There are far too many kids everywhere,' she said, her eyes flashing. 'And too many in this house as well. You won't catch me being a mother.'

She gave me this mouthful on the day we were watching the Pope's visit, back in 1979. Do you remember, Jack? The fever of those days, the whole country in a state of excitement. You'd taken Tess and Sheila with you to the Phoenix Park, and I'd kept the younger ones at home.

There was murder over that, of course. Eoghan sulked, MylesandConor never shut up about always being left out of the good stuff, and Eleanor just wanted to be with her big sisters. I shouted at the lot of them as they fought over space on the sofa, watching the Pope on the telly the following day.

I flipped my tea towel at Myles's arse once I'd had enough of his lip. 'Be quiet, the lot of you! Is it not possible to get one minute's flamin' peace and quiet in this house.' That's when she turned on me, Tess. Giving out about too many children. About never wanting any of her own. I can still see the way she looked: her bright green eyes flashing, that lovely tumble of wavy auburn hair that she always hated, the energy crackling off her like electricity.

Her anger felt adult. It wasn't just common-or-garden cheek, or back talk. It was genuine, grown-up anger. And so I kept my counsel. I mostly kept my counsel around Tess in those days, as you used to keep advising me. I didn't say to her that one day she'd change her mind. That one day she'd see how worthwhile family was. That one day she'd understand what I understood – even though I never had the chance to choose my own knowledge. Back in our day, there were no choices around having children or not having children: not for people like us, anyway.

I've since learned that the world isn't shaped to fit the things I once believed in, the things I was once taught. Maybe it never was, and sometimes that thought makes me feel cheated. I can still see those men who stood beside the Pope in the Phoenix Park that day, telling the rest of us how we should behave.

Father Cleary. Bishop Casey. Each of them with a secret family of his own. And then all the others, who did worse, so much worse, to other people's children over the years. I don't want to think about that, not anymore.

But these nights, when I allow myself to think about our life, our world, our time, I begin to understand Tess a little better. We had six children, Jack – seven if you count little Frances, who didn't make it. I do. Either way, that's an awful lot of children. And now you're gone and I count those children and their lives. I wonder at all they have become. I don't mean I question it; I mean that I feel something like wonder when I think about all of these adult men and women who came from us.

Eoghan, a mathematician in San Francisco. MylesandConor, our 'Irish twins'. Barely ten months between them. Myles born in January,

Conor in December of the same year. I hardly ever think of them as separate people, but as one unit, one word. Trouble. They're both in New York. At least I think they're still in New York, moving from one building site to another. 'We're in the construction business, Mom,' they both insisted, last time we spoke.

Yeah, right.

They couldn't come home for you, of course. If they had, they'd have run the risk of not being let back into the States again. It's not the life I'd have chosen for them – but what can you do.

And our Sheila. A doctor in London, working for the NHS. Who'd have thought it? As wild as she was – and in fairness, Tess was a wonderful big sister to her. Kept her on the straight and narrow when I couldn't. Then there's Eleanor, quiet, shy little Eleanor, a librarian in New Zealand. She was always the bookish one, the one who got picked on because of her glasses.

These days, those memories bring other, new hurts along with them, dragging them by the hand whenever they come to visit. The way five of our children moved so far away, for one. Was it to be far away from us, Jack? Or just far away from me? And none of them with any children of their own: or none that I know of. In one of life's strange twists, Tess is the only one who gave us grandchildren. And she was the only one to stay here in Dublin as well. What would we ever have done without her?

Tess with her gentle husband and her two sons, the lights of my life. I love both of those boys, fiercely. Aengus is pure kindness, and he adored you, Jack. You did so many things with him. Bowling, kite-flying, mad fishing expeditions, until you fell into the Irish Sea, off the quay at the North Wall. You could have crowned yourself on the rocks.

And then there's Luke. Beautiful, bright-eyed, angel-faced Luke. I know you don't want to hear me say it, Jack, you never did, but that boy is trouble. I know this, with a knowledge that has grown deep inside me, in the very marrow of my bones.

I'm beginning to understand Tess better, the older we both grow, the less she needs me as a mother. I was too hard on her, Jack, I know that now. Because she was the eldest, I expected too much of her, made her mother the smaller ones because I couldn't, because I didn't have time, because I was tired, because I was fraught, because I was poor, because I was stressed.

I don't know how to make that better for her, even now. I don't know what use words would be, or even what words to use. But I keep my eye on Luke. That's one thing I can do.

Maybe that way, if I can help her at all, she might learn to forgive us, forgive me.

4

Eileen, 1960

When the train pulls into Euston Station, I wake with a jerk. I wake in the same way now, all these decades later, after one of my bad dreams. They always start at the same place: seeing myself as I step out onto that platform, into the freezing, clattery November air, leaving the steamy heat of the carriage behind me. My suitcase is heavy, and I stumble as I try to get a hold of it. My hands are shaking, and I can't get a grip on anything.

Not the handle of my suitcase; not myself; not my own life.

'Hello, dear.'

Startled, I look up and a woman in a navy coat and sensible shoes is standing in front of me. I look around, confused. Is she speaking to me?

'My name is Majella. I'm a Sister at Maida Vale Hospital. What's your name?'

I am suspicious. Kevin has warned me to be careful in London. There are a lot of conmen around, he's told me. Later, I think how rich that is, coming from him.

'Eileen,' I say, careful not to give her my last name, just in case there are conwomen around, too.

'Well, Eileen,' she says. 'And how far along are you?'

I gape at her. 'What?'

'Ten, eleven weeks?' She smiles. 'I meet this train, three days a week. I'm from Kildare, originally, but in London for the past twenty years. I know why Irish girls take the boat.'

I try to take in all these pieces of apparently unrelated information.

'It's all right,' she says. 'Please don't worry. I have a place for you to stay. You'll be safe.'

I already have a name and an address in Camden written on a page torn out of a notebook. Kevin had handed it to me the previous week. 'It's my sister's address,' he'd said. 'She's agreed to help you. You can stay with her until you find your feet.'

He gave me that piece of paper at the same time as he gave me fifty pounds, in an envelope. He wouldn't look at me. It was the same evening he'd told me he wasn't ready to be a father.

'What do you mean?' I said – stupidly, as I soon came to realise. It was perfectly clear what he meant. And fifty pounds repeated it for me, loudly, in case there was something I hadn't understood.

There I was, just twenty years of age, head over heels in love and thinking my life was sewn up forever. All sorted, pins on paper. Kevin told me so many times how much he loved me, how we were meant to be together, man and wife. And I fell for it. I loved being with him, loved the way sex made me feel. It was whole lifetimes away from my mother's mutterings about men and what they wanted to do in the dark.

I loved Kevin. I loved the heat and the joy and the intimacy we shared. The knowledge that this man was mine, and I was his in all the ways that mattered. Kevin and me, marriage and babies: that's what I believed in. We'd both grown into our brand-new selves together, at the same time. I saw our whole lives stretch out before us: years and years at each other's side until we reached the gentle sunset of our old age.

And his sister had *agreed* to help me?

It's the same old, same old story. I took the mailboat a week later. And by the time the train hissed its way into Euston, the certainty had begun to shock me: I was on my own. I had to find a job, fast. Fifty quid wouldn't last long.

I felt a rush of savage satisfaction afterwards, tearing up that envelope and Kevin's mean little bit of paper. I tore them both to smithereens, tossing the shreds into the fire, watching as my old life went up in flames. They were bitter reminders of the relief I'd seen in his eye when I accepted, so quietly, all that he'd handed me.

Majella takes me back to Maida Vale and the Matron there, a severe-looking woman whose uniform includes a bow under her chin, takes one of my hands in both of hers.

'Another Irish girl to stay, Sister?' she enquires, hardly looking at Majella, her shrewd eyes on me.

'Yes, Matron.'

'Very well, then. You're welcome, my dear.'

And just like that, she's gone.

It is Majella who teaches me about kindness. The practical robustness of it. 'Just pass it on, my dear,' she likes to say. 'Just pass it on.'

*

It wasn't her fault – hers or Matron's – that what happened afterwards, happened. I wanted to keep my son; I really did. They did

37

their best to help me. But it was a circle I couldn't square: the work, the money, the baby's needs.

I reserve the whitest heat of my anger instead for those who came afterwards. For the ones who handed my son over to a 'respectable family' without any proper paperwork. Who blocked all my efforts to find him. Who sent him out into the world without knowing who his mother was, or even how to contact her.

Those are the ones I will never forgive.

5

Aengus, Summer 2019

'...Luke might have done something really bad.' The words hover between us, floating on the suddenly thickened air of the kitchen.

I don't try to talk anymore after that. Instead, I focus on the toe of my trainer, as if it's getting ready to do something amazing and unexpected. I just continue to let the silence fill the space around us. I can sense the shock my mother is feeling. In a way, it's kind of satisfying. I've watched Luke get away with so much for so long, that today feels as though it has been waiting to happen.

Finally, she's the one to break the thread of tension between us. She asks me, again, what I think has happened to bring the cops to our door.

'I don't know,' I say. 'Luke didn't go into details.' I'm deliberately not looking at her. I know how anxious she is, how anxious she always is around Luke. I hear her breathe deeply, trying to calm herself.

I can write the script. I've had plenty of practice over the years. Luke and I have never got on. I recall one really vivid moment from my sixth birthday, when he was three. It's my first standout memory, and it's been a kind of template for how things have been between us ever since.

We were getting ready for my party. My mother was organising a big birthday cake, goody-bags, party games, the whole kit and caboodle. I was on the kitchen floor, building some kind of complicated space station out of Lego when Luke woke from his afternoon nap and began howling.

My mother brought him in from the sofa in the living room. She sat him down beside me. Then the phone rang, or the doorbell – I'm not sure which, and it doesn't matter anyway – and she left the room. I stood up to get more Lego from the box in the corner of the kitchen.

When I turned around, Luke was smashing all before him. Lookout towers toppled; astronauts became headless; trees and dinky cars scattered everywhere. I flew at him in a rage. The next thing I remember is my mother pulling me back, scolding me. Telling me that I was six, that Luke was only a baby, that I knew better than to behave like that.

I've never forgotten that day.

Afterwards, Luke was the one who was comforted. Childish of me, to hold on to that, all these years later? Probably. But it's one of many moments that have left me with a lingering sense of resentment. I see it as the start of what became our unshakeable family structure: Aengus the well-behaved. Luke the forgiven. Luke the indulged.

Finally, I begin to speak.

6

Maeve, 1979

The next morning, Belle woke at six. She hardly ever cried, even as a tiny baby. I always had to encourage her to feed. I didn't understand why until a long time afterwards.

That morning, a nun I'd never seen before, Sr Lucia, was on early duty. She was young, and even the veil that shadowed so much of her face couldn't hide how pretty she was. She surprised me by telling me her name. None of the others had ever done that. And although she seemed kind enough, I was suspicious. I still wonder what sort of disappointment had made someone like her end up in a place like St Brigid's.

'How's baby doing?' she asked.

She laid the back of one hand on Belle's cheek. She was gentle, but nonetheless . . . As she began to stroke my baby's face, I saw the glint of her nun's wedding ring. I snatched my daughter away from her.

'Don't touch her. Don't go near her again.'

Her smile faded. 'It's all right, dear.' Her voice was low, soft. She had the trace of an accent that reminded me of Joanie's. 'I don't mean you any harm. We'll get to know one another, in time.'

No, I thought; no, we won't. Because I won't be here long enough.

She took a step back from the bed. 'What's your name?'

'Maeve,' I said.

'Maeve, like the Warrior Queen of Connacht.' She was smiling again. 'A good name to have.' She wrote something in a notebook that she pulled out of the pocket of her habit. 'And your baby?'

'Her name is Belle.' Then, because I was grateful she'd taken that step back from us, I added, grudgingly, 'It's French for beautiful.'

'A fine combination,' she said. 'Strength and beauty.'

Sr Lucia must have known I was trouble. Maybe they sent her to me because she was still new, still kind. Maybe they thought she'd have more luck, that she'd manage to weasel her way around me the way none of the others had.

She must have known about the day before, too. Because when they'd come to take Belle away, only hours after she was born, I fought them. I bit and I scratched and I screamed. The whole house was in an uproar, but there was no way I was letting her go.

Belle was the most beautiful thing I'd ever seen, and she was mine. I wasn't going to let what happened to Joanie happen to me. I refused to let my daughter out of my sight.

My daughter! The words felt so good that I kept repeating them to myself.

My.

Daughter.

Or I whispered them to Belle, pressing my lips lightly against her perfect little ears. Each time I said her name, I felt a small, sad upswell of consolation. And no matter what anyone said to me –

about how I needed to rest, that the baby needed to be weighed, how I really needed to behave myself – I wouldn't let them take her away to the cot in the nursery. I held on to her, even when I slept.

I knew what they were up to. I knew they were waiting for me to weaken. But I also knew that I needed only another couple of days. Two, maybe three at the outside. I may have been slight for my age, but I was strong. As well as determined.

I'd already clocked the lay staff's routines, the changes of shift, the girls working in the kitchen who were none too bright. I'd been watching them all for more than six months. I could take advantage of their dullness, slip myself into the gaps that opened up between their duties and their vigilance. I'd escape through the scullery, out the back entrance and across the fields. I had no clue where I'd go after that, but I didn't care. I'd manage, somehow.

Georgina guessed. 'You're goin' to make a run for it with your baby, aren't you?' she asked. We were folding nappies and sheets in the laundry, a few days before Belle was born. 'I see the way you watch everybody.'

Georgina's son was already on his way somewhere, to what they called a 'new life', probably in America. They took him from her one morning while she was still feeding him. She didn't howl like Joanie, she just collapsed in on herself, into a hollow, tearless silence.

Her cubicle was next to mine and so I'd slipped out of bed a couple of times and tried to whisper to her, after they switched out the lights. But she never answered. She didn't say a word for weeks. I began to wonder if she'd been struck dumb. When she did speak, that day in the laundry, she spoke softly, and only to me.

I was wary, though. I had learnt not to believe anyone. Afterwards, I remembered someone telling me that the nuns at St Brigid's were hard. That the softest part of them was their false teeth.

Sr Lucia had only just arrived, so she hadn't had the chance to become like the rest of them, not yet. I remembered the whiteness of her hand, the way she'd touched Belle's cheek with a gentleness that seemed real.

Of course I knew she couldn't be trusted, none of them could. But her arrival had made me think. Maybe I could gain *her* trust, use her kindness to my own advantage. I started to cobble together my plan of escape.

7

Betty, Summer 2019

Ah, Jack.

I'll never forget Tess's face that day, the way she stumbled across our porch step, looking like a lost child. When I saw the way she looked at me, I thought someone had died.

'Tess, love,' I said, 'come in,' and I steadied her, and held on to her hand. I took her umbrella from her and propped it up in the old ewer inside the door. Her face was grey with shock and something else, something more. I learned quickly that it was disbelief.

'I'm pregnant,' she said.

I held my breath, and my delight along with it. I locked it down hard inside me. I was terrified that if I exhaled, my happiness might escape, and it might upset her, or make her angry. I thought of asking, How? or Are you sure? But I stopped myself, just in time. I could hear your voice, Jack, saying for God's sake, woman, you've had seven of your own, you know well how it happens.

But that wasn't what I meant. Tess had always been so certain that she didn't want children. She'd come to see me, years earlier, shortly after she'd met Mike. It wasn't just a preference, she'd said, it was a decision. Her decision. And Mike was happy to go along with it. Apparently, he had no strong feelings either way.

'Why on earth would you want to decide something like that?' I remember asking her. I think I told her it was selfish, not to have children. Or words like it. I wish I hadn't said that, but I was so dismayed I couldn't stop myself. I'll never forget the way she looked at me. So I tried to make up for it that April afternoon, when she stumbled across our threshold, seeing how ravaged she looked. Our eldest child, Jack. My heart went out to her.

But I was careful. It wasn't my life, it was hers. I took her jacket and her handbag from her and sat her down on the sofa. She didn't say anything else, just sat there, and I waited for a bit and then I said: 'So, you have a decision to make, haven't you? There are choices – hard ones, but choices nonetheless.'

I'd watched that poor anonymous child – and her parents – back in 1992. We never knew her name. She was just 'the X Case'. I'd watched in horror as she was hauled back from England; watched the almighty row that followed. No matter what, I was going to support my daughter. If that was Tess's decision, no force in the world, legal or any other kind, would drag her – or me – back to this country, taking my child's choices away from her. My mind went racing to Sheila. She would help. And that way, I'd be sure that our Tess would get the best of care.

She looked up at me then, in surprise.

'Thank you for saying that,' she said. 'Thank you, Mum.'

I moved towards her at once. She hadn't called me that in years. We were Betty and Jack to her and Mike. I think it happened after they bought the house from us and settled us here in this grand little bungalow. No stairs. Only two bedrooms to be cleaned. And a modern delight of a kitchen with everything built in. I couldn't believe my luck: a proper kitchen at last. No more gaps and corners. How I'd have loved something like it when the kids were small.

I held Tess while she cried. My heart was beating fast, though. I couldn't help it. A baby. A grandchild. I could be useful again.

She wiped her eyes. 'I'm okay,' she said, 'really, I'm okay. It's just the shock. I think I need a bit more time to get used to the idea.'

'I'll make us a cup of tea,' I said. I straightened up and left the room to give her time to compose herself.

But the joy, Jack, oh the joy. I fair skipped my way to the kettle.

*

Afterwards, when she looked as though she was back to normal again, I asked her if there was anything at all I could do for her.

She smiled at me and refilled her teacup. 'You can show me how happy you are, Mum. You don't need to hide it. You and Mike can share all the delight between you until I'm ready. And Dad too, I'm sure.'

I hadn't wanted to ask, but I was glad. If Mike was happy, I knew our girl wouldn't be far behind.

'He got home last night,' she said. 'And I told him. He's thrilled – he said I was the one who'd always been so dead set against it, not him. He's looking forward to being a dad.' She sipped at her tea. 'I will be okay with it – but right now I'm swinging from one extreme to the other.'

She put down her teacup. 'To be honest, I haven't slept.' Her eyes filled. 'I couldn't go through with it, going to England, and all that awfulness. I spoke to Sheila yesterday. She was so kind, but I just couldn't do it. I can't even bear the thought of it.'

She wiped her eyes then with the heel of one hand. 'But I'm terrified. I've been remembering all of us as kids.' She shook her head, no longer meeting my eye. 'I don't want to be swallowed up, Mum. I really don't.'

Not like I was, I thought. She doesn't want to say it, but that's what she means. And she wasn't wrong.

I took her hands in mine. 'You don't have to be,' I said. 'And you don't have to be like me. These are different times, Tess. You don't need a houseful. You'll be a brilliant mother.' I stopped for a minute, filled with sudden regret. 'I made you serve a long apprenticeship. And I'm sorry about that.'

'Oh, no, that's not . . .'

I couldn't help smiling at her, remembering our baby-sitting battles. 'I don't blame you for feeling it, not one little bit. I'll help out in any way I can. I can promise you that, and so will your dad.'

She stayed all afternoon. We talked. I don't think Tess and I were ever closer. I didn't really understand it, but she told me something about antibiotics interfering with the pill she'd been taking, and so she'd been caught.

Caught! I tried not to look too happy, I really did. I didn't care how it happened; I was just glad that it had.

And of course, little Aengus was a joy, right from the start. I know it's never fair to call a baby 'good' for sleeping, feeding, smiling, giving no trouble. We had plenty of 'bad' babies, if that was the case, Jack, you and I. But Aengus was such an easy-going child – you couldn't make him up.

And Tess and Mike took to parenthood like ducks to water. As for us, well, I don't need to remind you of how we felt. You, a man of few words for so much of our life together, you were unstoppable on the night of the christening. I know, the couple of Jemmies helped loosen your tongue, but you were more emotional than I'd ever seen you. When we got home, and I made us tea, you told me your heart was 'very full'. You even shed a few tears.

A couple of years later, it was no surprise to me that Tess was pregnant again. She wanted to give Aengus a brother or a sister, she said. This time, she was radiant.

The old, superstitious part of me raised its head from time to time. I never said anything, but I couldn't help remembering what had happened to us, Jack. Such perfect happiness began to feel fragile to me. I'd lie awake at night, worrying in case there was something wrong with the baby that was coming.

You and I had been so ignorant in our day – but we were ignorant of all the things that could go wrong as well, and in a way, that was something of a blessing. After we lost little Frances, of course, things were different. How could they not be?

And so, when Luke was born, healthy, beautiful, lusty, I did something I hadn't done in years. I got down on my knees and I prayed.

I was filled with gratitude. As I moved towards my seventies, I remember thinking that my life was complete. Nothing but gentle years lay ahead.

Like you, as I held this little boy in my arms only hours after he was born, my heart was very full.

8

Tess, Summer 2019

For a moment, neither Tess nor Aengus says anything. He keeps looking down at the kitchen floor, his arms folded tightly against his chest. She swallows. The words won't come; her throat has closed over. And anyway, she doesn't know if there *are* words that would make this – whatever it is – feel any better. So she waits, hoping that something will offer itself as an answer to the question she doesn't know how to ask.

Through the open window, she can hear someone call a child home; a dog barks; the clock in the kitchen ticktocks along as though nothing at all has happened. These are ordinary sounds, but it's as if she's never heard them before.

After a long silence, Aengus speaks. 'All I know is, Luke went to a party last Friday night. He took my blue shirt without asking. I bumped into him on his way out and we had words.' He shrugs, glances over at Tess. 'I decided to leave it at that, but I was pissed off at him. He said he was going to a party in a friend's house. And before you even go there,' he says, 'I don't know what friend, and I don't know where the party was. All I know is I heard him come in around three on Saturday morning. He wasn't exactly quiet.'

Tess had heard Luke, too, as he stumbled his way up the stairs. She is unable to sleep until each of her sons is home, safe, under her roof. Mike continually teases her about it. They're not kids any longer, he keeps telling her. They're young men. But still. She can't help it.

Mike. Jesus. She sits suddenly upright. He doesn't know yet. She has to tell him.

'Aengus, I need to call your dad.' She rummages in her bag for her mobile, finds it at last, and glances at her watch. It's almost seven o'clock. Mike should be back at the hotel by now, or at least on his way there. She brings up his name, presses the call button, and prays that he answers.

'Hi, you've reached Mike McGrath. I can't take your call right now, but . . .'

She waits impatiently for the end of the recording. 'Mike,' she says tersely, 'call me. It's urgent.' As an afterthought, she adds: 'Nobody's hurt, but you need to get back to me as soon as you pick this up.'

Aengus looks at her. 'What are you going to do now?'

'I don't know, Aengus. I've never had the guards at my door before.' She stops, takes a breath, tries again. It's so tiring these days, the way she keeps having to bite her tongue. 'I think Luke might need a solicitor, but I don't want to do anything until I talk to your dad.'

Aengus is about to reply, but his phone beeps and he walks away, signalling to Tess that he'll be back in a minute.

She tries Mike's number again. Same message. Angrily, she throws her mobile across the kitchen table. It skitters across the polished surface and crashes to the floor. She ignores it, opens the kitchen cupboard instead and takes out a glass. Then she stoops, picks her phone up off the floor and makes her way into the living room. Her laptop is there, along with a half-full bottle of red wine. A leftover from Saturday night, the night she and Mike had had the row.

Or maybe the bottle's half-empty, she thinks, sourly, as she sits on the sofa and makes sure her phone is still working. Then she switches on her laptop and enters a search into Google.

'Informal interviews with guards ireland' she types. The first site that comes up is Citizens Information. She scrolls immediately to 'If you are 18 years old or over' and the room around her begins to chill. There is nothing here about an 'informal chat'. There are only words such as 'caution' 'interview' 'arrest'. With each new search, Tess grows more anxious.

Instinctively, she raises one hand and rests it at the base of her throat. She can feel the heat of her flesh, the steady underwater pulse of her own heartbeat. Someone once told her how a hand flying to the throat like that is a primitive gesture. That it's an ancient instinct, one that protects our most vulnerable artery from attack.

If only things were that simple.

She takes a mouthful of wine and tries Mike again. This time, he answers on the third ring. 'Mike,' she says, almost weak with relief. 'Thank God I've got you.'

'What's up?' he says. 'I've just seen your missed calls.'

He's still guarded, still wary of her. Saturday's row hasn't gone away.

'Mike, I don't know what's going on. But I need you to listen while I tell you what's happened. It's Luke.'

Now she has his attention. 'Tell me,' he says. 'What is it?' He finally sounds like himself. 'What's happening, Tess? What has Luke done now?'

9

Maeve, 1979

I hadn't slept properly since the morning Belle was born.
I was exhausted. She fed restlessly. She hardly ever seemed full or contented. Even her protests were feeble little cries. I fretted that my milk wasn't good enough. That I wasn't a good enough mother.

But my one, fierce focus was keeping her by my side. I never took my eyes off her. I'd been watching what happened to the other girls. Once they were back at their chores, they were allowed to see their babies for just twenty minutes each day, until the inevitable happened.

And it wasn't long before the inevitable happened to Grace.

It was late in the afternoon, a few days after Belle was born. It was that dull, tired hour when everyone trudged up the back stairs, their work over for another day. I heard their booted feet, noisy on the wooden treads. I heard dozens of girls calling out, their voices loud, sometimes harsh, competing with one other; there was the occasional short burst of laughter.

Then silence, as sudden as a stone. A hush that was followed by a piercing, unearthly scream. There were the sounds of struggle, of small fists hammering on useless windowpanes, of all the clamour of dozens of voices.

'No, no, don't take my baby! Please don't take my baby!'

I recognised Grace and felt a hot rush of guilt. I'd been angry with her for not fighting for Joanie that night, and now here I was, clutching my own daughter tightly to me. I didn't need to be on the half-landing to know what was happening.

I'd seen it too many times before. We'd crowd around that tall window, tight knots of us, watching as somebody else's little girl or boy was taken away to a waiting car. I'd hear the scrunch of tyres on gravel as the cars sped away, circling the manicured green spaces of the driveway.

Now, I don't believe that such a memory is possible. How could I have heard a car as it drove away, when all the windows were bolted tightly shut? Maybe I used to imagine the sound of spitting stones: maybe it was a welcome relief from what I heard all around me.

I was frozen on the day that Grace's son was taken. I don't think I have ever felt so powerless.

But there was one thing I was sure of.

What had just happened to Grace was not going to happen to me.

*

During the days that followed I was more watchful than ever. For night-time, when sleep often crept up on me, I had transformed the bottoms of a pair of pyjamas into a kind of baby sling. My sewing kit was one of the few things I had taken with me from home.

Making the sling for Belle was easy. And satisfying. Not just because of the sling itself, but because the stitching of it had felt all along like a small act of resistance.

Years and years later, Aafreen would tell me about the Canadian, Ethel Mulvaney, and the hundreds of women imprisoned in the Changi prisoner of war camp during World War II.

Ethel persuaded the guards to allow the women to sew quilts for the prisoners in the camp hospital. On their individual squares of fabric – sixty-six of them in total – the women sewed something of their own stories. A flower representing love, or a butterfly dreaming of freedom, or a ship to symbolise going home. Sewing became their own secret language, a way to escape their imprisonment.

The night I'd finished sewing the baby sling, and just as I was about to tie the two ends of the pyjama fabric around my neck, I was overcome by a sudden swell of memory. Its arrival out of the blue was so vivid it took my breath away.

An evening in May. Jeans rolled up. The shock of cold water around my ankles. Waves frothing forward, then dragging back again. Around and above us, the dusky pink of the sky against the dark grasses of the dunes.

We were all there that summer, evening after evening, the same crowd of us. Maggie. Ruth. Geraldine. Terry. Tess. And Fiona; shy, hesitant, awkward Fiona. Always wanting to be one of the crowd but never quite managing it. Always hovering on the outskirts, waiting to be asked.

And then there were the boys. Loud, pushing and shoving each other, sharing cigarettes. Calling out to us, their voices rising high above the waves. The way we all ignored them. Until we didn't.

My hands started to shake as I placed my daughter in her new seat. She rested there, on my knees, trusting me. I kept telling myself: this is what matters. Never look back.

Sr Lucia found us, just as I'd finished making the baby sling. Her eyes widened. 'Maeve,' she said, 'you look very flushed. Have you a temperature?' She stood back from my bed. She didn't touch either Belle, or me. She'd learned that much; how to keep a respectful distance.

'I'm fine,' I snapped. 'We're both fine.'

She took a step closer. 'I promise you,' she said, 'if you will let Belle come to the nursery with me tonight, I will bring her back to you in the morning.' Her eyes were troubled. I remember being surprised by that. 'You're beyond exhausted, Maeve. Let me help you.'

'What?' I said. 'Like the way all of you helped Georgina? Or Joanie? Or Grace? Get away from me.'

She raised both hands in surrender. 'I will not insist,' she said. 'But I mean you no harm.'

Sister Lucia left the dormitory then. I watched her leave and bit my lip to stop myself from crying. I ached for kindness. But I couldn't trust it. I couldn't believe in her, even though I wanted to.

The more exhausted I became, the less hope I had that my plan of escape would ever work. I wouldn't let it go, though. I thought about the story of Pandora. How she released all sorts of evils – sickness, death, pestilence – to rampage their way around the world, but she kept hope for herself, stowed away carefully at the bottom of an ancient jar.

I looked down at Belle, at her peaceful, sleeping face. And so I made a huge effort to hold on to hope. I needed stories now more than ever.

I needed hope enough for both of us.

10

Betty, Summer 2019

When I said to you, Jack, just before Luke was born, that I was afraid for Tess, that her happiness might be fragile, I was thinking about our Frances.

The pain of losing her doesn't last as long as it used to – and softer times quickly follow – but when it arrives, well. It's like arrows shot from the past, fast-moving, unexpected, life-stopping.

I remember the silence above everything else. In those days, nobody spoke about it. I don't think it was unkindness, Jack, I really don't. I think we just weren't able. We didn't have the words. For feelings that were strong and complicated and full of pain, or longing, or joy, feelings that fought for some sort of shape to be put on them, but the language wasn't there, or if it was, it wasn't enough, or we didn't know how to take hold of it. I didn't know how to name what was happening to me.

It was like living two lives. One where I took care of Tess, shopped, cooked, cleaned, did all the ordinary things that are the scaffolding of every day. And then there was the other life I stepped into each morning when I woke, heavy with dreaming. The life that felt like it had no future.

Once, in the vegetable shop, Mrs Kirwan put her hand on my sleeve and patted my arm. I looked up at her, surprised. Her eyes filled. 'I'm so sorry, pet,' she said. Those words shifted a whole silted river inside me. From that moment, my life began to flow outwards again. The relief of it. I've never forgotten that, the power that lay in those few quiet words. The acknowledgement: the simplicity of kindness. It taught me something.

And I've not forgotten the way you minded me, Jack. Comforted me as best you could. I'm sorry that I didn't see your loss to be as great as mine. Different, but still huge.

You said, and I saw how careful you were with every word, that our babies were real to you only after they arrived. You knew it wasn't the same for me. You knew how much I wanted her; how real Frances was right from the very beginning.

Like Mrs Kirwan's words, yours sparked some new understanding inside me. I didn't know how to say that to you back then. You kept telling me how grateful you were that I was alive, that I hadn't been taken from you, too. It took a long time for me to feel that way, and I know there were days when we fought, each of us trying to carve a path of our own out of those dark and dangerous woods.

I raged at the way daily life went on afterwards as though nothing at all had happened. Raged as the trees burst into blossom, the April showers came and went, the sun rose and set. But I've learned that we always, somehow, look for ways to recover. Because staying sad, staying the same, is just too hard.

Tess helped to show me that. As a toddler, she'd take my hand, silently, if I wept. She'd crawl up onto my knee, rubbing the corner of her blanket against my cheek to comfort me. 'Play, Mama,' she'd whisper. And I would, literally, pull myself into standing, kiss the top of her head and take her out into our back garden.

You'd made a swing for her during the days when I was all but frozen. I used to watch you from the kitchen window as you hammered and sawed and Tess followed you around, her blanket trailing against the ground so that it became a mucky square of grubby, grinning teddy bears. I had to wait until she was asleep so that I could steal it away from her and wash it, drying it overnight on the handle of the range.

And so life went on. It wobbled for a bit, to be sure. When it did, I'd think about my mother's words from years earlier. Just do your best, Betty, love. And if you can't do that, then do what you can.

Later, there was Sheila. And all the others, and the busyness, and you and me and the unstoppable everyday demands of family.

I know I've always said you were a man of few words, Jack, and you were, back then. But the words you did say were worth waiting for. With six children to feed and clothe and discipline and look after, a lot of what we talked about was who needed what, which bills needed to be paid, which ones could be put off until next week, what broken things around the house and garden needed to be mended.

But after we lost Frances, every night of our life together ended with the same words. Even if we disagreed over something, you never failed to say *Well, Betty, that's that, now. Tell me about your day.* Together, we continued that small conversation, each asking the other as the days slid away into the stillness of night, for nigh on sixty years.

And you made me laugh. With your stories about gobshites, and windbags, and working companions who didn't know their arse from their elbow. 'It's one thing,' you used to say, 'to be born a gobshite. It's another thing to die one.'

We got better at talking over the years, didn't we? And once the kids were gone, there was no stopping us. It's like we stored it all up during the busy times, and it poured out of us once we were on our own. Torrents of words.

On the odd time we went out together for a cuppa or a nice meal, I was proud of the way we chatted. There were so many others around us – younger people, too – who sat in stony silence or looked down at their phones. We still looked at each other, liked each other.

Go on out of that, woman, you used to say. You're turnin' us into a pair of romantics in our old age. I was, and we did.

I remember Tess coming in one evening when we hadn't heard her opening the door. You and I were on the sofa together. You were watching the snooker. I was knitting. I think it was Ronnie O'Sullivan who hit some extraordinary sort of shot and you let a roar out of you and grabbed my hand, waving our arms in the air, up and down, up and down together as though we were working the handle of some old pump.

'Look at that, would you, Betty! Just look at that!'

I never understood snooker, but it didn't matter. I enjoyed your enjoyment. I put down my knitting and held on to your hand with both of mine. It was one of those moments that was filled to bursting point with affection and familiarity, stitched together into the seam of intimacy we'd shared since I was twenty, you thirty.

Imagine that. Twenty. What a child I was. I laid my head on your shoulder and that's when Tess walked in.

For a minute, she looked embarrassed. As though she'd interrupted an indecently private moment and didn't know whether to come in or go out again. You turned to her and your face lit up, as it always did. 'Tess! Come on in. Boys with you?' you asked, as usual.

'I'm on my own, for once,' she laughed. 'This is a child-free visit, just to say a proper hello.'

It was right after the incident with the magnifying glass. I knew why she had come. 'Great to see you, love,' I said, and stood up. I gave her a hug. 'I'll go and put on the kettle.'

You patted the sofa beside you. 'Sit down there, Tess, like a good girl,' you said. 'And tell me all your news.'

11

Tess, Summer 2019

'And that's it. That's all I know. That's all Aengus knows. And I don't think he's hiding anything.'

For more than an hour, Tess and Mike have replayed everything that happened earlier. They're going around in circles, so she forces herself back to the centre. 'Do you think we need to get a solicitor for Luke?'

'Absolutely.' He is emphatic. 'I have Matthew Kerr's mobile number. I trust him. If he can't help, he'll recommend someone who can.'

This is real, Tess thinks. She is filled with something that feels like wonder. This is really happening to us.

'I'll give Matt a call as soon as we hang up,' Mike continues. 'And I'll get home as quickly as I can. If not tonight, then first thing tomorrow.'

'Are you sure? I mean, it may turn out to be . . . I don't know, not serious . . .' Her voice fades away as she remembers Burke's almost benign expression. How he seemed to look at her kindly. 'Maybe it *is* just an informal chat?'

Mike is silent for a moment. When he speaks again, his voice is gentle. She is almost undone by the remorse she can hear in every word.

'I should have listened to you, Tess. I'm sorry about Saturday. You've been right about Luke before. I've been caught up in my own stuff and maybe I've taken my eye off the ball. One way or another, I need to be home.'

She stands up, walks around the room as she speaks. 'It'll be good to have you here,' she manages, at last. 'Keep me posted about your flight and I'll pick you up at the airport. And Mike?'

'Yeah?'

'Saturday doesn't matter. I'm sorry, too. I said some things I shouldn't have.'

'It's okay. It's behind us. And don't worry about coming to the airport. I'll get a taxi. You need to stay at home for Luke.'

'Of course. I'm not thinking straight.' She drags one hand through her hair. It feels matted, sticky. She needs a shower.

'Did the guards say what station they were taking him to?'

'God, no. I never even thought to ask. I'll find out and let you know.'

'Text me. I'm going to call Matt now. See you soon.'

'Bye. Travel safely.' She hangs up.

Aengus puts his head around the door. 'I'm heading off now. You sure you're okay?'

Tess waves him away. 'I'm sure. Dad's on his way home.'

'Really?' He looks uncertain again.

'Yes. Tonight or first thing tomorrow.' She waves at him again. 'Go. Go on. I'll be fine. Enjoy your movie.'

'Are you sure?'

'Yes.'

Finally, he says: 'Keep in touch, then, won't you?' But still he hesitates.

'Of course.'

She sits down and begins a search for the Garda station phone numbers. She keeps busy, giving Aengus the message that he is free to go. She jots some numbers down on the notepad she keeps beside her laptop.

After a moment, he leaves the room, pulling the door shut, quietly, behind him. She puts down her pen with relief. It's going to be a long night.

The front door closes now, and she watches as Aengus makes his way down the garden path. At the gate, he turns for an instant and waves. He knows she can see him, even though he can't see her. It's the way he's always left the house, ever since he was a child at primary school. His departing back makes Tess feel a sudden longing for the days when he and Luke were children, and everything felt filled with possibility.

She sits down again, and her hand shakes a little as she reaches for the bottle of red and starts to refill her glass. She rests her head against the back of the sofa and closes her eyes. She can see herself, with brittle clarity, just as she was, almost twenty-three years ago.

Sees herself on the day when her life changed forever.

*

Helen had looked at her, over the tops of her reading glasses. 'So,' she said, 'what do you want to do now?'

Tess watched the careful, professional mask settle across her friend's face.

'There is not a lot I can do, as you know, but there is plenty of information out there if . . .'

'No, no, it's okay,' Tess said, quickly. 'I wouldn't dream of compromising you. I just need to know if there is any chance this result is a false positive.' Desperation pulsed beneath the surface of her words.

'Highly unlikely. With the test, and your symptoms, it's pretty conclusive.' Helen tapped her pen on the sheaf of papers on the desk in front of her. 'You're six or seven weeks' pregnant, Tess. I don't think there is any doubt.'

'I can't believe it,' she said. But she could, really. The first, faint suspicion of a couple of weeks back had grown into certainty even before she reached the doctor's consulting room.

There'd been the suddenly puzzling, disconcerting smell of onions in the kitchen last week – even though she hadn't cooked any. The heave of nausea in the early morning. The bone-crumbling exhaustion that lasted all day, followed by hours of muddy sleep that brought no rest.

Tess shook her head. 'I need to take some time. I have to think about this. I can't decide right now.' She stood up, gathering her bag and her jacket and letting her umbrella fall, twice. Her hands were shaking.

'Don't take too much time.' Helen's voice was kind.

'I know. I know. I understand. I just need to try and get my head together.'

'Is Mike home?'

'Tonight. I'm heading to the airport to collect him now.' She stopped what she was doing. 'Jesus Christ. What a homecoming.'

'If you want to see me together,' Helen said, 'I'll make the time for you. You know that. No matter when it is.'

'Thanks.' A sob started somewhere under Tess's throat. She wanted to get out of there before that happened. 'I'm going now,' she said. She pulled open the door of the surgery, not even hearing what Helen called out to her.

Afterwards, she thought it was something to do with being careful.

Careful?

It was a bit late for that.

*

She made her way back to the car and sat, resting her head on the steering wheel. The car filled with the remembered shrieks of Myles and Conor, squabbling as children. With Eoghan shouting at them both, trying to be referee, or peacemaker. She could see Eleanor's pleading eyes, watched as the little girl with the elfin face and the huge glasses searched for the comfort of her big sister's hand. And Sheila, beside her as always, sighing her constant refrain of *Jesus God but I'll be outta here as soon as. Can't wait to be shut of this lot.*

Tess was startled by a tap on the driver's window. She looked up to see a woman peering in at her. It took an instant before she recognised the brown uniform of a traffic warden. Christ, she thought, my parking ticket must have run out. She rolled down the window, ready to apologise.

'I'm sorry,' she began, but the woman cut her off.

'Never mind that,' she said, 'I just wanted to make sure you were okay. You weren't moving and I was afraid that something was wrong with you.' She looked embarrassed for a moment. 'I had somebody go into a diabetic coma last week. I'm not the better of it yet.'

Tears came to Tess's eyes at the woman's gruff kindness. 'No,' she said, 'there's nothing wrong. I've just had a bit of difficult news.'

The woman nodded. 'Okay, then,' she said. 'Are you sure you're well enough to drive?'

'Yes, yes, I'm fine, thanks.'

'You're a little over your time, so . . .'

'I'm going now. Thank you. Thank you so much.'

She rolled up the window, checked the mirror, indicated and pulled out into the traffic. The streets were getting busier now, gearing up for the evening rush hour.

'Keep your wits about you, Tess Doherty,' she murmured to herself. 'This day isn't half over yet.'

12

Maeve, 1978

My father drove me to St Brigid's. All through the journey he didn't speak one word to me. Even when we stopped at traffic lights, he stared straight ahead, as though he couldn't bear to look over and see me sitting beside him. I tried to tell him, as I had tried so many times before. But eventually I gave up.

It was a beautiful day at the end of June. The sun was high, hard and bleak against a bright blue sky.

I cried for most of the trip, my face turned away from him, my head resting against the passenger-side window. I don't know which was worse: being betrayed by the boy I loved; feeling frightened about what lay ahead; or knowing that my father was lost to me for good.

Back then, in those early days before my arrival at St Brigid's, I had gone into hiding somewhere deep inside myself. I survived by carving out a distance between me and what was happening to my body. I even began to think of myself in the third person, a person with a new name. And once I walked into that mother and baby home, a different life began. A different *me*. I can't explain it any better than that, even now. But that's what happened.

A nun ticked me off as if she was checking an item on a laundry list. She told me I would not be using my own name. She would give me a new one, she said, in due course. Because the girls 'preferred anonymity', she said.

Even then, I understood that it wasn't the girls who preferred anonymity. It was families like mine. Mothers and fathers terrified of having a daughter who had sinned.

What would the neighbours say if they found out? They wanted us to keep their secrets for them. And we all knew that Ireland was a very small place, already stuffed to the gills with other people's secrets.

'I know what name I'll use,' I said. I drew myself up to my full height, planted myself on the polished floor, my legs strong and steady. I imagined the soles of my feet sprouting pale, sinewy roots, forcing them underneath the floorboards, down into the cool darkness of the earth below. I was remaking myself into something fixed and unshakeable.

The nun – her name was Sister Raphael, I later discovered – looked at me sharply. The parlour door opened, and someone called out to her, said that she was needed elsewhere.

'It's Maeve,' I said, with a firmness I didn't yet feel. 'My new name is Maeve.'

She shook her head at me, impatient to leave, but not wanting me to have my own way. Still I stood my ground. Someone called out to her again, louder this time, and she sighed. I watched as she quickly noted my new name beside my old one. She handed me a slip of paper. B-23-9. I looked at it, at her, not understanding.

'Your dormitory number,' she said impatiently. As though I should have known. 'Bed number nine.' Then she waved me away from her, the way I later saw the kitchen girls flap their hands, shooing away a misbehaving hen.

But as I left, I felt a small shoot of triumph. I had my name.

Fuck doing what I'm told, I remember thinking. Fuck silence. And shame. It was all of those things that had brought me here in the first place.

This new girl, the one fizzing with defiance and energy and rage – she would survive this.

She would get out of here with her child, or she'd die in the attempt.

13

Betty, Summer 2019

Well, Jack.

Today wasn't so bad, after all. It's funny the way the big days, the significant ones, are often softer, kinder than I'd have imagined. They don't trip me up the way I expect them to. It's not your birthday, or our wedding anniversary, or the anniversary of the day you slipped away from us so quietly that are the harshest ones to get through.

It's more what happens on the ordinary days, the way unexpected sharp corners of grief catch me out in the simplest of things.

Your reading glasses that day, lit up by the barest glint of dusty sunlight. Or coming across your free travel pass in a jacket pocket, with your photo grinning up at me. Or finding daffodil bulbs in the cloakroom: the ones you never got to plant.

There they were, sprouting away in the dark. I was never the gardener you were, Jack. But I stuck them into a pot of compost and fed and watered them as thoroughly as I'd seen you do so many times and I decided to wait and see what would happen in the spring.

Up they came, their yellow heads bobbing away in the breeze. Seeing them there one sudden Saturday morning took my breath away. And then I couldn't stop smiling: there was something so gleeful about them, the way they were showing off their long legs. Almost bold, as though they'd just got away with something. I could see you, too, standing over them, pulling up the stray weeds, clearing away the last soggy bits of winter, caring, minding.

You did so much work in the garden, planting potatoes, carrots, turnips, peas. Feeding all of us, year after year. We'd never have got by otherwise. I used to see you through our kitchen window, every time I lifted my head from the Singer. You dug, and I sewed, making or mending or altering the children's clothes.

That sewing machine was something our kids used to rage against from time to time because it meant they rarely got anything new. It used to upset Sheila in particular. She hated wearing hand-me-downs. Once, to my surprise, I heard Tess hiss at her to be quiet. 'Eleanor can hear you. How do you think you'll make her feel, getting stuff third hand? Don't be so selfish.'

Tess would have been about fifteen at the time. I said nothing, but I bought a remnant of bright green cotton the next afternoon at Hickey's sale and ran her up a little summer dress. I think shifts were more or less in fashion back then, and I knew the colour would be spectacular with her auburn hair. When she came in from doing the grocery shopping for me the next day, I told her I had something for her.

'What?' She looked suspicious. She rarely got anything that hadn't once belonged to me.

I handed her the parcel I'd made up earlier, tied with a green satin ribbon that was an exact match for the dress. It was an apology from me, as well as everything else. She and I had had a fight the previous day. About those little brats, the Chawke brothers, and the way they'd bullied Eleanor. Tess was determined to fight back. I didn't want her to: I didn't want her scrapping on the streets. She was furious with me, said I thought far too much about what the neighbours would say. And in those days, in all honesty, she wasn't wrong.

She ripped off the brown paper and gasped when she saw what was inside. She shook out the dress and held it against her, smoothing the fabric with disbelieving fingers. 'For me? Really? Just for me?'

'For you.' I pulled her towards me and kissed her on the forehead. She didn't pull away. 'Just to say I really appreciate the way you help me out, and the way you stand up for Eleanor.'

She hugged me then and I could see her eyes brimming. She ran upstairs at once to put on the dress. And I was right: she looked wonderful in green, with the ribbon in her hair. Tess wore that shift dress until the material grew so thin you could see right through it. It was no use to even *think* of handing it down to Sheila or Eleanor.

That, I'm sure, is the point Tess was determined to make.

I've been very grateful to my sewing machine over the years. I was careful to do something for each one of our brood from time to time, something to help them feel special.

It drew us all closer together. I loved that feeling of binding them to me – loosely, but binding them, nonetheless. I like to think of those sewing moments as threads of connection. That was how my own mother used to describe them.

Threads of connection. Threads of love.

14

Tess, Summer 2019

It takes Tess three phone calls to find out where they've taken Luke.

'How much longer will he be?' Nobody's offering her any information.

'I understand Luke McGrath is still being interviewed. Would you like to leave a message?' The guard's tone is detached, impersonal. He sounds almost bored.

'Has his solicitor arrived? Matthew Kerr? Is he with him now?'

'I really can't say. One moment, please.' There's a pause, a muffle, as he puts his hand over the receiver. And then: 'I've just come on duty. But I can take a message, if you like?'

'No, thank you.' Then: 'Yes, yes please – just ask Luke to contact home as soon as he's free.'

She hangs up. Luke has already been gone for more than three hours. Mike isn't answering his phone. She hopes it's because he's already in the air, on his way back to her. She can feel that old anxiety begin to spiral again.

She pulls her notepad towards her and writes down the time of her phone call to the Garda station. Taking notes about such small events might make her feel less powerless. But she already knows what an illusion that is. She's had to learn that karmic lesson many times.

Karma: it's one of Luke's favourite words, particularly when something catastrophic happens to someone he doesn't like. A gleam in his blue eye. A smirk. He never tries to hide it. Just shrugs whenever Tess can gather enough energy to challenge him.

'That's very unkind, Luke,' she said once.

He shrugged. 'What good would my sympathy do him?' he asked. 'Anyway, he deserved it. It's karma. If anybody had it coming, he did.'

She hadn't known what to say. Luke often did that – challenged her at some deep, disturbing level that she had difficulty articulating. His lack of empathy frightened her. On that occasion, his blue eyes dared her to continue, but she knew where that would lead.

She turned away from him for a moment. When she looked up again, he'd left the room. His ability to arrive and leave like that, stealthily, silently, has always startled her.

Tess wishes Mike was here. This is too much for her to handle on her own. The screen of her mobile lights up. She grabs it, without looking. 'Luke?'

'No, Mum. It's me, Aengus. I'm just ringing to see if there's any news?'

'No, there's nothing. Luke's still in Clontarf Garda Station. I can't get any information.' She tries to be patient, to hide her disappointment. She needs to get him off the phone.

'Is Dad there?'

'No, but he's on his way.'

'Do you want me to come home? It's okay if . . .'

'No, no, don't do that. There's nothing to be done here. I'll call you if there's any news. I have to go.'

She hangs up as she hears the beep of an incoming call. 'Mike?'

'Yeah. I've just arrived. Waiting for a taxi now. Any news?'

'No. And I can't find out if Matthew Kerr is with Luke at the interview. They're not telling me anything. I'm terrified at the idea of this so-called "informal chat". Do you know what's going on?'

'I'll call him again now. Don't worry, Tess – Matthew is reliable.'

'Yeah, I'm sure he is, but did you get to speak to him, or did you just leave a message?'

'We spoke. Just before I boarded. He was making some calls. I'll get in touch with him now. I should be home in forty minutes; the queue is moving quickly.'

She hangs up. There's nothing to do but wait. That's always the worst part. The waiting.

She starts to pace around the room. She's restless, and when she's restless, memories begin to raise their heads. One day in particular has become insistent. She might as well let it come; get it over with. She sits back down, pours the remains of the wine into her glass, watching as the lees settle at the bottom.

But then there is the sudden sound of a car pulling up outside. A door slamming. She stands up quickly and moves towards the living-room window. But it's not Luke. It's not Mike's taxi. It's Mary from next door.

Tess lets the blind fall back at once, embarrassed. She can't bear the thought of being accused of nosiness.

When she sits down again, the images of that day jerk into life. She sees herself as she reaches the landing and makes her way to Luke's bedroom door.

15

Maeve, 1979

When Belle was just five days old, I had a visitor.
Sr Marguerite came hurrying into the dormitory to get me.
She was cross. Even the folds of her habit looked sharp, irritated.
'There is somebody here to see you,' she said, fingering the beads at
her side.

Was this a trick? I knew that adoptive parents arrived at St
Brigid's like this all the time. We girls knew that they swooped in at
any hour of the day or night, that babies were snatched away from
us without warning, that those who fought back never won.

I picked Belle up from the bed where I'd been changing her. 'I'll
protect you,' I whispered into the softness of her neck. 'I won't let
anything happen to you.' Then I straightened up and, at my own pace,
followed Sr Marguerite out the door and down the empty corridor.

I couldn't possibly have a visitor. Nobody knew where I was. St
Brigid's was miles away from home and my parents had made it very
clear they would not be coming. But maybe they'd changed their
minds? Maybe they'd come to rescue us, after all? For an instant, I
allowed myself to believe they were here to take us home.

Sr Marguerite was waiting for me now, impatiently, at the top of
the stairs that led down to the entrance hall. 'There's a woman here

to see you.' She lifted her head as she spoke, so that she was looking down at me. 'She says she's your aunt. Now hurry up, I haven't got all day.'

I was about to say something, but instead, I kept my mouth shut. A woman? My mother would never have come for me on her own. I kept my disappointment to myself and followed Sr Marguerite down the long corridors of the ground floor.

Georgina and I used to polish that parquet, on our hands and knees, before our bellies got too big. Once they did, we were sent to work in the laundry instead, washing the avalanche of nappies and sheets and baby clothes that piled up on a daily basis.

All my senses were firing now. I was ready for battle. Whoever this woman was, she would not be taking my baby away from me.

Sr Marguerite waved me into the parlour. Once I was inside, she closed the door behind me. I glanced back at where she had been, surprised that she hadn't stayed. There was no such thing as privacy at St Brigid's.

A woman was standing there, with her back to the fireplace. My first thought was how beautiful she was, in her long green coat and her bright pink scarf and her hat with its light, gauzy veil. Afterwards, I learned about her love of Bermona hats, of silk and style and elegance. But on that day, all I could see was how different she was. Everything about her was the opposite of this grey place. She looked fragile even then, her cheekbones sharp, her hands thin and restless. She seemed to study me for a moment and then nodded her head.

'You're very like your father,' she said.

That was not what I expected her to say. Not even close.

I took a step back. 'What?' I said. 'Who are you?'

Belle began to whimper. I rocked her gently, still keeping my eye on this strange woman. She started to walk towards me, and I backed away even further, towards the parlour door. I stretched out one hand.

'Stay away from me,' I said. 'I'm not giving you my baby.'

She held up both hands. 'That's not why I'm here. I don't want to take anything from you.' She looked at us, in silence. After a minute, she said: 'What's the baby's name?'

'Belle. Her name is Belle. It's French for beautiful.'

I waited for her to say something. But her eyes filled and when she did speak, her voice was shaky. 'I've come to take you home with me. To take you as far away as possible from this place, you and your little girl.'

Was this some sort of cruel joke? Home: with her? Both of us?

I didn't believe a word of it. But she used my old name, the one I'd left behind when I came to live here. The one that belonged to that other girl, the one I no longer was.

'My new name is Maeve,' I said. I tried to sound defiant, but I was close to tears. 'My *only* name is Maeve.'

'And I'm your father's sister,' she said. Her voice faltered. 'I'm your aunt, Eileen.'

Then I knew it was a trick. 'No, you're not,' I said, 'you can't be.' I could hear the triumph in my tone, my contempt for all the lies she was telling me. Did she think I was stupid? I could see right through her. 'My aunt is dead. She died in England, years ago.'

She shook her head. 'No,' she said. 'That's not true.'

Spite rose in me. I knew what she was after. She couldn't take her eyes off Belle. 'It *is* true,' I said. 'My father said his sister was long dead.' I paused. I'd learned how to wound. 'He said it was for the best.'

For a moment, the woman didn't move. When she spoke again, her voice was even softer than before. 'Let me show you something.' She put her gloves down on the table and reached into her handbag.

I noticed then that she wasn't wearing a wedding ring and I began to feel confused. All the women who came here looking for babies wore wedding rings. They couldn't have babies of their own, and the world had told them they were entitled to ours.

I was furious all over again: I could see Joanie's face, and Georgina's, and Grace's, and all the others who'd had their whole lives stolen from them. I was not about to be tricked. Not by this woman, not by anyone.

She handed me a photograph. 'Take a look.'

But I wouldn't. I didn't want to take my eyes off her, in case she suddenly moved against me. I glanced around the parlour, suspicious that there might be someone else there, in hiding, ready to pounce as soon as I became distracted.

She seemed to understand. 'I'll not come anywhere near you; I promise. Look, I'll move back again to the fireplace. Take your time and just look at the photograph. That's all I ask.'

I glanced down at it. Then I looked at her, and once again at the black and white photograph. It was a picture of my parents' wedding. There was a young woman to my father's left, leaning towards him to kiss him on the cheek. Her face was half-turned, laughing, towards the camera.

'I don't understand,' I said. 'You're supposed to be dead.'

She pulled out one of the heavy chairs that surrounded the long table. 'Won't you sit down for a few minutes?'

She was no longer looking at Belle. Now she had eyes only for me. At that moment, I believed her, although I wasn't going to show her that. I sat on the edge of the chair, soothing Belle, who had begun one of her thin little cries again. It was almost time for another feed.

'My name is Eileen,' she said. 'I'm your father's sister. Yes, I went away to England many years ago, around the time you were born. But I didn't die. I had a baby there. A little boy. I named him Cillian.'

I could feel my mouth open. I glanced down, again, at her left hand.

She smiled at me. 'No,' she said, 'I'm not married. I've always been on my own. My family would have nothing to do with me when they found out I was pregnant.' She shook her head. 'They surprised me; they really did. I'd grown up believing that all of us were kind. But my own brother wouldn't even speak to me.' She clasped her hands together and her knuckles showed sharp and white. 'And I gave up my boy for adoption. It is the biggest regret of my life.'

The day began to fill with a brittle, white light. I felt suddenly weak, with black spots dizzying before my eyes. The woman called Eileen looked alarmed.

'Put your head down,' she said, 'I'll get you a glass of water. Let me hold the baby for you.'

I clutched Belle closer. 'No,' I said. Now I was terrified that I had been lulled into letting my guard down.

She said nothing, just poured me a glass of water from the jug on the parlour table. She poured one for herself too and sipped. She moved back again to stand in front of the fireplace. I noticed that her hand was trembling.

I sat up straight and studied her face once more over the rim of my glass. I could see then how like my father she was – the same colouring, the same family nose. When my vision settled, I asked her: 'How did you know I was here?'

She took a deep breath and shook her head. 'Let's just say for the moment that it was coincidence. We'll have plenty of time to talk later on. We can share the whole story then.' And she looked at me. 'That's if you want to.' Her eyes were kind, filled with a compassion I had not seen since walking through the front door of St Brigid's.

'What do you mean?'

'I want to take you home with me . . . Maeve.' And she smiled. 'You and Belle. You can come and live with me and stay as long as you need. You're no sinner, no matter what they tell you here. You deserve to have a life. You don't have to give up your daughter.'

'What?' I stared at her. Was she even real? 'How do you know that?' And then: 'Are you sure?' My words were tripping over each other.

But I was filled with doubt. It couldn't be that easy just to walk away from St Brigid's, could it? Wouldn't somebody try to stop us? Wouldn't they send the guards after me to bring me back, the way they did when Georgina made a run for it?

I'll never forget her face. The way she crumpled, wailing, stumbling along between the two guards, her clothes creased and filthy.

'Am I really allowed to leave?'

'Yes,' Eileen said. 'You can walk out of here right now with me, with your daughter. Without a backward glance. You don't owe anybody a thing.'

And she lifted her head and looked straight at me. Her expression was proud. There was a kind of defiance to it that I had never before seen on an adult's face. On a child's, yes. And very occasionally, on one of the girls' at St Brigid's, even if it was a wordless kind of defiance. But I'd never seen challenge like this, carved into the bones of a grown woman's face.

I stood up. I still wasn't sure of what she was offering me, but anything was better than St Brigid's. We'd take our chances with this woman, Belle and me. Once I got on my feet, then we'd see about what to do next. Little by little.

I learned afterwards about the many times Eileen had come to get me, about how long she'd fought to see me. She didn't stop until her presence brought me down the stairs at last and along that polished corridor.

I thought above all of Monaghan Joanie. She'd come to me so many times when she needed a bit of comfort. And I thought, too, about Grace and Georgina. About all the others. About leaving them behind me in that place, and I almost weakened. Then Belle woke up and looked at me. In the clear blue of her eyes, I found the answer I was looking for. There was nothing else to be done.

'I'm ready,' I said.

'Do you want to collect your things?' she asked. 'I'll wait here for you. You'll be safe. Don't worry.'

One part of me wanted to run out the door, right now, stripping away every single memory of St Brigid's as I ran. The other part remembered the doll I'd almost finished making for Belle. I was proud of that doll: the way it came to life under my fingers; the way the other girls praised the neatness of my stitches, the cleverness of my design. All of these things became part of my very own Raggedy Ann, part of her cobbled-together fabric. There was too much stitched into that doll to abandon it here, to St Brigid's. I hesitated.

'Go,' my visitor said. 'I'll be waiting. You've nothing to be frightened of. Not anymore.'

I hurried up the stairs. Belle began to whimper against me. 'Ssshhh,' I whispered. 'I'm taking you home.' A sudden sense of possibility took hold of me as I said the word.

Home!

None of the other girls was around. They were all in the kitchens, or the laundry. Or away polishing floors somewhere. I pulled my holdall out from under the bed. I gathered my clothes together, my knitting, my sewing kit, my Raggedy Ann. I pushed everything into the depths of the bag. I hesitated over the pyjama-sling for a moment. Then I remembered how useful it was, particularly at night, and I stuffed it in, too.

When I made my way back down to the parlour, the empty silence was quickly becoming my last memory of that place.

Eileen was still there. She smiled at me as I opened the door. 'Ready?' she said. 'Here, give me your bag. You take care of Belle.'

I handed over the holdall.

At that moment, the parlour door opened. Sister Fidelma was standing there, her hands folded in front of her. She looked sterner than ever, her whole body taller, stiffer.

Before she could say anything, Eileen turned to face her.

'What?' she snapped.

I was startled. I'd never heard anyone address one of the nuns like that.

Sister Fidelma looked taken aback, too. I watched as she seemed to gather herself back together again. 'Before you leave,' she said, coldly, 'there is the matter of the outstanding…'

Eileen took a step towards her. 'There is nothing outstanding here,' she said. Her voice was quiet, controlled, but it was as though a river of rage was underneath her words, keeping them flowing freely, keeping them steady. 'I will pay you nothing. This girl owes you nothing. Not one young woman here owes you a thing.' And she turned back to face me.

'This holdall feels very light,' she said, calmly. 'Are you sure you have everything? Isn't there anything else you need to take with you?'

'No,' I shook my head. I glanced over at Sister Fidelma. We used to call her Fido, behind her back: the name you'd give a dog. It made us giggle, that small act of rebellion. Remembering it now made me want to laugh out loud.

I turned my whole body back towards Eileen. 'No, I don't want anything else from here. Not one thing.' I held Belle even closer. 'We're ready.'

Eileen nodded. 'All right, then. Follow me.'

I walked after her, down the steps, onto the gravel and over to the waiting car. I was frightened: something terrible was about to happen. I was terrified that someone would swoop down on us from above; that they'd snatch Belle from my arms; or at least they'd try to stop us from leaving. I felt Fido's eyes burn into the back of my neck.

But nothing happened.

It was only when I sat into the back seat of Eileen's car that I began to tremble.

16

Betty, Summer 2019

When I made the green dress for Tess, that Singer was the second sewing-machine you'd bought for me. We left the first one behind us in the flat in Kilburn, when Tess was a year old.

Do you remember that poor girl, Jack? Eileen, her name was – no more than a child herself, really. She lived on the third floor, and I met her on the stairs one day. She helped me carry Tess and the pram down to the hallway. The lift was broken again.

'You're Irish!' she exclaimed, after I thanked her for taking hold of the two back wheels, and most of the weight as well. She stopped then at the top of the flight of stairs, even before we got going, and looked at me in delight.

All I'd said was 'thank you' – but she'd caught the lilt anyway. It's funny, I'd become attuned to accents as well, in those days. They brought with them an echo of everything familiar. Eileen and I reminded each other of all that we missed.

Soon after we'd met on the stairs, I invited her into the flat for tea and barm brack. It was the end of October, almost Halloween. I'd felt the need to bake something that reminded me of home.

She and I became friends. We spent a lot of evenings together, when you were working. We even kept the spare key to each other's flat. We knew we could call on one another in times of emergency, or for a favour, or out of plain old loneliness.

Over tea and buttered brack that first time, she told me of the little boy that she'd had to give away. Her story didn't surprise me. As I boiled the kettle and made tea and listened to her chat, I'd been watching the way she looked at Tess. There was a hunger in her eyes that I recognised.

She'd called her son Cillian. Her family disowned her when they discovered she was pregnant. Her boyfriend didn't want to know, so she took the boat to England, like so many others. She got a job in the Schweppes factory in West Hendon – the same place where you were working before I followed you to Kilburn in 1959. Another one of those funny coincidences.

She told me that after her baby was born, she couldn't manage it all – the job, the child, the money. She'd asked her family for help. But they refused. They told her she'd made her bed; they wanted nothing to do with her.

'I kept hoping they'd be kind, that they'd change their mind once they saw photographs of their grandson,' she said. 'They surprised me; they really did. Particularly my brother. We used to be close, and I thought he was better than that.'

So she had no choice. She gave Cillian up for adoption. She cried when she told me what her parents had said to her: that she could never be a good enough mother. That she could never give her son what a proper family could. That she had sinned, and this was her repentance. She'd caved in when she no longer had the strength to fight them.

I was conscious of our Tess fast asleep in her cot in the second bedroom. Every time I was with Eileen, I thought about how you had stood by me, that I had a ring on my finger, that nobody had cut me off for bringing shame to my family. Everyone got over our quiet wedding in Quex Road church, as well. They forgave us eventually. And once we took Tess home, all of it was forgotten, just as you said it would be.

I still remember Schweppes, Jack: the name picked out in big, bright red letters against the high, white wall. And the fountain outside. I'll never forget my first sight of it. There was that delicious smell, too, as soon as you'd get off the bus. I never liked the Underground, but I used to take our Tess on the bus the odd time, to meet you after work. I remember the way the air would be filled with the sweet smell of strawberries, or sometimes, cream soda.

We took Tess there together at Christmastime to see the huge tree outside the factory walls with all the twinkling lights. She was mesmerised. They were good enough days, Jack, despite everything. Just half an hour for you on the Northern Line from Kilburn High Road; good money, good conditions. And the English foreman didn't care where you came from, as long as you did your job.

Still. I couldn't ever manage to make myself feel at home there. It was all too different. I was glad when we'd saved enough to go back to Dublin. By the time we did, I no longer cared whether anybody remembered, or suspected, the reason I'd left.

These days, I've been thinking about all the cruel details of Eileen's story. We used to talk about it during the months we lived in Springfield Lane. It must have been painful for her, watching me with Tess. I was living the life that might have been hers.

Eileen was a dab hand at the sewing, and I taught her how to make patchwork quilts. The day we were leaving, I let myself into her flat with my bags of remnants. I'd yards of stuff I'd bought at markets all over London, but mostly at Camden. There was one stall I really liked, run by a lovely young Indian woman. When I got to know her over the weeks and months, she saved offcuts for me. Some studded with beads, some with tiny mirrors attached, others with sequins.

And the colours! I can still see the rainbow of shades – from red to purple to burgundy; from lovat green to jade; from kingfisher to cornflower to midnight blue. While Eileen was at work that day, our last day in London, I spread those pieces of fabric on her bed – dozens of squares of cotton and silk. The whole room was transformed. The tiny mirrors sparkled. The walls and ceiling of that grim flat all shimmered together, like a floating, light-filled skin on the surface of the sea.

I never said anything when I saw Eileen keep the children's quilts she made. I watched her fold them into tissue paper and place them in a holdall she kept at the side of the sofa. I knew she was holding on to them in the hope she'd get her son back.

I hadn't wanted to part with my Singer, but you said we'd never manage it on the mailboat, along with Tess, the pram and all our luggage. I only agreed once you promised to buy me another, once we got home.

Seeing Eileen's face on the evening before we left, when she walked into her bedroom and saw what I'd done, I was glad you'd encouraged me to be generous. She was so grateful. You were a good man, Jack. I still miss you.

I hadn't thought of those days in London in a long time. Now, though, since you've been gone, I think of nothing but the past. It's not a sad remembering – more a nostalgic one.

I'm liking the way the memory loops draw me in, each one connecting with the other like a slow, careful backstitch so that everything that happened then and everything that happens now draws closer and closer together.

It's like there's no separation between the past and the present, no real dividing line. In a way, the past has rooted itself inside me, insisting that I pay it proper attention, no matter how much I try to focus on today.

And I never let myself think about tomorrow.

I don't want to tempt fate.

17

Tess, Summer 2019

*Y*ou've been right about Luke before.

Mike's words make the memory begin to unpleat itself. As she waits for him to arrive home, the stuff of Tess's memory spreads itself out before her.

She pushes open the door to Luke's room and calls out his name. She's crept quietly up the stairs so that he'll have no warning of her arrival. This time, she wants to be the one with the advantage of surprise.

There's no answer and she hasn't expected one. Luke has been giving everyone the silent treatment ever since he was grounded.

'I need to speak to you, Luke,' she says now as she steps into his bedroom. 'And I need you to speak to me. You can't stay silent forever.'

To her surprise, the curtains are open. Sunlight streams in through the open window, blinding her for a few seconds. For several days now, Luke's chosen surroundings have been dark, airless, closed off from the outside world as well as from the rest of the house. Closed, but not locked. Tess had confiscated the key to his bedroom, once what had happened last week, happened.

When her eyes adjust, she sees that Luke is not lying on his bed, tapping something into his phone, ignoring her. Nor is he hunched over his laptop, sitting at the desk to her right, ignoring her.

Instead, she sees a chair by the window. The net curtain is blowing towards her, billowing outwards with the airy news of his escape. She understands what has happened even before she thinks it.

'Jesus *Christ*,' she says now, running towards the window. But the stillness in the room tells her that Luke is long gone. There is not even the shadow of his presence. It frightens her: this feeling that Luke has never really been here. Or if he has, that he has only ghosted his way through this family; that he belongs somewhere else.

Quickly, Tess leans out the window and scans the back gardens in either direction. Nothing. She runs downstairs, pulls her mobile out of her handbag. She calls Mike.

'I don't know when,' she says. 'He was there before lunch. There's no sign of him now . . . No, there's no point in you rushing home. I just wanted you to know. Yes, yes, of course I'll call you if he turns up.'

Tears well: of anger, frustration, disappointment. 'Jesus, Luke, what am I going to do with you?' she says out loud to the empty hallway.

*

She'd asked him that same question the previous week, too, as he sat sullenly in front of her at the kitchen table. On its surface she'd placed the old-fashioned blue and yellow metal box, the tobacco box that had once belonged to her father. Luke's face darkened. 'What were you doing in my room?' His words were tight, his jaw clenched.

'You think *that's* the question we should be asking here?'

Tess leaned down, her face deliberately close to his. Let him feel the anger. He flinched, pulled back, looked away from her.

'But in case you really do need to know, I'll tell you. I went in to pick up your school uniform off the floor so that you don't make a show of yourself at the end of term in a couple of days' time.'

She saw herself, bending down to gather up Luke's trousers. As she did so, something fell out of one of the pockets. A small Ziploc bag. It was crammed with pills. Twenty, thirty, maybe more: yellow triangles with some brand name stamped on them, a logo she recognised but couldn't place. The warm day grew chill around her.

She searched the other pocket. It was empty. She glanced around the room. Luke had never been tidy. He was careless with his things, but she suspected he might be careful about this.

I can't pretend it isn't happening, she thought. She could hear Betty's voice in her head, a long-ago memory of one of the many noisy, furious rows she used to have with Myles and Conor.

'I don't care about your "rights",' she'd say, angrily, as she emerged from their bedroom with more evidence of their shoplifting. 'Safety is my only concern. Yours, and the safety of this family.'

Tess crossed the room quickly now. She pulled open the top drawer of the wardrobe, shoving the socks and underwear to one side. The drawer was littered with neat, glossy rectangles. As though someone had cut up the pages of a magazine into carefully sized packages, folding the paper over and over, like some kind of ironic origami.

Her fingers fumbled as she unfolded one of them. White powder gleamed up at her.

She pushed the drawer shut, opened the next one. In the middle of a pile of tee-shirts, she saw her father's box. 'Mayo's Tobacco Is Always Good': the yellow centre to the blue metal box was as vivid as ever. She opened it. It was crammed with Ziploc bags.

She remembered the day her father had gifted the tobacco box to Luke, when he was still a small child. The way he had managed to admire it every time they visited, until he got what he wanted.

As Tess stood in Luke's room that morning, anger came: a physical blow to her chest. She picked up the box, closed the drawer. She scooped up all the rectangles of laminated paper and took them with her into her bedroom. Her throat felt as though it had filled with grit.

And Mike wasn't here. He was off somewhere in the vastness of Silicon Valley, absorbed by a whole other life. He was so far away from her right then that his absence had the clarity of truth. Tess felt that he was no longer real.

But this was. This tobacco box was real. So were its contents. And she had no idea what she was going to do next.

*

Later that same night, Luke was sitting across from her at the kitchen table. He refused to meet her eye. He turned his head and stared out the window instead.

'Look at me, Luke!' she shouted.

Startled, he turned back to face her. She rarely shouted at him, not these days. 'And when I picked up your trousers, these fell out.'

She slammed the bag of pills onto the table in front of him, narrowly missing his hands.

'And then,' she continued, keeping her voice steady, 'I didn't have to look too far before I came across these.' She shoved her father's tobacco box towards him, scattered the shiny rectangles across the kitchen table.

Luke was starting to say something. His anger began to rise. She could see the flush of heat on his jawline. Good. A reaction at last. That was all she wanted. Some thread of connection that she could tug on to call him back, to bring him safely home.

But in the end, he stayed silent.

Tess went on the attack. Hoping she wouldn't get it wrong. 'And before you start giving me any shit about the privacy you might feel yourself entitled to, imagine what *I* feel entitled to as the *owner* of this house?'

He looked at her, steadily. This time, he did not flinch.

'You're *seventeen*, Luke. Have you any idea what this could do to your life? Not only taking it – getting *caught* with it?'

She picked up one of the Ziploc bags, waved it in his face. Now she was desperate. 'What the *fuck* do you think you're doing, dealing this stuff?'

For a second, she saw something like fear cross his face. A shadow, a fleeting one, but it was something. She felt a flicker of hope. This was more of a response than she'd had in years. If she could push just a bit harder.

At that same moment, the kitchen door opened. Aengus's face appeared, looking white, bewildered. Oh for Christ's sake, she thought, of all the times. He opened his mouth to say something, and she snapped at him, in a fury.

'Not *now*, Aengus. Luke and I are in the middle of something. Go away and shut the door.'

When she turned back, she saw Luke smirk. His expression had returned to normal. He was his usual nonchalant self. As though he'd just got one over on his brother. As though he'd just got one over on her.

Tess lost it. Without thinking, she slapped him hard, her hand connecting with greater force than she'd intended. Horrified, she took a step back from him. Then she burst into tears.

'What are you doing, Luke?' she cried. 'What are you doing to yourself, to us?'

He stood up from the table. With a shock, she saw the imprint of her hand, visible across his cheek. He turned his face away from her.

'I don't fucking care,' he said, shrugging. 'And it's none of your business, anyway. I'm nearly eighteen. I'll be outta here as soon as I can.'

And then he left the room.

*

Afterwards – but there never was an 'afterwards' with Luke. There was no uneasy reconciliation, or apology, or half-hearted explanations. Things just reverted to how they had been beforehand: silent, sullen.

Mike quizzed him, of course, when he got back, about a week later. Too late, Tess thought, bitterly. The heat had gone out of it all by then. At least for Luke.

Mike had looked at her in despair. 'What do you want me to do, Tess? I have to earn a living, and this is how I earn it. Brexit is a looming shitstorm, and we're up to our necks in it, trying to salvage something.'

'I know,' she said. 'I know.' She'd tried to compose herself. 'But this is hard, Mike. I didn't sign up to doing this stuff all on my own. It's too much.' She bit her lip, turned away from him. What she didn't say lingered in the air between them.

You're never here when I need you.

He looked at her. There was a sadness to his face that was new. He sighed. 'I'll go up and talk to Luke now.'

'Okay,' she said. 'Just don't let him do a snow job on you.'

Mike checked whatever response he'd been about to make. Then he left the room, closing the door quietly behind him. When he came back downstairs afterwards, he wondered aloud to Tess whether, you know, maybe, Luke really *was* minding the stuff for a friend?

'Bullshit,' she said.

Mike looked off into the distance. His eyes were troubled. 'I'm not sure I believe him either, but I got nowhere, no matter what I said to him.' He hesitated. 'We don't want to alienate him even further.' Then, quietly, not looking at her: 'He feels very humiliated that you struck him like that.'

Tess looked at him in astonishment. 'What?' she said. 'Wait – Mike – he's playing you. He's pitting each of us against the other.'

He didn't answer.

'Now he's made this about *me*, rather than about *him*, about what he's done. Mike, he's dealing. He's seventeen. What would have happened if he'd been caught?'

Mike still wouldn't meet her eye. 'We have to try to find some way of handling it so that we don't lose him.'

'What we have to do is have a united front,' she said, forcing herself to speak quietly. 'Can't you see that?'

He sat down, heavily. He hunched forward, elbows on his knees. This is what fights about Luke always do to us, she thought. They push us further apart every time.

'This isn't just one thing . . .' she began.

Mike interrupted her. 'What?' he said. 'What else do I not know?' A surge of anger made his face tight, closed.

The suddenness of it took Tess aback. 'I'm not keeping anything from you, if that's what you mean. I just have this awful feeling—'

Mike didn't let her finish. 'He's a teenager. Teenagers do stuff, hide stuff, get up to all sorts.' He ran one agitated hand through his hair. He stood with his back to the fireplace, stuck his hands in his pockets, glared at her. 'How many stories have you told me about your own brothers, about Myles and Conor? For Christ's sake, stop getting this out of proportion.'

She heard the steel in his voice. 'What if he'd been caught?' she asked again.

'Well, he wasn't,' he snapped. 'And I'm sure that Aengus got up to things we don't know about. You're too anxious around Luke. You hover over him, all the time.' He stopped.

'So this is my fault?'

'Don't put words in my mouth.' He shook his head at her. 'But you always think the worst of him.' He looked down at the floor. 'I don't want to repeat my own father's mistakes.'

Tess didn't answer. It always came back to this. She took a moment and then, quietly, she said: 'He's getting harder to deal with all the time, Mike. He keeps pushing things. It's not just this one . . . event. It's that I feel him pulling away, becoming someone I don't like.'

She stopped, shocked. She had never said that out loud before. 'I love him, of course I do,' she said quickly. 'I'd lie down and die for him. I'm his mother. But I don't like the person he's turning into. I'm not able to handle him. He's selfish. Cruel, even. He likes it when he hurts me.'

Mike sighed. 'You're looking at things through the wrong end of the telescope. I think you expect him to be like Aengus. Well, he's not. And we should really stop wishing that he was.'

We?

Mike's face suddenly sagged. She felt the old familiar ache of tenderness. She went to him, took one of his hands in hers. 'Mike, love, you're freezing,' she said.

He didn't seem to hear her. 'I'm terrified, Tess. Of pushing him so far away from us that we'll never get him back.'

She thought it was already too late. That Luke had long since abandoned them. Not the other way round.

Tess wished she could talk to her mother. Betty would know what to do.

*

The room grows darker, but Tess doesn't bother switching on the lights. Mike will arrive home from the airport soon. Then it will really begin: the rest of their lives. Maybe until that happens, she can pretend that it is still possible for them to be an ordinary, unremarkable family. That life can continue in all its messy possibilities. A life in which it still matters to pull across the curtains, switch on the lights, boil the kettle.

In the meantime, she'll sit and count her new fears. Among them, old ones stir. They begin to reappear, stealthily, one by one. They make their way to the surface from that part of her she thought she had silenced, all those years ago.

The part that knew, the part of her that had always known at some visceral level, that she never wanted to be a mother.

Part Two

SUMMER *2019*

I find myself at the railings of Ice House Hill Park. I used to come here a lot when I was a kid. But the gate is closed; of course it is. Part of me knows that I shouldn't be wandering around the city like this at two a.m.; part of me doesn't care. I've followed a strangely compelling need: to sit by the pond, to listen to the water, to stand on the grass in my bare feet. To be five again.

I hear a noise behind me. I turn, my heart instantly pounding. It's an elderly man, walking an elderly Labrador. Both of them shuffle along, arthritic. The man nods in my direction.

G'night, he says. And then, as the dog stops and cocks one leg: Are ye a wee bit lost?

No, I say. I'm on my way home. I just wanted to sit by the lake.

He seems to consider that for a moment. Then he looks right at me, his eyes pale blue and watery. The Labrador gazes at me, too. For a mad moment, I feel like laughing. These two even look like each other.

Dear girl, the man says at last, away home wi' ye now. Don't go lookin' for trouble.

That makes me angry. I almost snap: Too late; it's already found me. But I'm suddenly not able to say anything at all, so I half-raise my hand in farewell as I walk away.

Take care o' yersel', he calls.

*

The house is in darkness. I let myself in and climb the stairs, knowing what creaky treads to avoid. I manage to get into my own room without waking anyone. I kick off my shoes and, still fully dressed, I climb under the duvet and allow the weight of exhaustion to overwhelm me. All I want is oblivion.

*

I wake around five. It's already light. I make my way to the shower and stand under the hottest water I can bear and I scrub and I scrub and I scrub, punishing my skin, stripping away the shame.

I pull on leggings, trainers, a baggy tee-shirt and I race downstairs, ignoring the voice that now calls my name, slamming the front door behind me.

And then I run. The city streets are still Saturday-morning quiet.

I run until I can no longer breathe. I run until I am soaked in sweat. I run until finally, the memory-loop starts over and I can smell his smell; see him again; feel his hands, feel his weight; and then I break.

18

Tess, Summer 2019

Tess leaps to her feet as soon as she hears a key in the front door. She stumbles on her way to the hall. Everything around her seems to be shifting, changing.

Old photographs, showing a life that now belongs to someone else; a careless pair of trainers in one corner of the room; a plate with a discarded half-slice of old toast. They should all be familiar, ordinary: but it's as though she has never seen them before. Fear is the only thing that's keeping her upright.

'Luke?'

She steps into the hallway just as Mike dumps his case on the floor and throws his coat over it. 'Mike, oh Mike.'

She puts her arms around him and he pulls her close. Finally, he steps back. He looks as though he's aged. His eyes are bloodshot and the skin beneath them is painfully transparent, etched in thin grey lines. Tess can see her own fears in the way he's looking at her.

'Any news?'

'Nothing. I'm really scared, Mike. I've got a bad feeling about this.'

'Let's go inside and sit down. Tell me exactly what happened.'

She starts over, telling him unimportant details this time: the sergeant's comb-over. The detective's calm, almost morose way of speaking.

Finally, Mike interrupts her. 'I managed to get a hold of Matthew again for a couple of minutes earlier this evening. Just after you and I spoke. He said he'd call us back at ten o'clock.' He glances at his watch.

'What else did he say?'

'That he'd go straight to Clontarf Garda Station to represent Luke and would fill us in just as soon as he could. I've left him a couple of messages. But there's nothing yet. We just have to sit tight, Tess. That's all we can do.'

*

When Matthew Kerr calls, Mike puts him on speakerphone. 'They've released Luke, but it's not over, Mike. They want to interview him again. I'll represent him, if you still want me to, although this isn't exactly my area.'

'What area are we talking about?'

Mike gives Tess a look. Her question has had a sharpness to it that she hasn't intended.

There is a pause. 'Hasn't Luke been in touch?'

'No, not yet. Tell us, please. What's going on?'

Mike's hand creeps up to the back of his neck. For a moment, Tess feels almost sorry for Matthew Kerr, a man she has never met. What must it be like, she wonders, to be so often the bearer of bad news?

'Luke's been accused of sexual assault. A young woman has named him and one other person. Something that allegedly happened last Friday night.'

Tess grows cold. She sees, all over again, Luke's face as the guards are taking him away. She sees Aengus standing in the kitchen, not looking at her. She hears his words that Luke may have done 'something really bad this time'.

'What kind of sexual assault? I mean, specifically?' She does her best to keep her voice neutral. It's not Matthew's fault, after all.

'That's not clear, just yet. That's why there will have to be another interview, sometime in the next couple of days. It's not helpful to speculate right now.'

Helpful to whom, she wonders. His reticence irritates her but the expression on Mike's face is enough. She says nothing.

'So, talk us through what's likely to happen, Matt,' he says.

'One step at a time. The next interview will be a formal one. I'll get in touch with the guards first thing in the morning and I should know more after that. Try to get Luke to talk to you whenever he gets home.'

'Is there anything else we can do, anything we should do, in the meantime?'

'Not a thing, apart from that. It would be helpful to know Luke's version of events. I'll be back to you as soon as I can.'

'Okay, Matt, thanks for the call. We'll talk again tomorrow. Did Luke say anything to you afterwards?'

'No, he didn't. He said very little, full stop: apart from denying the accusation. He said he was there, all right, at the party, but that he had done nothing wrong. I offered him a lift home but either he didn't hear me or he didn't want to take me up on it. He was out the door of the station like a shot.'

Yes, Tess thinks, that sounds just like Luke.

'We'll let you know when he gets here. And we'll try and get him to talk to us.' Mike gestures to Tess, urging her to say something.

'Thank you, Matthew.' She is not reassured. 'Thank you for your help.'

'No problem. Talk to you soon.'

She calls Luke's mobile. It goes straight to voicemail again. She leaves another message, forcing herself to sound calm, motherly. 'Luke,' she says. 'Please call us. We're worried. Whatever it is, we love you and we'll figure this out together. Just come home to us.' She breaks on the last word.

Then she turns to Mike. 'What does Matthew Kerr mean, "not his area"? If he's not an expert, then do we need somebody who is?'

Mike's mouth is set in a thin, grim line. His hands clutch each other, fingers intertwined. She sees the taut whiteness of his knuckles. He doesn't know what to do, either, she thinks, with a suddenness that takes her breath away. Of course he doesn't, he's just as much at sea as I am.

And then she begins to wonder. What do the words 'sexual assault' mean, legally? What's going to happen to Luke? And finally, ashamed, because it hasn't been her first thought: Has their son really hurt some unfortunate young girl?

She says none of this aloud. No matter what he has done, Luke will need them in his corner. 'Should one of us go and look for him?' she asks at last. Her voice sounds steadier than she feels.

Mike shakes his head. 'No, I don't think so,' he says. 'I think we should wait.'

'And if he doesn't come home?'

'We'll give him another hour or so. Then we'll decide.'

Mike opens his laptop and Tess gives him the list of the sites she's already looked up earlier that evening. She suddenly doesn't want to be in the room while he searches. 'Do you want something to eat? There's some casserole left over from last night.'

'Yeah, that'd be good, thanks.'

He takes her hand as she's about to leave. 'We'll get through this. Just because Luke's been accused of something doesn't mean he's guilty.'

19

Maeve, 1979

The last time I'd been in a car was with my father on that silent journey to St Brigid's. I cried and he kept acting as if I wasn't there.

Now, with Eileen, with Belle, I had to figure myself out all over again. I wasn't sure who I was, the mother-me who sat in the back seat with a baby in her arms. Already, St Brigid's was beginning to feel like a dream filled with noise and confusion. It was becoming someone else's story, not mine.

As we drove away from that place, I thought about one of those endless tales from the Bible that we'd had to listen to most evenings before bedtime. The one about Lot's wife being turned into a pillar of salt. It was supposed to teach us about obedience: Lot's wife was punished by God because she didn't do as she was told.

But what made the deepest impression on me was how Lot behaved. When the evil men of Sodom came to take away the two strangers who had visited his home, Lot offered them his own daughters instead.

My head shot up from the text. 'He was going to sacrifice his two *daughters* to the men of Sodom?' I said. 'His own *daughters* instead of two men he didn't even know?'

Sr Fidelma was taken aback at the challenge. She turned to look at me and the light glinted off the thick lenses of her glasses. 'It was the lesser of two evils,' she said. But she looked uncertain. As though she'd never thought of it like that before.

'Not for the girls it wasn't,' I said. I felt my fury grow. 'It wasn't any the less evil for them.'

Georgina's elbow dug into my side. 'Why salt, Sister?' she said. 'Why was Lot's wife changed into a pillar of salt?'

There was more I wanted to ask: how come Lot's wife isn't even given her name in the story? How come she's the only one to be punished? But I didn't. I stayed quiet because Georgina's question had got us onto safer territory.

The further Eileen drove us from St Brigid's, the more settled I became. I didn't know what lay ahead and I decided not to care anymore. The motion of the car soothed my little daughter, and eventually, it soothed me, too, and we slept.

*

It was almost eight o'clock in the evening when we pulled into a small side street, on the southern edge of Dundalk. Eileen turned around to face me. 'Welcome to Willow Grove,' she said, smiling. And then: 'Welcome home, both of you. Come on in. We'll get your stuff from the car later.'

I couldn't wait for her to open the car door so I did it myself, Belle tucked under one arm. I stumbled against the kerb in my hurry to see what coming home looked like. Eileen opened the front door of the house and we stepped inside together.

'Give me a minute,' she said, 'and I'll put on the lights.'

I waited in the hallway. After months of cold, cold rooms, the speckled green lino of the dorms, the brownish walls of that place we'd left behind us earlier in the day, I was afraid. I had a stark memory of my parents' kitchen on the evening I told them about Belle. I saw the dull tiles, the functional chairs, the absence of cheer everywhere. All those drab surfaces.

When the lights came on, I saw how different this home was. Slowly, I took in the warmth of it all. The paintings, the rugs, the gleaming ceramic lamps. There were no dark corners here. I didn't know what to say. Or I did – at least, I knew what I should say – but I wasn't able to speak.

'Let me show you to your bedroom, first. Then we'll have something to eat in the kitchen. You must be starving.'

I wasn't. Besides, I didn't trust the lump that had taken over my throat. I wouldn't be able to fit anything around it. So I said nothing. I just clutched Belle to me all the more tightly.

'This way, Maeve.'

I followed Eileen up the stairs and she opened the second door on the left. I'll never forget my first impressions of that room: all that clarity and calmness. I saw a large window, with the gently moving shadows of trees outside. I saw a wardrobe, painted blue: blue! Just imagine! All of its panels were sprinkled with tiny red, lacquered flowers. A dressing table with three mirrors. A bed, with a riotous patchwork quilt, filled with the colours of autumn.

It was when I saw the Moses basket with its tiny matching quilt that I broke. The shimmering bees and dragonflies pierced my heart. I kissed Belle's forehead over and over and sobbed in a way I hadn't done since my earliest days in St Brigid's, when I hid under the blankets, my face pressed into the lumpy mattress. This wasn't real. It couldn't be real. Something would wake me up in a minute and the shadows of that place would close in on me, all over again.

Eileen put her arms around both of us. Belle whimpered but didn't wake. It was strange, the way she'd been so quiet in the car, not at all her usual restless self. Maybe the motion of the journey had soothed her, but I like to think that she knew we were on our way to somewhere better, together.

Eileen held both of us, Belle and me, until I'd finished sobbing, until I could finally trust the ground beneath my feet again.

'How can I thank you?' I managed at last.

'You don't need to,' she said. 'This is nothing more than you deserve.' She looked at me, in that steady way she had. 'Do this for somebody else, one day, that's all. Someone in need of a bit of kindness. Just pass it on.'

She stepped away from me. 'And now I'm going downstairs to make dinner. We'll get you sorted tomorrow with clothes and whatever else you need. In the meantime,' – she reached over to the dressing table and picked up something from a small glass dish – 'you might want to wear this.'

I looked at her, not understanding.

'It's a wedding ring,' she said. 'It's up to you, but it might be a good idea.'

'But . . . but . . . I don't . . . I don't have a husband,' I stammered.

'He's dead,' she said, bluntly. 'You're my widowed niece and you have nobody else in the world. We'll figure out your story together, later on. But that's why you've come here to live with me.'

I could feel my life taking flight. A bright new map was spreading out before me. 'I can change my name,' I said. 'I mean, properly change it – both names. Become a whole other person.'

Eileen looked at me for a moment. Her face was sad. 'I think you've had to do that already,' she said. 'But yes. You can.' She paused. 'I know you're a fighter, Maeve. And you can change your name either way. Take your time to decide about wearing the ring.'

I took it from her and slipped it onto my ring finger. As I did so, I remembered the glint of the nuns' silver bands. Brides of Christ.

It was a perfect fit. 'I'm a bit tired right now of fighting,' I said. 'And of feeling ashamed. And this might make things easier for Belle, too, mightn't it?'

She squeezed my hand. 'Yes. This is not a forgiving country, Maeve. Not for so-called "illegitimate children", and certainly not for "fallen women".'

It was a phrase I'd heard before. Father Farrell had used it often enough, on the days he'd visited St Brigid's. Fallen from what? It had always puzzled me. But it was clear from what he said that whatever heights we'd fallen from, it was all our fault.

'Why are we the ones to have fallen?' I asked. 'We did nothing wrong.'

'Keep that fighting spirit in your back pocket,' Eileen said. 'You may need it again.'

20

Betty, Summer 2019

I've been two years without you, Jack, and if you told me it was two centuries I'd been on my own, or two months, I'd believe you.

The other day, I caught sight of myself in the dressing-table mirror and was brought to a halt, stunned at what I saw. That face: wrinkled, slack, surrounded by grey. Age spots dotted here and there, a generous sprinkling of fading freckles. The eyes were still mine, though, and I was glad of that. Because inside, I feel much the same as I did when I was young.

I hate the amount of 'olding' that goes on in the world. It makes me angry. The way some people, in their own lazy way, continue to match age with invisibility, or stupidity, or lack of energy. Not physical energy, of course – that does change. But the inner energy: I think that might burn even more brightly now, the older I get.

And as for stupidity. Well, that's got nothing to do with age. The things I've seen.

Anyway, I listened to someone on the radio yesterday morning talking about the modern craze for 'upcycling'. Except that it isn't modern at all: we spent our lives doing it, you and me – but we just called it 'make do and mend'. Nonetheless, it got me thinking about all the old belongings I have around me, including things that used to be yours.

Don't worry: I did as you asked. Aengus has your watch. And I gave Luke your father's magnifying glass. I think he was surprised. I certainly was – surprised at how he reacted. His eyes filled and he turned away from me. I went to say something to him, to call him back, but Aengus put his arms around me just then and whispered 'Thanks, Gran. I promise I'll always look after Granda's watch.'

When I looked around for Luke, he was gone.

Tess told me afterwards that they were each glad to have something belonging to you. I said that your wishes had been very clear: the boys should have something tangible of yours, something you yourself had used or worn. *Memento mori*, you used to say. Then Tess and I looked at each other and had a little weep. Just a little one, Jack – I well remember what I promised you. But still. Then Tess put on the kettle and we had tea.

So, after the radio programme yesterday, I decided that it was time to give your clothes away to the charity shops, so that some poor soul might get a turn out of your jackets and coats. Winter's coming and this city can be cold and unforgiving.

So many homeless people everywhere these days. Sitting on concrete pavements, begging. Huddling in doorways, trying to shelter from the rain. And I see too many in sleeping bags, lying on layers of cardboard to keep out the cold. Or else, there are whole families staying in some hotel or other. Mothers and fathers and toddlers and teenagers crammed into one room with all their belongings.

In anybody's language, it is nothing short of criminal. Those in charge should be ashamed of themselves because something in this country has changed, and not for the better.

We weren't well off, Jack, but we were always able to keep a roof over our children's heads.

*

Once I started poking about in the cupboards, I came across so many things I'd forgotten – bits and pieces that came with us from our old house, things I wasn't ready to let go of back then. You told me, more than once, that I shouldn't cling to the past.

But that's not it. It's as if I keep coming across random bits and pieces of furniture in the wrong place: I keep banging my shin against them. It feels important to rearrange them, to find somewhere to put them so they won't be in my way.

At the bottom of your wardrobe, I discovered an old Afternoon Tea biscuit tin. I hadn't thought about it in years, but I recognised it at once. I took it with me to the kitchen and put on the kettle. This couldn't be managed without a sit-down and a cup of strong tea.

When I took off the lid, there was a smell of cold dust and old paper, but everything inside was perfect. As well as certificates and guarantees for stuff long bought and long gone, there were random bits and pieces that filled me with unexpected delight.

A picture, painted by Eleanor. Faded and crackling, to be sure, but I remember well the day she gave it to me, her fingers stained with poster paints. 'I Love You Mam' in shaky letters with a big, colourful rainbow above them. That brought the tears to my eyes.

There was an old envelope, too – one of the sort we used to dread. If there's a window on it, you used to say, there's nothin' good inside. But this time, there was: I could see the shade of the satin ribbon through the cellophane.

Still bright green, as though I'd put it away yesterday. It made me think of the dress I'd made for Tess, as a thank you for looking out for Eleanor, for protecting her from the neighbourhood bullies when I couldn't. I must give that ribbon back to Tess. I think she'd like to have it.

There was a key ring in the biscuit tin, as well, with a big brass 'B' for Betty. I don't remember which one of them gave it to me. Probably Eoghan. He always was a thoughtful child, sensitive.

He thought I didn't know, but of course I did, I always knew. You and I both knew, although you didn't want to talk about it. I knew you couldn't accept it, not that. It was a bridge too far. I didn't argue with you. I just wish Eoghan had felt able to tell me.

In the end, I told *him*, the day he left to go back to San Francisco after you. I told him what I knew, said I didn't care whose arms he had around him, man or woman's. I told him what I'd learned over the years: that love takes its own shape. I think I surprised him.

'I want you to be happy,' I said. 'That's all any mother wants. For her children to be happy.'

We were standing in the kitchen and he had me locked in this huge hug. I was glad to have had these quiet minutes with him before he left. And he said his partner, Paul, is a good man, that they live a rich, full life together. They plan to marry in 2020.

Why not here, I said, in Dublin? That way, I can be with you, we can all be with you. You can be a June bride: I'll even buy a hat! We laughed at that and I think he was pleased; I hope so. I thought you would like to know, Jack.

Seeing him and Eleanor again after so long did my heart good. She's happily single, just like Sheila. Her latest project is running support clubs in the evenings for disadvantaged children. Why does that not surprise me. She's quiet and contained but she has the heart of a lion. Both of them had only loving things to say about you.

It feels important to tell you all of this, before I forget. My memories are wandering all over the place, Jack. It's a mystery to me. These days, things that happened long ago become bigger, brighter, more rounded out, the further back they go. They have much more substance to them than anything recent.

I feel as if I'm in the middle of those moments, living them again. They come to me with their own colour, with shape and with sound, and they draw me in, as though I belong to them, and not the other way round.

The last thing I found in the biscuit tin was a tarnished silver bracelet, given to me by my best friend Margaret, when I was fifteen. I laughed out loud when I saw it. I could see the two of us, clear as day, back in the mid-fifties, with our forbidden lipstick and our eyeliner and our teased hair. I used to sneak into her bedroom to get ready to go out. Margaret's mother was a lot less eagle-eyed than mine.

Last night, just before I slept, as well as taking me back to my own fifteen-year-old self, that bracelet took me back to Tess at that age, and then to the sudden memory of her best friend, whose name is on the tip of my tongue. She and Tess were inseparable. Even their birthdays were within days of each other.

That young girl just disappeared one summer. We never saw her again, and her parents moved away from the neighbourhood soon afterwards.

I must ask Tess about her. Such a lovely girl, she was. She was with Tess the night of Conor's accident. Tess always envied her her long, straight, brown hair. I couldn't convince our daughter that she, Tess, was every bit as gorgeous. She wouldn't believe me, no matter what I said. You used to shake your head when you heard us talking about it.

Women, you'd say, yiz are never satisfied.

21

Eileen, 1960

I took to Betty straight away, the minute I heard her accent. I helped her carry the pram down the stairs in Springfield, one of the mornings when the lift didn't work. She was kind, like Majella. And Betty's husband, Jack, was a lovely, gentle man. A devoted father. Little Tess's face would light up every time he walked into the room.

He worked in Schweppes, too, but in the engineering department, not on the factory floor, so I hardly ever saw him during the day. But it was one of those coincidences that Betty and I enjoyed as we sat and sewed together in the evenings.

She was the first Irish person who knew about Cillian. Apart from the other girls at Maida Vale. Telling Betty was such a relief. She didn't judge me. And she was honest. But for Jack being Jack, she told me, she'd have found herself in the same predicament as me. She let me cry, made me tea, trusted me to mind Tess on a few occasions.

I remember, even at the time, feeling that she made up those appointments of hers, just so that I could enjoy time on my own with her little girl.

*

During those evenings with Betty, I started at last to look forward. I didn't try to bury the past, I could never do that, but I was able to see that there might be another life ahead of me, if I had the strength to choose it. I'd never stop looking for Cillian. Never. But in the meantime, I needed a plan. I needed to get out of London.

'Where will you go?'

We were sitting on the living-room floor, surrounded by multicoloured pieces of fabric. Betty had promised to show me how to make a quilt. Something inside me took flight at that offer: I'd always been good at sewing. Maybe this was something I could do to help heal the hurt; a new skill that might keep me busy until I was ready to go home.

'I'm thinking of Dundalk,' I said. 'I've never been, not even once.' My parents were wary, suspicious of the goings-on that they believed took place so close to the border. They'd heard tales of smuggling, of occasional outbreaks of violence, of lawlessness. Drogheda was as far north as they were prepared to travel. I knew I'd be safe from them in Dundalk.

'Majella knows a nurse there,' I told Betty, 'someone she looked after a few years back. She said she'd contact her and ask for her help.'

I was grateful, all over again, for Majella. We'd kept in touch, even after Cillian's adoption. There were times when I didn't know what I'd have done without her.

'What will you do when you get there?'

I hesitated. 'It's maybe a daft plan, and I've no idea if it would even be possible, but . . .' Betty herself had sown the seed. 'It's really more of a dream.'

'Go on,' she said, softly. 'You're anything but daft. You're clever and resilient and courageous. I really admire you.'

I looked at her in surprise. Her face had flushed a little. She reached over and took my hand. 'Look at what you've survived,' she said. 'You can do anything you set your mind to.'

I was warmed by her words. It was a long time since anybody had praised me. Even before Cillian, it was my brother Frank who made my parents proud – not me. Betty's words set free a surge of optimism and I began to speak, hurtling as fast as I could over the surface of the words, in case I lost the courage to say them.

'I want my own shop. I want to make quilts and children's clothes, with appliqué and embroidery and . . .' I stopped. What I really meant was, I wanted to make beautiful things. I didn't want to do any of the functional sewing that had been around me all my young life.

Hems being let down on coats. Dull, homemade cotton dresses for the summer. Clothes I had to 'grow into', swamped in shapelessness for a year or more, until I filled them. Drabness revolted me now. I dreamt of silk and merino, of cashmere and colour. I hungered for them.

'I think it's a wonderful idea,' Betty said. 'And you're so talented – a natural. Don't let all of that go to waste.'

Almost without my noticing it, talking to Betty in the evenings helped my plan to take shape. In London, every pram, every go-car made my heart lurch. The familiar streets were reminders of how often I'd walked them, filled with hope that I could do it. I could take care of my son, on my own. I could be a good enough mother.

The pull of home grew stronger.

Little by little, Majella got in contact with several women in Dundalk. First Nora, a district nurse. Then a librarian with the beautiful, exotic name of Freya. And then Maria, of course. Maria who was a leading light in the local Chamber of Commerce.

'Maria is the fiery one,' Majella said. 'She takes no nonsense from anyone. Nora tells me she has all the men on the Chamber terrorised.'

I had to ask. 'Did all of them have . . .' I couldn't say the word 'babies'.

'Yes,' she said, gently. 'They've all had babies they couldn't take home.' She paused for a moment. 'They know about you now. They're waiting for you to call.'

She pulled a sheet of paper from her pocket. 'Here are their phone numbers,' she said. 'Go do it.'

And so I did. My days began to fill up with possibility. Hope became a bright blur, the colour of sunflowers. At the same time, I kept thinking about this secret army of women. All of them – all of us – all over Ireland. Mothers of lost children.

I owe them so much, every one of them.

22

Tess, Summer 2019

Sometime after midnight, they hear the sound of the front door slowly opening. Tess and Mike stiffen.

'Let's just wait for a second,' she says, quietly. 'It might be Aengus.'

They hear footsteps, the creak of the last tread of the stairs.

Mike looks at her. 'That's not Aengus,' he says. He stands up quickly and reaches for the handle of the half-open living-room door. 'Luke?'

There is no answer.

She hears Mike take the stairs, two at a time. She hears him call Luke's name, again and again. Unwillingness keeps her in the armchair. Nausea shifts inside her at the thought of this new scene. It feels like so many others.

There are raised voices now, but she can't make out the words. Eventually, footsteps make their way downstairs. More than one person. She sits up straight, forces herself to be present.

Mike holds the door open and Luke walks in. Everything about him spells reluctance. He lowers his eyes, refuses to meet Tess's gaze.

'Sit down, Luke.' Mike's voice is firm. 'Your mother and I need to know what's going on.'

He stands, his back to the fireplace. His hands are shaking. He becomes aware of Tess watching him – although his eyes are on Luke – and he quickly puts his hands in his pockets.

Luke is sitting on the edge of the sofa. For a minute or two it seems that he's begun examining his fingernails. The air in the room feels brittle; it might shatter at any moment. Suddenly, he begins to speak. He raises both shoulders, spreads his hands wide, his face a mask of incomprehension. 'It's just some stupid mistake,' he says, looking at Tess. 'No biggie. The cops just needed me to clear something up.'

'And did you?'

Luke shrugs. Just one shoulder, this time. 'I told them everything I knew. And then they let me go. That's all there is to it.'

She waits. He must know another interview has been scheduled. They have not 'let him go'. His ability to lie saddens her.

'What I'd like to know, Luke,' Mike says, 'is why the guards wanted to speak to you in the first place. And why you've been gone for several hours.' Something hovers between Mike and Luke, sharp as a blade.

Tess tries again. 'Luke, help us to understand what's going on here. Please. Our hands are tied if you won't be honest with us.'

Still nothing.

'Luke, we've already been in touch with Matthew Kerr. We know you're facing another interview. A formal one, this time. If not tomorrow, then probably in the next couple of days.' Mike pauses for a moment. 'We're paying him to look after you. We'll know what's going on, eventually. So you might as well tell us.'

Tess wonders about that. Luke is an adult. Maybe she and Mike won't have the right to know what happens between their son and his solicitor. Maybe they will both be forced back onto the sidelines, while Luke keeps his secrets. They'll have to stand there, helpless. Looking on.

Luke glances up at his father, his face a blank. 'I won't need a solicitor,' he says. 'They've got nothing on me. Besides, I'm over eighteen.' His tone, the words he chooses, make Tess's heart beat harder.

'Nothing on you regarding *what?*' Mike's anger is growing. 'And what's that supposed to mean – that you're over eighteen? What has that got to do with anything?'

No answer.

'Luke?' she says. 'It's a reasonable question. What did the guards want to discuss? We'd rather hear it from you.' She's sure Luke has a good grasp of his rights, but she says it anyway: 'We'll ring Matthew now if you won't talk to us.'

Luke looks down at his hands again. She watches him weighing something up. He is anything but stupid. Finally, he speaks, with a sigh that says *all this trouble for nothing.*

'It was just an incident with a girl. Someone I know from college.'

He shakes his head in disbelief. His gesture seems to say how trivial this all is. How annoying. 'She made a complaint against some of us. But the guards know it isn't true. She's a flake.' He picks an invisible thread off the surface of his jeans.

The force of Tess's anger takes her by surprise. 'What reason did this girl have to make a complaint against you, Luke? And she's not just "a girl" or just "a flake".' She glares at him. 'She has a name. What's her name?'

He looks at her. 'What?'

'The girl you know from college. The young woman you clearly had *something* to do with. I'm asking you: What is her name?'

He swallows. 'Annie, or Amy, something like that. I don't really know. I hardly know her at all. She made a complaint, but it just isn't true.'

He hardly knows her at all? Tess is getting angrier by the minute.

'What kind of complaint?' Mike's voice is quieter now, but he has begun to clench his jaw. 'Luke?'

'She said we assaulted her . . .'

'We?' The word explodes into the living room. Mike takes a step towards where Luke is sitting.

Tess watches as Luke runs his tongue around his lips. Finally, he is looking nervous. His careful facade has just developed a hairline crack. Maybe the truth will begin to leak out from this tiny opening. Strength begins to return to her spine, just when she needs it. But she's been here before. And Luke is a master at keeping it all together.

'Are we talking about a sexual assault, Luke?'

'They're saying . . .'

'They?' The word cracks like a whip. 'Who are "they"?' Mike takes two large steps away from the fireplace. He takes his hands out of his pockets and grabs Luke by the shoulders. He shakes him. 'Tell us what's going on, Luke. Tell us why the guards have interviewed you. Tell me or I swear to God I'll beat it out of you.'

Tess looks at him in amazement. He has never laid a hand on either of their sons. He's always sworn never to repeat his own father's mistakes. She is startled to see how changed he is. His body is tightly coiled, poised to strike.

Luke turns away, shaking his father's hands off his shoulders. 'I'm going to bed now,' he says. And, as she and Mike watch, stunned, disbelieving, he stands up and walks away.

'Luke!' Mike's voice shatters the air.

But he continues to walk away. Tess puts one hand on Mike's arm, holding him back. Together, they watch as Luke opens the living-room door and closes it ever so quietly behind him.

Mike turns to her, his face ashen. 'What the *fuck*?'

'Leave it,' she says quickly.

She knows this mood of Luke's. He will give them nothing more, no matter how hard they push. He has retreated to that strange home where he belongs much more fully than to this one.

Mike lowers himself onto the sofa. When he looks at her, his face is pleading. 'What do we do now?'

'We wait,' she says. 'We try again in the morning. But we have to accept that we may get nothing more from him.'

He looks at her, stricken. 'Then what?'

'We'll just have to be here for him. Pick up the pieces afterwards. I don't know, Mike. The only thing I know is that we have no power right now. We'll have to trust Matthew – or whoever – to steer us through it all.'

'Jesus Christ,' he says, quietly, letting his face fall into his hands.

'I know.' After a minute she says, 'I think we should go to bed. I really don't want to get into it with Aengus when he gets home. I don't think either of us is up to it. I'll text him.'

'Yeah, you're right.' Mike stands up and brushes down his trousers with trembling hands, as though this were suddenly an important, all-absorbing act.

'You go on ahead,' Tess says. 'I'll switch off the lights.'

'Okay.'

She watches as he leaves the room. He looks hunched, defeated.

She looks around her for another few minutes. She sees the room as it used to be, decades earlier. Crammed with kids pushing, jostling, each one shouting to be heard above everyone else. She sees her mother, snapping her ever-present tea towel at somebody's bare legs: usually Myles's, or Conor's, shouting at them to behave.

But those days taught her that above everything, family is about protecting the ones you love – isn't it? Family is family, Betty used to say. You fight with them, you fight about them, but above all you fight *for* them.

Tess stands up. She needs to find her fight again. Needs to access that spirit that will help her to reach Luke. No matter what he's done.

Then she switches off all the downstairs lights and follows Mike up the stairs to bed.

23

Maeve, 1979

B elle was just over three months old. We were all together in our tiny back garden in Dundalk. I was helping Eileen to hang out the washing.

She turned to face me, a clothes peg between her teeth. 'What did you say?' It sounded like 'Wass?'

I pointed to the billowing sheet, the grass underneath my feet, to Belle, right beside me in her bouncy chair. Her cheery sun hat, patterned with cherries and slices of fruit, shaded her small face.

'This!' I said and flung my arms out wide. 'All of this, here!' My happiness was so intense at that moment, I didn't know whether to laugh or cry.

Eileen smiled. 'Good,' she said, taking the peg from between her teeth and fastening a pillowslip to the clothesline. And she bent down to pull something else from the wet tangle of clothes that filled the plastic laundry basket.

'I think this pyjama top has had its day, don't you? Looks a wee bit faded to me. We can do better.' She was facing the other way, absorbed once again in this everyday task.

And then I couldn't speak.

A blue clothesline. Yellow clothes pegs from the bright, red basket at her feet. The intense green of the grass. All at once, everything around me looked raucous: the noise of all those colours was blinding, deafening.

And it was as if I was inhaling it all over again: the salty, feminine smell of the sea. Because she had her back to me, Eileen couldn't see how I was suddenly rootless, rudderless, afloat in that ordinary suburban garden.

I began to imagine the texture of the material, its softness against my skin; the bright bloom of scarlet poppies in their ever-repeating pattern; the harsh memories that were stitched into the seams. I had cried that night, my face pushed deep into my pillow so that my parents wouldn't hear.

They were still downstairs, drinking tea and eating cake in one of their many unchanging Sunday night rituals. But soon, they would be in their bedroom, right across the landing from mine. My mother heard everything in those days, saw everything – or so I used to believe.

Eileen turned back to me, still smiling. Then she must have seen my face. I watched her, in slow motion, reach out one hand, walk towards me, her eyes large and anxious. 'Maeve, what is it? Tell me.'

She told me afterwards that I opened my mouth, closed it, opened it again. No sound came out. She said: 'Let's go inside. Come on, just one foot in front of the other. Lean on me.'

I began to resist and she said, quickly, 'I'll come back out for Belle. It'll just take a second. You need to sit down.'

I allowed myself to be led into the kitchen, where I sat on the edge of one of the painted wooden chairs. I sat where I could see, through the open door, that Belle was still there, that she was safe. I saw her kicking, the bouncy chair moving up and down with her delight.

'You okay for a minute?' Eileen stroked my hair. My face was wet. I hadn't known I was crying. I nodded and she ran back out to the garden, picked up Belle and hurried back inside again. She set the bouncy chair down beside me and closed the kitchen door. 'I'm going to make you some tea, okay?'

What I remember next is sipping strong, scalding, over-sweet tea. I must have made a face because she said: 'It's for shock. Sweet tea is good. Drink up.'

Gradually, I felt myself return from the outside in. And then I began to shake. Eileen wrapped the throw from the couch around me. She closed the windows. Then she stood behind me, her hands on my back, soothing, warming. She never said a word.

And just as suddenly as it had begun, it was over. I felt warm again, too warm. I shrugged off the heavy quilted throw, dragged my fingers through my sweaty hair. I felt weak, embarrassed at my own weakness, angry that memory still had the power to derail me like that.

'Do you want to tell me?'

I always loved that about Eileen. Her directness. I never knew it was possible to live with such openness: there were clean spaces everywhere, room to breathe. She had no time for even the occasional kindliness of evasion.

I looked out the window then, towards the clothesline. Everything was moving gracefully in the sudden mildness of a summer breeze.

*

An evening in late May. Jeans rolled up. The shock of cold water around my ankles. Waves frothing forward, then dragging back again. Around and above us, the dusty pink of the sky against the dark grasses of the dunes.

We were all there that summer, on Dollymount Strand. Inseparable, the whole lot of us: a shifting, changing web of friendship. Some stood out: above all, Maggie. She was the best-looking of us all. She didn't know we called her Mad Maggie. Then there was terrible Tess – and she *did* know we called her that. She was always getting into trouble. And then there was Fiona, shy, bookish Fiona. Always on the outside, always wanting to be let in.

We were mostly local: we knew each other by sight, or we knew each other's brothers and sisters. Except for one. None of us recognised him. He sidled up to us one evening and his presence caused a flutter. His name, we learned, was David.

He made his way over to my side, and he stayed there. Maggie looked daggers at me that evening. She never forgave me.

I loved looking at David: at his dark hair, the startling blue of his eyes, his tanned skin that was so luxurious beside my freckled whiteness.

*

During the next week or two, I thought about David every minute of every day. I couldn't eat. I lost weight. I bought remnants and ran up summer dresses on my mother's Singer. I wore my hair differently.

I'd learned to be wary of my mother, though, and so I was careful not to start using makeup, as some of the other girls had. But

I didn't need to, because I glowed and the world glowed with me. David and I kept on meeting, without the others knowing. I didn't want them to know. He was my secret. I wanted to keep him to myself.

One evening, we met in the dunes. He whispered he'd be careful. 'Come on,' he nuzzled my neck, 'you've kept me waiting for ages. It's only natural that I want it.'

'I'm afraid,' I whispered back. 'We'd better not go all the way.'

I tried to push him away, as gently as I could.

'It's not fair,' he said, 'you've been saying no for too long.'

And all at once, he was no longer whispering. There was an edge to his voice that hadn't been there before.

'David,' I said. 'Please.' I struggled to get out from under him, but he pushed me back down into the sand.

This was my fault. What did I expect?

'Come on,' he said, and his tone was wheedling again. 'Come on, I'll be careful. Besides,' he whispered, 'you can't get pregnant the first time, right?'

And so I let it happen. I didn't know how to say no. Even at the time, it felt like it was happening to someone else, to that girl I was hovering over in the sand dunes. I was looking down on her now, on that other girl, and on him.

It hurt and I started to cry.

When it was over he kissed me. 'It'll be easier next time,' was what he said. I watched, as though from some faraway place, as he zipped up his trousers, dusted the sand off them and held out one hand to me.

I looked at the blood on my thighs, my underwear, and I panicked. How was I going to hide those stains from my mother?

'Well,' he said, 'are you coming?'

*

When we met again, three terrifying weeks later, I told him. He stuck the butt of his cigarette into the cooling sand and stood up. 'I have to get back,' he said.

'What?'

'I'm on the late shift. I won't be able to see you for a week. We'll talk then.'

'When? What night will we meet?'

'Sunday,' he said, without hesitation. 'At the bridge. I'll see you there at seven, okay? Usual spot. I have to run.'

'Promise?' the girl was so stunned at his calmness she couldn't think of anything else to say.

'Yeah, promise.'

When he didn't turn up by nine on Sunday, she made her way home, each footstep filled with lead. She ignored the relentless voice inside her. It kept asking her how she could even *think* things would be okay. Things wouldn't be okay ever again: *you're pregnant.*

Her father met her in the hallway, making his way back into the living room with a tray set with teacups and a plate of cake. Sunday night domesticity. Her stomach lurched, sickened at the sight of it.

She didn't feel well, she told him, and went upstairs immediately. She pulled her favourite pyjamas out of the chest of drawers, smoothing the soft fabric, tracing the shape of the glowing red poppies until finally, she started to cry.

Then she got into bed, pressed her face into the pillow and turned herself towards the wall.

24

Betty, Summer 2019

Well, Jack.

It must have been giving away some of your coats and jackets to the charity shops a few weeks back that did it. I was finally able to face the tidying, and now I can't stop. The other day, I began to go through the bookshelves in the living room. I haven't had the heart to go near them since you.

On the top shelf, lying on its side with the spine facing the wall so that I couldn't see the title, was what turned out to be a photograph album. It was Kilburn, Jack. A peeling label on the front said *Springfield, 1959–1961*.

I thought I'd lost it, years ago. I remember going looking for it to show the boys pictures of Tess when she was a one-year-old. It was nowhere to be found. And now, it's made its way into my hands in a way that I still feel is strange. I've no idea what drove me to stand on the kitchen chair and start clearing that particular shelf, rather than any of the others. I was careful but Aengus would have had my guts for garters if he'd seen me.

'Gran!' he'd have said. 'You know you only have to ask.'

And yes, I do know. But there are times when having to ask is the last thing I want. Instead, I have this fierce need to hold on to *me* and my ability to take care of things for myself. Just like you did. 'Use it or lose it' you used to say, as you made your way into the garden once again, to dig and plant or prune, and sweep up the leaves that always swirled around the same spot once autumn came: a red and gold tornado. You'd always find something to keep you busy, even in our small back garden.

When you retired, you told me that you were not going to sit in a chair and wait to die. That shocked me, until you reeled off the names of the men you used to work with who had done just that: retired, sat back, and died a year or two later. What a waste, you used to say, shaking your head. What a terrible waste. I was glad that you knew how to potter. It's a skill. One I'm becoming more and more grateful for as the days go by.

I used to find it comforting to hear the noise of the metal bolt as you opened the door of the garden shed. It made a good, solid sound: the certainty that everything was the right way up. I'd spotted you through the kitchen window one day, the can of WD 40 in one hand, poised for silence. I opened the back door and asked you, please, not to do it: not to kill the bolt's protests. I liked its rough music.

Once I got safely down off the chair, I sat and opened up the Kilburn album. The pages creaked; it was that long since they had been turned. And there I was: more than sixty years ago. You took this first photo at Euston Station, the day I ran away to be with you. I was terrified you mightn't turn up and what would I do then? But you did. You were a man of your word. I spotted you on the platform as the train snaked into the station. I was filled with the most extraordinary sense of peace. I knew we'd be all right. Coming to you felt like coming home.

I see that I'm wearing the blue costume I made myself. I'd only finished it the night before. When I tried it on, I knew I'd have to alter the skirt. And so I'd put in a bit of elastic at the waistband, because I could feel myself already beginning to swell. Nobody else had noticed. Not Lizzie, not Mary. They were hawk-eyed around everyone else on the shop floor, but I somehow managed to fly below their radar. That's always amused me: the more we look at the people closest to us, the more we stop seeing them.

I loved that dark-blue costume. I'd even bought a bit of faux fur for the collar of the jacket and it made me feel like a film star. I think I'd seen a photo of Grace Kelly wearing something like it, or maybe it was Audrey Hepburn – it doesn't matter. I was delighted with myself, thrilled that I was escaping Dublin and moving to the bright lights of London to be with you.

I know, I know – but sure, I was only a child, we both know that. At thirty, you were a man of the world, although neither of us was cut out for life in London. I knew it in my gut, knew that England wasn't where you wanted to be. At first, I looked on it as a bit of an adventure. I felt safe because we were there together and so I had the best of both worlds. But I also knew we had no choice. We couldn't go back home, not then, and so we stuck it out.

Turning the creaking pages of this old album reminds me, too, of the first time we'd gone looking for a flat, just days after I arrived at Euston. You had circled the Flats to Rent section of the *Evening Standard* and we began to tick them off our list, one by one. After the first place we saw, you turned to me very gently and said: 'Best to leave the talkin' to me, pet.'

I was stung. What had I done wrong? I knew I was by far the more talkative of the two of us, the friendlier. Had I spoken out of turn? 'But she was nice, that lady,' I protested. 'She was happy to talk.'

You stopped in the street and tucked my hand into the crook of your arm. My cheap not-quite-wedding-ring gleamed in the light of the streetlamp.

'It's your accent,' you said. 'It might go against us.' And you squeezed my hand.

I learned to be silent after that. Learned not to speak until I was safe, until we were among our own. The next landlady stared openly at my stomach, although I still wasn't showing. She wasn't taken in by my ring, either. I could see by the way she glanced at my hand.

Getting the flat at Springfield was a relief. Nobody there seemed to care who we were or where we were from, as long as we did no damage and paid the rent. We stayed there until a few months after Tess's first birthday when we made the grateful journey back to Ireland.

You took me to Mayo a couple of years after we settled in Dublin. It was then that I really understood the pull of home: understood it with my eyes and my head, as well as my heart.

*

The room has gone cold. I've no idea how long I've been sitting here, the photograph album of Kilburn open on my knee. I get up, a bit stiffly, and make my way to the kitchen, where I boost the central heating for another hour. I'm not ready to go to bed yet. There's no way I'll sleep anyway, not after London has crept up on me and opened a door into a part of the past that I wasn't expecting.

I pull the tartan blanket from the back of the sofa and tuck it around my knees. I pick up the photo album again and find it's warm from being in my hands for so long.

There's a large picture here that I can't take my eyes off. It's a photo taken the year before we lived in Kilburn, the year you and I first met at the Galtymore. Mary and Lizzie and I doing our Christmas shopping in Oxford Street. We must have been snapped by one of those street photographers – you know, like that man who used to stand on O'Connell Bridge? Arthur Fields was his name. He took photos of passers-by for more than fifty years. Imagine that: him standing there, winter and summer, rain and shine, handing out his little numbered tickets, hoping that enough people would buy his photos so as he could keep body and soul together. He was an immigrant, too, if I remember: from the Ukraine, of all places. Maybe he didn't feel the cold of Dublin too much, coming from all that snow.

I'm astonished, all over again, at the things I remember. And also at the things I forget – day to day things that keep me retracing my steps. I have to go back and stand in the same place where I had a thought, before I can remember what it was, and what I need to do next. I have to coax it out of the air, where it's managed to hide, mocking me. I know this will be familiar to you, Jack: I used to tease you about it in your later years. And now here I am, just the same.

The three of us, Mary, Lizzie and I, were modern young women back then, earning our own money as Clery's salesladies. We were dizzy with the grownupness of it all. Our shared flat, the dances at weekends, our new clothes, all the possibilities of travel. And what an adventure a weekend in London was! Lizzie's patient sister, Jenny, in her little house on the Edgware Road, allowed us to take pillows and blankets downstairs to sleep on the floor by the fire on the Friday and Saturday night.

You and I fell for each other at once. The Galtymore was heaving; the huge glitterball kept showering the dancers below with splinters of coloured light. And there were familiar accents everywhere. It was like another Irish county. Mary and Lizzie envied me; I know they did. I think we all felt that I had begun to pull away from them once that weekend was over and the three of us were back home again.

We knew that another kind of life was beginning for me. But they were generous, all the same. They teased me on the boat home, agreed that you were a good 'catch'. You were a good-looking man, Jack: strong, with that dark thatch of hair and sea-green eyes. 'You'd stand in the snow to look at him,' Lizzie said, once, wistfully. Poor Lizzie. She wasn't so lucky – not in any of the ways I was.

I still have your letters, Jack, from those early months. They're tucked into the back flap of the album. But it's getting late and I think the photos are enough for one day. Tomorrow, I'll read the letters tomorrow. I already know what they say.

And there's the picture of Tess – the one I wanted to show the boys. There she is, blowing out the candle on her first birthday cake, clutching her new doll. You made the little cot out of offcuts of wood and painted it pink. I made the tiny quilt, and some clothes for the doll. Tess had endless fun, putting her baby to bed, waking her up, and later, when she got a bit more dexterity, dressing and undressing her over and over again.

Eileen came to that birthday tea. I've always thought that was very brave of her. Tess loved her, trusted her, would sit on her knee for the longest time while Eileen read her the story books she'd bought her as a birthday present.

I rang Tess again yesterday afternoon, as soon as I came across the album, told her what I'd found. She sounded preoccupied. But I can't push her, no matter how worried I feel. Something is going on. I have to try to be patient. Aengus let something slip the other day, something about a party and Luke, and then tried to cover it up. I think he thought I already knew. But I didn't and then he looked embarrassed. He changed the subject, explained to me how he could do something with the snaps on the computer so that we'd always have them, and stop them from fading.

I didn't tell him that these are the sorts of memories that never fade. They just get brighter, stronger, more filled with colour with the passing of every year.

25

Aengus, 2015

It started off like any other ordinary evening.

I got in from Gaelic practice around five. Mum usually got home from work between six and half past. Luke was probably in his bedroom with his headset on, oblivious. That suited me fine.

At half past five, I got her usual text. *On my way.* Then, a few minutes later: *Luke's not answering his phone. Can you check that he's home?*

I stepped into the hall and yelled his name. Nothing. I raced upstairs and hammered on his door. 'Luke! You in there?' There was rarely any point in trying the door. If Luke was home, he'd have locked himself in, as usual.

No answer. So I tried the handle just in case, and to my surprise, the door swung open. There was the usual mess. Clothes all over the floor, plates with bits of toast stuck to them, crisp packets, chocolate wrappers. But no Luke.

I messaged her back, tried to make it sound casual. *Not home yet. Want me to call him?* I knew she'd be on the Dart, and she hates talking when she's on the train. Hates overhearing other people's conversations almost as much as she hates other people overhearing hers.

The reply was instant. *Yes, please.*

So I tried him and it went straight to voicemail. Then I WhatsApped him. Twenty minutes later, still nothing. Just those irritating little grey ticks to show the message had been delivered but not read.

By the time Mum got home, I'd already left Luke half a dozen voice messages and called two of the friends he hung out with most. No answer from either of them. I was furious by then. I couldn't help it. This was beginning to shape up like so many other times. There goes my evening.

'Let's give him another hour,' she said. 'Then I'll drive around and see if he's in any of his usual haunts.'

'I'll come with you,' I said.

She looked at me, in that level way she has. 'You don't need to do that, Aengus. Really.'

"Course I will. Two pairs of eyes are better than one.'

*

We drove around in the fading light. First to the seafront, where we'd found Luke before, sprawled on the grass that bordered the prom. He used to disappear like this from time to time, ever since he was thirteen. Sometimes, he'd hide out in the shelters beside the old swimming baths.

We used to go there in the summer as kids. The water was always freezing. Then the whole place was bought by developers who turned it into a restaurant. But we never called it anything but 'the baths'.

Mum parked and I legged it over to take a look. Nothing. So we tried the streets where some of Luke's classmates lived. But there was no sign of him, and the kids hanging around the corners, or sitting on walls sharing sneaky fags, hadn't seen him either. They looked genuinely puzzled.

By this time, the light was going fast.

'What now?' I asked her.

'I think we need to go to Clontarf Garda Station,' she said quietly.

No drama. I'd heard her yell at Luke many times over small shit, but this calmness really jolted me.

'Okay,' I said.

*

I don't think the guards took us seriously. A fifteen-year-old boy who hadn't come home after school? And it was only nine o'clock?

But I could feel my mother's fear. It was like some kind of weird scent that she was giving off. Something basic, almost animal.

And there was something different about this time. Before, Luke would only be missing for a couple of hours. I never found out where he went; he'd never say. He'd just disappear, even when he was grounded for some bad behaviour or other.

He always thumbed his nose at Mum's rules. He kept pushing against her, challenging her. I think her frustration amused him.

*

Well, Luke didn't come home that night. Mum and I called everybody we knew. Dad must've rung us a dozen times from wherever he was. We could only keep giving him the same answer. No, nothing yet.

Mum's mobile went at two the following morning. She snatched it off the table. 'Yes?'

Her face flooded with relief and I felt myself exhale. He was alive.

'Is he okay?' she asked. And 'Where?' Long silence. She dragged one hand through her hair, sighed and looked over at me. 'I understand,' she was saying. 'Yes, thank you. Thank you.'

'Well?' I was impatient. I needed to know what next. What *I* would have to do next. I was cranky, now that I knew he was safe. And I was wrecked. I needed to go to bed. Before I knew it, I'd be sitting at my desk, facing Mr Keogh's honours maths test. I'd done none of my last-minute revision, and on top of that, I wouldn't be getting much sleep. Thanks, Luke. Thanks a lot.

'They've found him. In Howth. He stowed away on a fishing boat with two of his friends.'

'He what?' I started to laugh. He really was safe. My brother was safe. The swell of emotion took me by surprise.

Her mobile rang again. Dad, this time. So I listened, getting my information second-hand. I didn't care. I was just glad for all of us that Luke was alive. I felt shaky with relief, at the same time as wanting to beat the shit out of him.

'Yes, on a trawler. No, Mike, just in the harbour. They got cold, apparently, and tried to light a fire on deck. Someone saw them and called the guards. They're bringing him home now. Yes, of course. First thing in the morning. We'll let him sleep tonight.'

She hung up. She looked at me and her face suddenly crumpled. 'I don't understand, Aengus. I just don't understand. Where did I go so wrong?' She started to sob, great, choking gulps and I went to her, pulled her to her feet and wrapped her in the biggest hug I could manage.

'It's okay,' I said. 'It's okay.' And I just held her while she wept.

I felt suddenly shy. I didn't feel I could say *It's not your fault. None of this is your fault. Luke is Luke and he's hard to be with. That's all. You're a great mother. I couldn't imagine being anyone else's son. You're the best.*

So I just hugged her all the harder.

*

I waited up until Luke got home. I expected him to make an effort at an apology, even a half-arsed one. But he didn't.

He smelt of smoke, old fish and cold air. He wouldn't look at me. I wasn't surprised: his pupils were huge so he had a lot to hide. I said nothing and left the two of them alone, at Mum's request. She said it would be better if she had a few words with him on her own.

That was fine with me. It was already four in the morning. There were faint traces of blue light in the sky as I crashed into bed.

Everything inside me felt empty. Hollowed out. I didn't even bother taking off my clothes. I pulled the duvet up and over my head.

My last thought was a shocked realisation. A fire, on deck, just above the diesel tanks?

For fuck's sake. All three of them could have been blown to kingdom come.

And then I slept.

26

Tess, Summer 2019

Tess wakes. For a moment, she can't move. Everything inside is tingling, on high alert: something has woken her. She glances over at Mike. He's asleep, after a restless, anxious, whispering night. She eases herself out of the bed and picks up her phone.

Five-fifty a.m. She pulls her dressing gown off the hook and steps out onto the landing. Closing the bedroom door quietly behind her, she waits until she hears the faint click of the lock.

Instantly, she recognises the sound: *that's* what has just woken her. Quickly, she makes her way to Luke's room. There is a thin line of yellow light where the door meets the wooden floor. So she's wrong, after all: he's still here. And he's awake. Maybe she can get him to talk to her, now that it's just the two of them and last night's charged energy has been filtered away by the hours of darkness.

She knocks, softly. Knocks again and waits while she counts to twenty. Then she turns the handle slowly. The door opens. The bedside light is on, but Luke's bed is empty. The room is empty.

She turns and hurries downstairs. His jacket is gone from where he'd tossed it the night before, carelessly, over the newel post. His backpack is missing. She pulls open the front door and looks in every direction. But there is no sign of Luke.

She closes the door and rests her face against the glass. It feels cool against the sudden heat of her cheeks: another one of those rushes that have been happening lately. Her face and neck are on fire. And then the anxiety begins to swell. Her heart races. She has the feeling of impending catastrophe that always grips her at times like this.

She stays by the door for a couple of minutes, waiting for the world to settle again.

*

In the kitchen, she boils the kettle and imagines Betty beside her, patting her on the hand, smiling in reassurance and saying the same thing she would say in the midst of any crisis, familial or universal: I'll go and make us a cup of tea.

Tess takes her cup with her into the living room and opens the curtains. She watches as the familiar Saturday morning routines begin to unfold all around her. There's Gerry from number twenty-four, leaving for the early shift. In another hour or so, a car or two will start up, Louise and Ruth will head off to their part-time jobs. Deirdre will call for Mary and they'll set off on their walk together. All the slow weekend rituals are beginning, as though nothing at all has happened.

Children will soon begin dragging out their portable goalposts onto the green space; others will ride their bikes at speed around the park, the younger ones staying safely on the footpath. It's all so ordinary. It's been like this for as long as Tess can remember. She feels a tug of fear as she thinks about the future. A future in which nothing might feel mundane, or safe, or uneventful ever again.

She tries Luke's number. Once more, it goes straight to voicemail. She'll give Mike another hour and then they'll have to try and figure out what to do next.

She sips at her tea, uncomfortably aware of her still-flushed face, the prickly heat all over her scalp. She looks out the window, hoping to soothe herself by gazing on all that predictable green.

A young boy dashes off the grass onto the road, chasing a bright red ball. He's up early. Tess starts as she sees him, and a bright hook of memory pulls her in. She sees herself, and Fiona – Fiona! She hasn't thought about her in decades – on the night of Conor's accident.

*

Tess and her mother were arguing again.

'You needn't glare at me like that,' her mother was saying. 'Dad and I need you to be here on Friday night. You can have Fiona over, if you like.' She pulled open the cupboard doors, began piling in bags of porridge and lentils, tin after tin of baked beans. 'But you have to be here to babysit.'

Tess stared at her mother, open-mouthed. 'You're jokin',' she said. 'A birthday dinner with Joe and Carol? You don't even *like* Joe and Carol.'

Her mother gave her a strange look. 'Joe's my oldest brother,' she said. 'What's liking got to do with it?' She stopped unpacking groceries for a minute. 'We don't see much of each other, that's true, but that doesn't mean I don't love him, or wish him well.'

'It's not fair.' Tess followed her around the kitchen table. 'You *said* I could go out on Friday.'

'Any other Friday, Tess, just not this one.'

'But Maggie's birthday party's *this* Friday. Everybody's going.'

Her mother didn't reply, just kept on taking things out of her shopping bag, arranging them in the kitchen cupboards, in that maddening way she had. As though nothing else but this mattered. As though this daily task took all her concentration and attention.

Tess tried again. 'What about Sheila?'

But her mother's expression began to settle into that determined look that Tess knew all too well, that firm set of the mouth. 'Sheila is far too young to babysit,' she said, shaking her head. 'She's only eleven, you're sixteen.'

Tess lost it.

'Fine!' she shouted. 'Then *you* stay at home and look after them! They're *your* kids, after all – not mine! This is *so* unfair.' And she slammed her way out of the kitchen, her eyes filled with tears of fury.

She stamped her way up the stairs and shoved open her bedroom door. It isn't even *my* room, she raged to herself. I've to share *that* as well as everything else.

Eleanor was sitting on one of the bottom bunks, reading *The Enormous Crocodile*. Eleanor was always reading and Roald Dahl was her current obsession. No matter what was going on, she'd manage to find a quiet corner for herself and her library book. Sometimes Tess forgot she was even in the house.

'Get out!' she shouted now at her little sister. She flung herself onto the top bunk, kicking off her shoes. They fell onto the lino with a clatter.

Startled, Eleanor looked up at her. Her elfin face was troubled. She moved closer to the door, her book clutched to her chest.

'What's happening? What's wrong with you?' she asked, her eyes owlish behind the cheap frames of her new glasses.

'Nothing,' Tess snapped. 'Mum and Dad are going out on Friday night and I've to mind all of you lot, again.'

'I'll help,' Eleanor said, her small face all eagerness. 'Conor likes me to read him bedtime stories. I can do that, once he's in his jammies. Please don't be cross.'

Tess began to soften. 'I know you will,' she said, at last, 'and I'm sorry for shouting at you. Just leave me alone for a bit.'

Eleanor moved away from the door and sat back down on the lower bunk. She didn't speak, just started reading her book again. Tess waited until the storm passed. Then she lowered herself to the floor and tapped Eleanor on the shoulder. 'Come on, let's go downstairs.'

She felt a stab of guilt as she looked at her sister's faded paisley-print summer dress. The once brave broderie-anglaise piping was grey and tired-looking. Tess used to wear that cotton dress; then it was Sheila's turn, now it was Eleanor's. It made her angry all over again. Too many kids, too little money. None of it was her fault: so why did she have to be the one to suffer?

Eleanor swung herself into standing and slipped her hand into Tess's. She squeezed her big sister's fingers, giving comfort. Tess looked down at her in surprise.

'It'll be okay,' Eleanor said. She nodded her reassurance, like a mini adult. 'Maybe Mum will let me bake fairy cakes. You can have the best one.'

Tess smiled at her. 'Yeah,' she said. 'Yeah, maybe she will.'

*

On Thursday night, Tess's mother relented a little and told her she could go to Fiona's house until seven on Friday. 'Don't be late back,' she warned her. 'Dad and I will have to leave the minute you get here. Don't delay us.'

'Okay.'

'Fiona is like your shadow these days,' Tess's mother commented. 'Is there a bit of hero-worship going on there?'

Tess, still furious with her over having to babysit, didn't reply. She wasn't going to give her mother the satisfaction of knowing that Fiona wasn't allowed to go to Maggie's birthday party, either.

'I don't want to go,' Fiona had said, quickly, to Tess, earlier that week. 'Maggie only asked me because of you.'

Tess didn't know what to say, because Fiona was right. She was too quiet, too serious for the other girls.

'Well, I won't be goin' either,' Tess said, 'so we can hang around together.'

*

She loved being in Fiona's house. Loved the quiet, the peace of it. Her mum was such a good cook, too. They never had to eat lentils and her Victoria sponge was heaven.

Fiona had a record player all to herself. Tess couldn't even begin to imagine such luxury: a room of your own, *and* a record player. Not to mention having just the one brother, and he was old enough to be hardly ever at home.

That day, Fiona put on 'How Deep Is Your Love' by the Bee Gees, then 'Night Fever', then 'Stayin' Alive'. She'd got the singles for her sixteenth birthday, a couple of months back. All the girls at school were talking about *Saturday Night Fever* and how deadly John Travolta was.

Most of them hadn't even seen the film, despite some of the boasting that went on at break time, but *everyone* was listening to the music. Tess knew the whole story second-hand, though, and wished she and Fiona were old enough to go to the local cinema and see it together. There were whispers that a few of the more daring girls had managed to slide into the cinema, that they'd done themselves up to look eighteen, but Tess didn't believe them.

'You're so lucky, having your own room,' she sighed now, trying on some of Fiona's silver nail polish. She was lying on the bed, sprawled. Fiona was sitting on the floor as they listened to 'Stayin' Alive' for the third time. 'I wish I did.'

'But your house is fun,' Fiona protested. 'My mum has started making me stay over at my cousins' most Friday nights. She says I need to learn how to share.' And she made a face.

Tess was relieved to see her cheeky expression. Fiona had been very quiet for the last few days, not herself at all. Tess grinned at her now. 'The last thing we do in my house is learn how to share. SOS – that's what my dad calls dinnertime: Stretch or Starve. At least you don't have to fight everyone else at the table for your grub.'

*

Later, Tess and Fiona were sitting side by side on the sagging sofa in Tess's living room. Eoghan sat quietly with his Lego, in the middle of the floor. He liked being where his big sister was. Myles was in the front garden with Conor, just underneath the window.

Tess could see his reddish hair along with Conor's fair head as they negotiated the rules of some private game. With only ten months between them, they were more like twins. As the two youngest, they'd mounted their own barricades, separating themselves from everyone but each other.

'Are they okay out there on their own?' Fiona asked. She peered over one shoulder.

'Yeah, as long as we can see them.' Tess did a quick head count. Everyone was where they should be. 'Want popcorn?'

'Yeah. Where's Eleanor, but?'

'She's gone upstairs to Sheila. We'll call them when it's ready. C'mon.'

Tess pulled the saucepan out from the cupboard under the sink. Fiona got the bottle of oil from beside the cooker and handed it to her. Tess measured carefully, then placed the pot on the flame. Fiona got the bowls from the shelf and put them on the kitchen table. She stood beside Tess, watching. But she seemed uneasy. She kept shifting from one foot to the other and her hands started fidgeting with the material of her dress.

'What's up?' Tess asked. She liked the way the hard little beads of corn rattled into the oily saucepan. She put the lid on, firmly, gave the pot a good shake, just as her mother had shown her, and placed it carefully back on the gas.

Fiona grew agitated. 'I . . . would you . . . can I tell you something?'

The kernels began to pop, pinging against the lid of the saucepan. The speed of their small explosions made Tess laugh. She turned the heat down low and looked at Fiona, waiting.

'Yeah, 'course you can. What is it?'

'It's just . . .' and she trailed off.

The popcorn was beginning to steady now, there was only the occasional mild pop. Tess turned off the ring and took the saucepan off the cooker. 'We'll leave it for a bit to cool.' She placed it on the draining board. She caught sight of Fiona's face then, saw the tears threaten.

'Hey, what is it? You can tell me anything, you know that.'

'Promise you won't tell anyone?'

'I promise,' Tess said, but warily. She was mindful of her mother's instruction to her. Repeated often, because as the eldest, she had responsibilities. So many, in fact, that she grew tired hearing about them.

Secrecy had no place if a child was in danger. All bets were off. Safety came first.

And so Tess waited, watching as her friend struggled to find whatever words she needed. 'Is there something going on at home?' she asked at last.

Fiona tilted her head to one side, as though considering. But she still didn't say anything.

Tess was mystified. 'At school, then? What is it?'

Just then, they heard screaming, coming from the street. Tess looked at Fiona in alarm, then she shot out of the kitchen, down the hallway, out into the garden. She noted in a flash that Conor was no longer there. She rushed out into the street and then, as though from somewhere far away, she heard another scream – perhaps Myles, perhaps Conor, maybe both.

She stood at the kerb transfixed. Her throat filled with panic as she tried to make out what she was seeing. The big blue blur of a car that had just screeched to a halt. Conor, lying in the middle of the road. And the red ball he got for his fifth birthday bouncing gently off the kerb until it rolled to a full stop outside Tess's gate.

Then she ran towards him. 'Conor!'

On the front step, Myles sat, now shocked into silence. Conor was screaming, a high-pitched, terrified scream, the like of which Tess had never heard before. But it filled her with relief. Thankgodthankgodthankgod he was still alive. She was by his side in seconds. One leg was twisted back under her brother's small body and she knew at once that it must be broken; the angle of his knee was all wrong.

'It's okay, it's okay, sweetie. We'll fix it where it hurts, we'll fix it, don't worry.' It didn't matter what she said. The important thing was – her first aid classes had told her so – that she remember to keep him awake, keep him talking to her.

Mrs Kirwan came running out from next door. 'I've called the ambulance, Tess – it's on its way now.' She struggled to catch her breath. 'Are you all right? Do you need any help?' She glanced down at Conor, saw that he was alive, conscious. After eight children of her own, Mrs Kirwan never panicked.

'Can you take Myles inside with you, Mrs Kirwan? Please? And keep an eye on the others? I'll go with Conor in the ambulance.'

'Of course, of course,' Mrs Kirwan said, at once. 'Don't you worry, Tess. I'll look after them.'

Conor's cries were whimpers now. His face was deathly white, his green eyes hazy.

The driver of the car was standing several feet away. He was in the middle of the gathering crowd of neighbours. The driver's door was still open, the engine running. 'I didn't see him,' the man kept saying. 'I never saw him.' Tess could hear the appeal in his voice. 'He was suddenly there, just dashed out in front of me. I didn't have time to stop.'

Fiona and Sheila were standing at the kerb, looking at them. They each had Eleanor by the hand. Both of their faces were terrified. Eoghan was just behind them, freckles standing out starkly against his suddenly white face. Eleanor's mouth was half-open, as though she'd started to say something and had forgotten how to finish.

Myles fought Mrs Kirwan with everything he had. When the ambulance arrived, Tess said to her: 'It's okay, he can come with us.' Myles clambered into the back with her. He didn't take his eyes off his brother all the way to the hospital.

His hand crept towards Tess, and she held onto it. It was hot and sticky and it felt rough against her palm. But she would not let go, not for the world.

'It's okay,' she said. 'Conor'll be fine. The doctors will fix him up and he'll be home again in no time, drivin' us all nuts.'

*

The rest of the evening passed in an uproar of activity: the hospital, their parents' arrival, Conor's leg in plaster. And then the slow, astonishing journey home by taxi. Taxi! Tess was too fraught to be properly thrilled by the novelty of it all. Myles fell asleep on her lap on the way home, his sturdy body smelling of sunshine and clay.

When she went into Mrs Kirwan's house to gather everybody for home, she was expecting to see Fiona there, too, waiting for her. But Fiona had gone.

She felt bad then. But she'd go looking for her tomorrow. Right now, she was so tired she could sleep for a week.

That night, her dreams were crammed with little boys and blue cars, bouncing red balls, the warm ping of popcorn, and the pinched, haunted face of her best friend.

*

Tess comes back to this morning with a start. Her eyes are still following the little fellow – Freddy, that's his name – as he races up and down the green space, kicking his red ball. His mother keeps an eye on him from the garden gate. None of the other kids is playing with him. Tess has noticed that before: he's a bit of a loner. Poor little fella. He reminds her of Eoghan.

It's almost seven o'clock. She has to wake Mike, but feels reluctant to start the day. These childhood moments go hand in hand with the knowledge that she's growing older. She misses Sheila. And Eleanor. And the boys: even Myles and Conor.

And perhaps more than anything else these days, she finds herself longing for the life she's never had. One filled with purpose, with definition: the kind of life that Sheila has carved out for herself. Sheila always had focus, determination. Her plan was simply one of escape. *I'm outta here soon as,* was her mantra as a teenager.

But she, Tess, has spent her life as the dutiful daughter; the responsible, caring daughter; the one who can always be relied upon. Resentment has crept up behind her while she has been looking the other way.

And she misses the friendships she's let slide over the years. Too much busyness. Her eyes begin to fill as she remembers the summer evenings with Fiona, Maggie and all the others on Dollymount

Strand. Gone, all of them, one way or another. And now there's Luke.

Abruptly, she stands up. I can't afford to go there. I have to keep it together.

Her tea is now cold. She makes her way back into the kitchen and throws the dregs into the sink. She lifts her hair off the back of her sweaty neck, twists it into a loose bun. Once more, she tries Luke's phone. Once more, it goes straight to voicemail.

She steps out into the hall and sees Mike, standing at the top of the stairs.

'Tess? What's happened? Where's Luke?' His face is even greyer than yesterday.

'I don't know,' she says. 'The front door woke me as he was leaving. I've phoned him several times. There's no reply.'

She climbs the stairs to where he's waiting. He puts both arms around her, kisses her.

'It's okay,' he says. 'We're going to get through this.'

She squeezes his hand but doesn't answer. Then she makes her way into the bedroom and this strange day begins in earnest.

27

Maeve, 1981

I was standing across the road from the shop, waiting. Waiting for the word. As excited as a child.

'*Now* you can look.' Eileen reached for my hand.

Before I opened my eyes, I pictured the three of us together. Three generations of family, holding on tightly to each other, with Eileen as the anchor.

When I did look, I saw a bright, sky-blue banner unfurling itself across the head of the plate-glass window. It looked real: as though it had been gripped by the wind and then moored in flight. The word '*Féileachán*' was painted there, in old Irish script. Butterflies of all shapes and sizes wound their way in and out of the letters, trailing flowers in their wake. The paint shimmered, making the wings appear translucent as they curved and dipped in flight.

'Look, Belle!' I pointed upwards. 'Butterflies!' Her small hand was cool in mine, her face made ruddy by the wind. She smiled. Her eyes shone and she let go of me and reached out, making small grasping movements, as though catching the butterflies with her fingers. With her other hand, she clutched her doll close to her chest.

Belle had been slow to walk, and her steps were still halting and unsure. Sometimes, she seemed to forget what she was doing. She would sit down abruptly, no matter where she was. Or she'd stop and look down at her feet, wondering what she should do next. Something nagged at me, too, when I saw her with other two-year-olds. She often stood to one side, disconnected. Absorbed in her own world.

The silence of that other world sometimes frightened me. Mostly, though, I pushed it all aside. She was fine. My daughter was fine. Children walked and talked in their own time.

'What do you think, Belle?' Eileen scooped her up. 'Will we go inside and see Mama Leen's new shop?'

For the past few months, Eileen and I had looked at every empty premises in Dundalk. Sometimes, her old friend Maria came with us. I learned not to disagree with her. She had five or six years on Eileen, but somehow she seemed much older. When it came to business, her word was law. 'This won't do,' she said, on more occasions than I could count. 'There's not enough footfall on this street.'

Once, when I'd fallen in love with a particularly spacious shop, Maria shook her head. It was a brusque, decisive gesture and I could see Eileen was torn. 'You're better off investing in somewhere more central.' Then she shrugged. 'But it's your decision, of course.'

Eileen looked at her as she spoke, with that direct gaze that I had come to know. 'You've never given me bad advice, Maria. That's why I asked for your help.'

I was surprised at how pleased Maria looked. I made sure to keep my views to myself after that.

Eileen handed me the keys now. 'Go on, Maeve, you open up.'

I'd seen this shop in its original, disappointing state. It hadn't been my choice and that still rankled. Eileen had kept the renovations secret. Time enough for you to see it when the work is done, she kept saying. I didn't know what to expect.

But I should have known.

I pushed open the heavy door. The interior was unrecognisable. The dim, fusty, damp-smelling place that I'd last seen was now transformed. The old counter had disappeared. Instead, multi-coloured painted shelves, like steps of stairs, climbed up one wall. They were filled with children's clothes, games, books. On the other walls, quilts of different shapes and sizes were displayed, all of them glinting, shimmering, lit by carefully placed spotlights. Racks and rails of children's clothes were arranged on all sides.

And there were butterflies everywhere: mobiles hung from the ceiling with delicate red admirals, made out of plywood. Huge crepe-paper orange monarchs fluttered above our heads, suspended on fine, barely visible wire. There were at least half a dozen dramatic yellow-and-black tiger swallowtails, painted onto the doors at the back of the shop.

'Eileen!' I found my voice after a moment and turned to look at her. 'I can't believe it! How did you do all of this? And how did you make all those butterflies?'

'You like it?'

'I *love* it. And look at Belle: she can't believe her eyes.'

Eileen bent down so that her face was level with Belle's. 'Do you like it, too, sweetheart?'

Belle stood completely still, staring straight ahead. For a moment, I was brought back to the day in Eileen's back garden, when the raucousness of all that colour overwhelmed me and plunged me deep into some other, darker, place. I understood my small daughter's silence. I turned her face towards mine. 'Belle,' I said. 'It's okay. Close your eyes.'

She obeyed instantly, and I lifted her, cradling her head against my shoulder. She was eerily quiet for a moment and then she began to wail. It was a high, desolate sound and it scared me. I walked outside with her, back into the ordinary noises of the busy street. Finally, she calmed. I whispered to her, held her close and waited. She began to struggle against me at last, and I knew it was over for now.

I set her down on the footpath and waited to see what she would do. She tugged at my hand and began to walk back towards the shop door.

'Will we go back in to Mama Leen, then?'

For an answer, she pulled even more strongly on my hand and I allowed her to lead me. Once inside, I saw that Eileen had dimmed the lights. Everything was softer, quieter. She looked at me questioningly and I said, 'We're fine.'

'So, Belle, do you think you'd like to see your room now, yours and Mama's?'

Belle nodded eagerly and Eileen took her by the hand. 'Follow me,' she said, glancing back over one shoulder.

My room? Our room? Eileen had said nothing about any room. I followed her up the stairs as she chatted to Belle. Watching the way my little girl planted both feet on each step, watching the careful effort she made to climb the stairs, one trusting hand in Eileen's, filled me with an inexplicable sadness. What was wrong with me?

'Are you ready?' Eileen asked.

'Yes.' I was curious.

She opened the door into a large room, painted in the lightest shade of green. In the middle of the floor was a brand-new sewing machine. All around were baskets of fabric, a jumble of colour and texture. To the right, there was a small sofa, a coffee-table and a tiny kitchenette.

'This is for you,' she said. 'Your own workroom, so you don't have to use the kitchen table anymore. It's time to separate work from home.'

I looked at her in disbelief. Then I began, slowly, to fill with delight. 'Really? This is for me?'

'Just for you. But you know there's no such thing as a free lunch, right?'

I laughed. 'Yeah, go on – what's the catch?'

'A pretty nice catch, actually. Look at the order book.'

On the cover of the blue order book – they had become familiar to me over the past two years – Eileen had pasted an image of my prototype doll. I'd called her Bellissima, after Belle, but also because I wanted her to be beautiful.

I'd noticed the way rag dolls frightened Belle: their expressions were too fixed. I understood why she didn't like them. I was reminded of the time Joanie had sewn buttons for eyes onto the teddy bear I'd once knitted for her; how blank and sinister those buttons had made the bear's face seem.

I'd long since hidden away the Raggedy Ann I'd made back in St Brigid's. As Belle grew, I no longer wanted any reminders of that place. We'd moved on, both of us, together.

For Bellissima, I'd used pastel fabrics, bright hair, wide, soft features. Everything about her was tender, appealing. My little girl slept with her every night, tucked around the doll's pliable body.

I opened up the order book. Inside, in Eileen's beautiful, copperplate handwriting, she had noted a dozen or so names, none of which I recognised. 'What am I looking at?' I asked her.

'I've been dying to tell you – but I decided to keep it as a surprise for today.' She was beaming. 'Those are the initial orders for your new customers' very own Bellissimas – and I have a waiting list as long as your arm. I thought these would be enough to get you started.'

'Twelve!' I stared at her. 'But—'

She already knew what I was going to say. 'There's no pressure. It's more than three months to Christmas. You can do it.' She placed both hands on my shoulders. 'And it's time, Maeve. Belle needs to be at playschool. You can't be everyone and everything to her.'

We'd had this conversation before. Eileen would start it, gently, from time to time. But I resisted. I didn't even understand my own reluctance until later. I tried not to see the anxious way she would sometimes look at Belle. It was always present between us, a silent undercurrent to every day. Mostly, I skated over the surface of it. Pretending it wasn't there.

'You can do it, Maeve,' she said again. 'You're clever and you're artistic and you're hardworking. Bellissima is only the start. You need to make room for yourself in your own life. Trust me.'

I understood what she meant, where that urgency was coming from. I knew that she, too, had had to make room in her own life for other things, other people. She had long ago exhausted all the crowded, lonely avenues that might have led her to Cillian. She'd knocked on so many doors over the years, made so many journeys back and forth to London, following even the slightest lead. It had worn her out.

She'd told me, maybe a year earlier, that she had done everything she could. She'd left letters and messages and invitations and contact details everywhere she could think of. Finally, she said, she'd had to accept that Cillian would need to come looking for her. She could do no more, and she was as much at peace with that as she could ever hope to be.

We'd made it easier, she told me. Having me with her, having Belle to raise together, helped. I knew she was concerned about us, her new family. But it wasn't a discussion I was ready to have. Not then.

On that day, though, our first day in that bright and lovely space, I knew it was time to start finding the way to write my own new story. To begin to accept that my life, and my daughter's life, were going to be different from what I had hoped, what I had planned on the day I'd made my exhilarating escape from St Brigid's.

28

Betty, Summer 2019

Well now, Jack.

There is a whole sea of trouble at Tess's. She hasn't told me anything about it, not yet, but Mrs Nosey Neighbour, the one who lives in Mary's pocket – you remember Mary, from the park? – she told me at the shops this morning that a Garda car was seen in the past few days outside our old front door.

I was quite sharp with her, told her she must have been mistaken, and then I walked off about my business. I made sure to hold my head up. But she'd started something churning inside me. Something that made me think of Luke.

I'm worried, Jack. What on earth can that young man have done to bring the guards to our daughter's door? I know, I know, MylesandConor brought them to us, to that same door, years and years ago, but I can't imagine Luke nicking stuff from a sweetshop, can you? Besides, Tess always makes sure both boys have enough money for whatever they need. Maybe even too much. But I'd never say.

She was here for a cup of tea earlier and I know she wasn't telling me the truth. The whiteness of her face, the strain I saw there, made me feel sad.

'Are you all right, love?' I asked her. 'You're looking very tired.'

I've found 'tired' to be a useful word over the years. It's like the set of Russian dolls I once bought in London, years ago, where one little figure nestles inside the other. In the same way, so many options nestle inside the word 'tired'. A listening ear, understanding, sympathy. But no judgement.

'Stressed', on the other hand, is not a good word to use with our daughter. Last time I blurted it out, a couple of weeks back, she just put down her cup and said 'I'm *fine*. Just *fine*,' when I knew by her tone she wasn't fine at all. But she was very prickly and so I pulled back. She murmured something about not having slept well the night before, and I let it go.

This afternoon, though, she waved one hand in the air, irritably, and said 'It's just more of the same – Luke and Aengus fighting all the time. It wears me out.'

'What happened?' And then I added quickly: 'Only if you want to tell me.'

But I wasn't quick enough to change the way I was looking at her: she saw my 'worry-face', as you used to call it. I know she did. She softened at once. She reached across the table and placed one warm hand on my cold one.

'It's okay,' she said. 'Truly. It's nothing for you to fret about. It's just that sometimes the pair of them do my head in.'

'Really?' I said. I let the word hang in the air for a bit. 'That's not something I'm familiar with. Our house was always such an oasis of tranquillity.' She smiled at that and the moment lifted a little.

I gave her every chance, Jack, but she never mentioned it. She never once said anything about the Garda car. So I allowed the fiction of Aengus and Luke and their fighting to continue.

She'll tell me, in time, I know she will. But I can't shake the feeling that something bad is making its way towards us, stalking our daughter and her family.

You brought us all closer, Jack, during those final weeks of your life. Particularly Luke. But I felt him slipping away from me afterwards, once you were no longer here. Gradually, even your shadow slipped away, too, taking with it your watch and your magnifying glass and your workshop in the shed at the bottom of the garden and all your small treasures.

You really understood Luke, better than any of us.

What was it you called him? Inquisitive, was it? No, acquisitive. That's the word. You said he was acquisitive. You called him that – but only to me – when you'd refused to give him your old magnifying glass, the one that once belonged to your father. He threw such an almighty tantrum that day that Tess took him home straight away.

I remember how upset you were, how upset we both were. I can still see that old magnifying glass in its faded black velvet sleeve. I can feel the weight of it on my palm. Your father brought it back from France, sometime in 1918. It was his celebration of making it back home safely after the War, unlike so many others.

He used it to compensate for his failed eyesight. You said he was an avid reader, always hunched over the kitchen table with a book. That's how you remembered him. And that's why the glass was so precious to you. You loved its heavy brass frame, its smooth mechanism, and the way your father's initials were etched onto the handle.

You'd taken both boys out into the back garden one bright summer Saturday. They were about seven and ten years old. You showed them how to harness the midday sunlight through the lens of the magnifying glass. They were thrilled when you set fire to a piece of paper as the highlight of your lesson.

Patiently, one at a time, you let them try, making sure that they each managed it, making sure they were both safe. Afterwards, you told me how Luke tried to hold on to the magnifying glass, insisting he be allowed to take it home.

'No, Luke,' you said, kindly but firmly. 'That stays here, with Granda Jack. It's not a toy. You can use it anytime you come to visit, but only when I'm around.'

Tess and I were inside, so we were unaware of what was happening until we heard Luke screaming.

She was up and out the door like a shot. Luke was beside himself. He was shaking, crying, his whole body rigid. Aengus was standing off to one side, looking bewildered.

Tess gathered them both to her and left immediately. 'I'll call you,' she said, over one shoulder, as she bundled the still-howling Luke into the car. And then: 'I'm so sorry.'

You told me over and over what had happened, as though trying to figure out what you had done wrong. 'I couldn't let him have it,' you said. 'Talk about playing with fire. What else could I have done?'

'Nothing,' I said. 'You did nothing wrong.' You were always soft-hearted, Jack, something that used to drive me mad when our own children were young. You left all the discipline to me. And that often meant I handed out enough punishment for both of us. I'd a temper on me in those days, and I'd lay out all round me. There were times when I was harsher than I should have been, I know I was. I regret that.

You were so tender with Tess's two boys. You refused to see any bad behaviour for what it was. They're just being boys, you'd say. I saw Tess give you a look when you said that, on more than one occasion. I don't blame her. She challenged you once, sharply. She said you shouldn't excuse bad behaviour with that tired old line, 'boys will be boys'.

Where did that leave the girls, she asked. I understood why she said that, and I silently agreed with her, but my heart went out to you because you looked so confused. As Aengus might say, you just didn't 'get it'.

Anyway, a few days later, after the incident with the magnifying glass, Tess brought Luke back to apologise. You took him by the hand and went out into the garden where he said he was sorry.

It was over, and we never mentioned it again.

29

Eileen, 1960

I knew who she was, the minute I stepped off the train from Amiens Street, lugging my case down the last two awkward steps. It was something about the way she stood on the platform, with that air of ownership that I would get to know so well. That day, I just hoped that some of her self-possession might rub off on me.

It was partly her coat that did it. Beautiful beige wool with a soft, dark brown mink collar. Up-to-the-minute London and New York fashion. The American style magazines were calling that kind of collar 'wedding band'. The coat sleeves were wide and wrist-length and she was wearing impeccable white gloves. I couldn't take my eyes off her. Pure film-star glamour.

This lovely woman smiled and made her way towards me. 'Are you Eileen?'

'I am. And you must be Maria.'

I stood up straight and held out my hand. Majella had told me not to be shy. Show this woman you're worth your salt, she said. Look her in the eye. You need her to believe in you.

We shook hands and I saw her appraise me. I was glad I was wearing gloves. I could feel how sweaty my palms had become.

'I've heard only good things about you,' she said. 'Welcome to Dundalk.'

'Thank you. It's lovely to meet you.'

There was only the slightest tremor in my voice. Had I passed muster? I wondered. Or was there something else I needed to do?

I'd made my own costume a couple of weeks earlier: dark navy bouclé wool, with a pink trim around the edge-to-edge jacket. Knee length pencil skirt, navy court shoes. I'd got the material in a sale, but those shoes had cost me a fortune. When I got dressed up to show Majella, I could feel the rush of confidence that my new outfit gave me. It was a kind of inner glow that made me feel I could do anything.

Best foot forward, Majella had said, nodding in approval. And remember: your shoes and your bed are investments. You're always in either one or the other.

'Come with me.'

Maria turned and walked towards the station exit, her handbag nestling in the crook of her left arm, her coat swinging smartly from side to side. Even the way she walked had purpose. People turned to look at her, some covertly, the more daring with open admiration. She was like a bright flash of colour, moving quickly across the concourse, making the shades of grey around her disappear.

I know I struggled with my suitcase, but I must have managed because the next thing I remember is sitting in Maria's car. I was surprised at the way Dundalk train station was so similar to the ones I'd got to know in London: same yellow brick, same glass and metal roof. I wasn't sure whether that was a good or a bad omen. I decided it was neither. This was my new life: just get on with it.

I'm no longer sure what Maria and I spoke about – nothing of what we had in common, I'm certain of that – but I have a vivid impression of that car journey from the station to what would be my first home in that unfamiliar city.

The wideness of the streets surprised me: I'd expected everything to be much smaller. But there were very few cars compared with London. I remember the imposing face of the town hall, as well as the library, and passing by a blur of green spaces.

Maria parked outside a small shop, with a tobacconist's on one side and a hairdresser's on the other. 'Here we are,' she said. 'Come and look at the space first, see if you can make it work.'

Make it work? What was she talking about? Wasn't she offering me a flat above a shop, at a modest rent, somewhere to live and be safe? Of course I'd make it work: I *had* to make it work. But I followed her and kept my powder dry, with Majella's advice ringing in my ears.

Maria opened the door and we stepped into a dimly lit room. The large window that gave onto the street was covered in that white-out stuff, painted from the inside so that nothing of the shop's interior was visible to the curious passer-by.

Her manner became brisk. 'The flat is upstairs. Run up and take a look at it and then come back and talk to me.'

I ran up the stairs and pushed open the door into a small living room, tiny kitchen, bedroom, bathroom. It was bright and it was perfect and it was mine. If I could afford it. The thought gave me pause. All over again, I calculated my careful savings from the past two years in London as I hurried back down the stairs.

'It's wonderful. I—'

But she didn't let me finish.

'It's yours to rent. And so is the shop.' She handed me a piece of paper. 'Here's the addresses of some of the best fabric suppliers, between here and Belfast. I understand you don't want to spend any time in Dublin.'

It wasn't a question. And even if it had been, I wouldn't have had the wit just then to answer it.

'Majella tells me that sewing is where your interest lies?'

She must have seen the shock on my face because she stopped and spoke more gently. 'Don't worry, if you can make the space work, we'll sort out the details between us later. It'll take you a couple of weeks to settle yourself.'

I looked around me, filled with a mix of excitement and terror. My own shop! As my eyes adjusted, I could see the sturdy counter, the shelves behind it, a door into what looked like another, smaller room.

'Well,' she said, 'are you interested?' There was a touch of impatience in her voice now, and it jolted me into speech.

'Yes, yes, of course I'm interested – but—'

'Details come later,' she said, firmly. 'Now, let's get your things from the car and you can start making yourself at home. We'll meet in the morning and discuss your business plan.'

I became aware that my mouth was open and I closed it, quickly.

'I've already done a bit of digging: we need an alterations service on this side of the city. That should help to get you started. In the meantime,' she handed me an envelope, 'this evening, you can get a bite to eat here. And the grocer's is just two streets away.'

There was a rough map on the front of the envelope. 'Dolores is the hairdresser – she's just next door. She's a good neighbour and so is Cillian, on the other side.'

The name gave me a shock. I hoped Maria wouldn't notice.

She helped me in with my suitcase and then she was gone, leaving a trace of perfume and powder behind her.

What was it Majella had said? That Maria had all the men in the Chamber of Commerce terrorised? I could well believe it.

*

For the rest of that day and night, I felt as if I'd been in the presence of a whirlwind. I was energised, fuelled by an optimism I had never known before. I couldn't sleep: didn't want to sleep. Nothing daunted me. I'd no clue what a business plan was, but I'd find out. Until I did, the ideas that were forming in my head would have to be enough to convince Maria that I was worth her investment. Majella had prepared me well.

After I'd finished unpacking, I sat on the two-seater sofa in my tiny new living room and allowed myself to fill with a sense of home. This was happening. It was really happening.

I took Maria's envelope out of my pocket to check the directions to the local café. When I lifted the flap, I saw that it contained one crisp, green pound note. The kindness of it took my breath away.

I remembered Majella's words. I promised myself, and her, that I, too, would 'pass it on'.

Right now, I needed to prove to her, to both these women, that I deserved it.

30

Joanie, 1980

Joanie is restless again.

Most nights, she spends hours wandering. She steals out onto the corridor as soon as everyone else is sleeping. By now, she has the nuns' night-time routines worked out, down to the last second. She knows when to slip into a doorway to avoid a patrol; she knows the exact moment to make her way back to bed when, on every third night, their rounds are more thorough; and she knows when to stay put in the dormitory.

The nights she doesn't wander are the times when a fight has broken out earlier, or one of the girls refuses to stop wailing, or somebody among them loses the plot. On those occasions, the nuns are all a lot more vigilant. They miss nothing.

Even on the ordinary nights, the quiet ones, Joanie is alert to the swish of habit against lino; the faint scent of antiseptic soap that each leaves in her wake; and the slowing down of her own heartbeat as, one more time, she finds herself safe, undiscovered.

Once, though, she got careless. She must have been distracted. That happens to her from time to time, most often on the days when one of the other girls has given birth. It's always harder to focus afterwards. Harder, too, to escape the ambush of Charlie's soft memory, his tiny fingernails. And that head of black hair! She can still feel the sleek babywetness of it as she pressed him against her cheek.

That night, Joanie had slipped off the corridor and into the sluice room, all her senses firing. She could hear the low voices that meant two of them were approaching, rather than one.

That was unusual. The night-time rounds were always solitary ones. Joanie had often wondered whether such solitariness was a punishment, although she couldn't imagine for what.

The girls were the only ones needing to be punished, as far as Joanie could see. The penitents, that's what they were called. Such a strange-sounding word. Joanie had never heard it before. Maeve told her it meant 'sinners'. Joanie imagined that the girls, the penitents, must use up every single punishment in the whole world, so that nothing was left over for the nuns.

That night, Joanie stood very still as she waited for the voices to fade. She hoped she'd be able to control the tickle at the back of her throat, the harsh cough that always wanted to break free whenever she was frightened or stressed. Her heartbeat began to pound at the top of her head and she wasn't able to make out the words that floated past the sluice room door, just the tone.

She didn't recognise the voices, either – everything was too muffled. But there was a sense of urgency to them that was unfamiliar. Joanie tiptoed her way towards the far corner of the room, and crouched there, her heart hammering. If anyone opened the door, she'd be safe: away off on the other side, hidden by the shadows.

While she waited for the danger to pass, Joanie looked out the window – but sideways, from her vantage point on the floor, in case anyone out there looked up. She took care to keep herself invisible, even from below. But people hardly ever looked up. Her big brother Eddie had taught her that, playing hide and seek in the orchard at home. He used to climb up to the highest branches of the apple trees. None of the other kids could ever find him. They looked everywhere except up. But even if they did, Eddie had a knack of hiding away, making himself invisible among the leaves.

He did it often enough at home, hiding from trouble, and so when it was a game, he always won. Thinking of him as she crouched by the window, Joanie was filled with a wrenching sickness for her home place. At least most of the unkindnesses there were familiar; bearable. She missed her mother, though. And she still didn't understand why they'd sent her away with hard hands and closed faces.

Warm up the bed for me, there's a good girl, he'd said. And she'd done as she was told, just as she always knew she must. That's what made it all so confusing. That, and the way her father turned away from her afterwards, as though she was nothing to do with him.

She still missed her brother Eddie, his rough tenderness, his wild sense of fun, his fierce protection of her. She'd love to see his cheeky smile again, just the once. And it still hurt, thinking of all the little ones growing up alone, without their big sister. Joanie didn't want to think too much about what would happen if she wasn't there to look out for them.

As she gazed out the window, she began to feel hypnotised by field after field of black, nothing much visible at first, then the sway of the wind as it flattened and raised the leaves of the vegetable gardens. Like a dance, she thought. It was as though the wind and the leaves had a shared rhythm, each one always in step with the other. It was peaceful here, and she leaned her head against the wall, gazing into the gradually lightening darkness as her eyes became used to the gloom.

Right below her, a sudden pool of yellow bloomed. A door opened. She heard voices again, indistinct words, then feet on gravel. Curious, she edged closer to the window, keeping to the shadows, just in case.

She recognised Billy, one of the gardeners, by his cap. It was tartan and so it always stood out from the others'. Delivery men, workmen, gardeners: they all wore flat caps, but Billy's was different. His was red, with faint blue, yellow and white stripes. It was a bright shout of colour as he moved about the vegetable gardens during the day. It was easy to tell Billy apart from the others and besides, he was tall, very tall, and skinny. He was also kind: he usually had nice things to say to the kitchen girls whenever he came to the back door. Beanpole Billy, Cook had christened him. He knew, but he didn't seem to mind.

Joanie saw him touch the peak of his tartan cap now, as he bent his head, holding out both hands for something that she couldn't yet see. Then he stepped back, and the wooden box he was holding became visible.

Joanie was puzzled. It was one of those rough, splinter-giving, slatted boxes: the ones that held onions, or carrots or potatoes. She'd seen them often enough during the times she was put on kitchen duty.

Why was Billy taking one of them away from the back door, rather than delivering one of them to the girls in the kitchen, a boxful of vegetables to be washed and peeled? That ordinary, daytime chore somehow didn't fit with what Joanie was seeing. And what was Billy doing here anyway, so late at night?

He touched his cap once again and turned away. The yellow bloom disappeared, and he made his way towards the wooden gate to the left of the main vegetable garden, the gate that was always locked. He held the box out in front of him, not up close to his body as he usually would. His tenderness confused Joanie. And so she watched as he rested the box gently on the ground, opened the gate, picked up the box again and disappeared from sight.

She waited for a minute or two to see if he might come back through the same gate, but he didn't. She stood up, suddenly nervous at how much time must have passed.

Slowly, she opened the door of the sluice room, slipped soundlessly into the corridor, and closed the door behind her. To her left, she saw the squat figure of Sr Marguerite disappear around the corner at the other end of the corridor.

Right on time.

She turned and made her way back towards her dormitory. If anybody had seen her, they'd have been surprised at the swiftness of her step. At night, she moved much more quickly than during the day. She was less aimless, too.

She'd found that a practised slowness during the working hours meant that everyone left her alone. It meant the other girls usually got chosen for the energetic stuff, and she could keep on doing kitchen duties whenever help was needed. That suited her, the peeling, scraping, washing. She could keep herself to herself. Besides, she didn't want to make friends, didn't want to get close to any of the other girls, ever again.

She misses Maeve, though. She was so much kinder than the others. Every time she thinks about her, Joanie gets a lump in her throat. She remembers the wee lemon-and-green-striped teddy that Maeve knitted for her. She remembers the way Maeve used to comfort her at night, rocking her back and forth in the glimmering silence of the dormitory. She'd let her cry, too, wiping her tears away gently, telling her stories until Joanie was calm enough to go back to her own bed.

But one day, just like that, Maeve disappeared, along with her wee babby, the one with the funny name. Joanie has decided to take heart from Maeve's escape. It means that one day she, too, might get out of here. And when she does, she'll not stop until she finds out where they've taken her son.

His name is Charlie. And it's a secret, her secret. She repeats the name she gave him, hugging it to herself, over and over as she walks.

She promises him she'll never stop looking.

31

Tess, Summer 2019

Tess ends the call to her mother and puts her mobile on the coffee table. She's called Betty to tell her that Luke is home again, safe. That he came back late last night and has been in his room ever since.

'He has to appear sometime,' Betty says. 'Hunger will drive him downstairs, if nothing else. Just wait him out.'

Tess bites back a sharp reply. It isn't always that simple, she wants to shout. Life is a bit more complex these days: not everything can be solved by a tea towel snapping against bare legs. Besides, you don't know the half of it. I shielded you for years; kept a lid on everyone's bad behaviour; made their antics fly below your radar. There were two mothers in our house, not one. So don't tell me that all I have to do is wait Luke out. Different times, mother. Very different times.

Tess leans her head back, sinking into the softness of the sofa cushion and closes her eyes. Maybe she'll just doze for half an hour. It would be good to escape, to somewhere she isn't needed.

She drifts into a hazy sleep. After a moment or two, she becomes aware of someone coming into the room – probably Mike: it sounds like his quiet step. She chooses not to open her eyes; allows herself to fade away even further into a deep, comforting nothingness.

*

A phone rings somewhere and Tess's eyes snap open. To her surprise, she feels refreshed. She sits up and sees that it's Luke who's sitting across from her, not Mike.

'Luke,' she says, 'I didn't know you were here. How long have I been asleep?'

'I'm here about half an hour,' he says. 'Dunno how long before that.'

He starts to fiddle with his phone, turning it back and forth but, oddly, not looking at the screen. 'It looks as though the guards are going to drop the charges against Hunter.' He blurts out the words, not looking at her.

'What?' something inside Tess leaps to attention. 'Hunter?' she asks, slowly.

Luke looks uncomfortable. 'Yeah. He was at that . . . party, the one I was at. You know.'

'He's the other person accused of assault?' She tries to take in the implications. She hasn't known the name until now. Matthew Kerr has been grimly, ethically silent.

'He can't tell us, Tess.' She can hear Mike's exasperation. 'You *know* that. We're not Matthew's client. There are boundaries.'

'He doesn't mind taking our money, though.'

Then Mike would sigh, shaking his head in a way that makes her even more angry. 'We've been over this before. I'm as frustrated as you are. But that's the way it is.'

Luke nods now, just the once.

'Answer me, Luke,' she says, sharply.

'Yeah,' he says. 'He's the other person.'

'And why,' she can feel her mouth go dry, 'why are the charges going to be dropped against him and I assume not against you?'

He shrugs. 'Dunno. Matthew called earlier. That's all he said.'

'Have you spoken to Hunter?'

'He's not answering his phone.'

I'll bet he's not, she thinks, furiously. 'Keep trying.'

He looks at her now, his blue eyes bluer than ever. 'I didn't do it, Mum. Honestly, I didn't do anything wrong.'

He lowers his head. His voice breaks. Finally, he sobs. She watches him, his bent head, his suddenly forlorn figure. His gelled hair now makes him look vulnerable, a caricature of cool, not even close to the real thing. Everything in her strains towards him, but she steels herself not to move.

'Talk to me, Luke,' she says. 'You have to talk to me, to us. This is torture. We need to know.'

He wipes his eyes roughly with the back of one hand. 'I'm ready,' he says. 'I'm ready to talk to you now.'

She stands up, rests one hand briefly on his shoulder. 'I'll get your dad,' she says. 'But only if you swear to tell us the truth, no matter how bad it is. No more lies, Luke. No more evasions. We'll stand by you no matter what, but do us the honour of telling us the truth.'

He looks up at her, his face still wet. 'I will,' he says. 'I promise.'

She opens the door to the hall and climbs the stairs. She taps quietly on the door of the boxroom, in case Mike is on a call.

'Come in,' he says, swivelling the chair to face her. The desk is littered with documents, printouts of Excel sheets, scribbled Post-its, random bits of paper. 'You okay?'

'It's Luke. He says he's ready to talk.'

'Is he now.' It isn't a question. Mike leans back into the chair again. His expression is grim; his face has set into hard, unforgiving lines.

'Let's just listen. Let's just let him speak.' Tess raises her hands, lets them fall again in resignation, or defeat, she isn't sure which. 'I don't know what else we can do.'

It's as though she and Mike have changed places since yesterday. He feels convinced that Luke is guilty as charged; she's willing to give him the benefit of the doubt.

'He says the guards are not going ahead with the complaint against Hunter.'

'Hunter? So that's his name.' Mike rubs his cheek with one hand. He hasn't shaved. 'Great,' he says, bitterly. 'So Luke is now the only one facing charges? Jesus Christ.'

In the noon light, Tess is shocked, all over again, at how suddenly old he looks. He stands up and she places one hand on his chest. 'I know this is a stupid question, but are you even halfway okay?'

He attempts a smile. 'I'll let you know after we've listened. We'll try to ask as few questions as possible, all right? Let's not fill any silences. He has one chance, just the one, to come clean.'

'You think he's guilty.'

Mike hesitates. He's taken aback at her directness. Indecision shadows his face. 'I wish I didn't, but part of me is beginning to believe that he is. Why else would he have run like that yesterday morning?'

'I don't know. I have doubts, for sure, but I honestly don't know. And just because he's behaved badly doesn't mean he's automatically guilty. I try to hold on to that.'

'I hope you're right. Let's do this and see what happens.'

*

'I understand you're ready to talk to us, Luke.'

Mike sits in the armchair; Tess takes the sofa. They've decided to sit separately, so that they can each see Luke from a different angle. It's Mike who's suggested it. 'Besides,' he's said, 'I don't want him to face a monolith. We want to encourage him to tell us the truth, not intimidate him into silence.'

He spreads his hands. 'Okay, son,' he says, 'we're here now and we're listening. This is your one chance to tell us what happened. We need to know what we're dealing with.'

Luke faces his father. He does not flinch. 'I didn't do anything wrong,' he says. 'Honestly, I didn't.'

'Okay,' Mike says. 'Well, we're here because we need to understand what *did* happen. So I'm going to put that to one side for the moment. And I'm not going to ask you why you ran away and stayed away all day yesterday. Not yet.'

'I was scared.' Luke looks down at the floor.

'Look at me, Luke. I said we'd leave all that aside for now. Why don't you tell us instead what happened at the party.'

Luke edges forward in the armchair. His face is open, earnest.

'The girl I was with is called Amy. I don't know her well – just from seeing her at college. But she was at the party that night and we got on well together. We had some drinks and she . . . came upstairs with me.' He stops.

'Go on.'

'Hunter came up as well.' Luke pauses. 'I mean, not at first, just a bit later on.' His face begins to flush. 'He had some dope that he didn't want to share with everyone, so it was just the three of us. He stayed for a while and then he left.' Luke glances over at Tess but she doesn't say anything.

He bites the inside of his cheek, abstractedly, and she stiffens. He used to do that as a small child, when he'd been caught red-handed, doing something forbidden. He used to lie so easily back then, even when it was clear he was in the wrong.

He starts to shrug. 'Then we . . . you know . . . we started getting together. Kissing and stuff.' He won't look at either of them.

His embarrassment doesn't feel real. Tess glances over at Mike, who's looking steadily at Luke. The tension in the room begins to build.

'That's not why we are where we are,' Mike says after a minute. 'Something happened that you're not saying. This is no time to be coy, Luke. This girl, Amy, is clearly saying that you had sex with her when she didn't consent.'

'But that's not true,' he insists. 'That's exactly what I'm telling you. She was as into me as I was into her.' He's almost shouting.

'So what changed?' Tess asks.

Luke turns and looks at her. 'I dunno. One minute everything is fine, and the next minute she's crying. I stopped when she asked me to, I swear I did. I thought she wanted it – we both did. I mean . . .' and his voice trails off.

There is silence for a moment and then Mike speaks again. 'I'm trying to understand this. So – what happened between the time that Amy seemed to want it and when she began to cry?'

Luke looks uncomfortable. 'I'm not sure. Hunter came back into the room. I think she might have felt embarrassed, or something.'

Every one of Tess's nerve ends is alight.

'So Hunter came into the room for a second time, after you thought he'd gone back downstairs?' Mike's tone is reasonable.

'Yeah.'

'Isn't that a bit strange? I mean, if it was clear you and Amy were together?' Now he sounds puzzled.

Luke shrugs. 'Everything was fine as far as I was concerned.' He looks first at Tess, then at Mike. 'Hunter didn't stay. He left us alone together.'

'As far as *you* were concerned, everything between the two of you – you and Amy, that is – was fine,' Mike repeats.

'Yeah but, I mean, *I* don't know – how am I supposed to know what she was feeling?' Luke is beginning to get agitated.

'Did you even ask?' Tess is furious. She can't help it. Mike glances over at her. He shakes his head once, almost imperceptibly.

'Can I go and get a glass of water?' Luke's voice cracks.

'I'll get it,' she says. She's glad of the chance to leave the room. The heat has begun to grow at the back of her neck, the flush is already starting across her cheeks. And her heart is racing again. She needs air. And maybe Luke will speak to Mike in a way that he mightn't in front of her.

In the kitchen, she lets the cold water run over her wrists for a couple of minutes. She opens the window and lifts her face to the breeze. When she can't delay any longer, she goes back into the living room. She hands Luke the glass of water.

'Thanks,' he says. He drains the glass quickly.

Mike is leaning forward, elbows resting on his knees. 'Are you sure that's everything?'

'Yeah. Swear. That's it. Nothing else happened.'

'Okay. We're not finished with this, Luke, not by a long shot. But that's enough for now. I think it goes without saying that you're grounded for the next few weeks. We need you to be here at all times, in case Matthew needs to speak to you again.' He pauses. 'And in case we need to speak to you again.'

'Okay.' Luke looks relieved. 'Can I go?'

'Unless your mother needs to ask you something?'

'Nothing else right now. You can go to your room.'

He stands up, makes for the door.

Tess waits until he's almost there. She judges the moment. Then she calls after him, sharply. 'Luke!'

He turns back to her, his face suddenly ashen.

'Take your glass back to the kitchen, please.'

He goes to where he was sitting, picks the glass up off the floor. Then he leaves the room, closing the door quietly behind him.

Tess and Mike look at each other. 'Well?' Mike asks. He speaks so softly she can barely hear him.

'He's not telling the truth.'

Mike waits, looking down at his hands.

'His face when I called him back to pick up his glass spoke volumes. He was terrified I'd found out something he didn't want us to know.'

'I agree.'

'What else did he say to you while I was out of the room? I hoped he'd open up more if I wasn't there.'

'Yeah, well, he said they did have sex. Unprotected, but consensual. According to him.'

'Anything else about Hunter? There is something very weird about him and his part in all of this.'

Mike sighs. 'I can't figure it. Unless . . .'

Tess feels cold. 'Unless what?'

'Unless they both tried to have sex with her – and Luke doesn't want to say.'

'Jesus Christ.' Tess runs her hands through her hair. A headache is beginning. 'I want to wake up from this nightmare.'

'We need to let Matthew know Luke's version of what happened. I don't think we'll get anything else out of him for now. He's decided on his story.' Mike pulls his mobile out of his pocket.

'We have to keep trying, Mike. We need to keep talking to him. Particularly as the charges have been dropped against Hunter.'

'Yeah, well.' He's searching for Matthew's number. 'Let's see what advice Matt gives us.' He presses the call button.

Tess waits, her stomach churning, while Mike leaves a message. Then he stands up. 'I'm going back upstairs,' he says. 'I have to work.' He shakes his head. 'There's such chaos brewing at work, I've no choice. I'll try Matt again later.' He looks at Tess. 'Unless you want to?'

She shakes her head. 'No. Let's talk to him together, when he gets back to you.'

She watches him leave the room. She can't move. Numbness crawls up her legs, across her shoulders. There is nothing she wants more than to climb between soft sheets and sleep for days.

But the fridge is empty. There is nothing for dinner. And the four of them need to eat. Their occasional family takeaways usually have an air of lightness to them, of celebration, particularly when Betty joins them. Tess couldn't bear that pretence right now.

She stands up and makes her way to the kitchen. She sits at the table and pulls the notebook towards her, unclipping the cartoonish pen.

She begins to make a list for the supermarket.

32

Maeve, 1983

It's six o'clock in the morning. Eileen and I are having our usual Thursday breakfast meeting. Belle is still asleep, but not for long. Ever since starting in the new shop, Eileen and I agree that early mornings are the best time for our catch-ups.

She spreads out the shop account books on the table in front of us. 'We need to diversify,' she's saying. 'This recession is really beginning to bite.'

Before I can say anything, there is a ring at the doorbell. It's an urgent summons, repeated in short, sharp bursts. I glance over at Eileen, puzzled, but she's already making her way towards the front door. I stand behind her, waiting.

'Paddy,' she says. I can hear the relief in her voice. Paddy is our milkman. He's part of our ordinary domestic routine of early morning deliveries. On Friday afternoons, late, he calls to collect whatever he's owed. He's a familiar neighbourhood figure, one who allows the kids, even the smallies, to 'help' him collect the empty milk bottles from the cluster of houses on our street.

I wonder what brings him to our door.

'Missis,' I hear him say. He's breathless.

I get a glimpse of his white face over Eileen's left shoulder. Then he whispers something I can't catch, although I see him glance over at me, just the once. He looks nervous.

'Maeve. Come with me. Quick as you can.' Eileen grabs me by the hand and pulls me along with her as she hurries towards the stairs.

I see how terrified she is. 'What? What is it? What's wrong?'

'It's Belle. Quickly.'

I follow her racing footsteps up to the landing. Something begins to fall inside me: that clutch of dread that has been with me ever since St Brigid's. It nests there, within some small internal space, folded away, silent. It maintains its own peculiar balance: until it doesn't.

Eileen opens the door and pushes me into Belle's bedroom. Inside is as I would have expected, at least at first. Lego bricks scattered all over the floor. A multi-coloured chaos of Sindy and Barbie clothes lying on the bed.

But the doll's house has tipped over; it's lying on its side under the bedroom window.

And then I see her.

Belle, in her My Little Pony pyjamas, is standing on the outside windowsill, her arms poised for flight. A silent, terrified scream closes my throat. I rush to the window at the same time as Eileen sprints from the room. I will never forget the sound of her footsteps hurrying down the stairs.

I have no idea what happens to time during those few seconds. I am aware of a tremendous stillness, a quietness into which everything around me disappears, sucked under some invisible surface. I have a sudden flash of understanding: this is what it means to have your heart in your mouth. Mine seems to stop beating for those few endless seconds, as I reach through the open window.

I clutch at my four-year-old daughter's pyjamas and yank her back into the bedroom by a handful of pink fabric.

She kicks and she screams and we fall together into a heap onto the bedroom floor.

'Jesus Christ, Belle, Jesus Christ,' I keep saying, over and over. I hold her close until she stops wriggling, her howls finally turning to whimpers.

'Belle, sweetheart, what were you doing?' I rock her back and forth and she calms. I kiss her beautiful face, her big blue eyes. Seeing the tiny veins on her closed lids makes me want to cry.

'I fly, like fairies,' she says. 'I have wings, Mama.' And she flaps her hands, preparing for flight.

I shake my head, barely able to speak. 'No, sweetheart,' I say. 'Only fairies have proper wings. Little girls have to stay on the ground, with Mama and Mama Leen, where it's safe.'

She frowns. 'No, Mama,' she says. 'Tinkerbell fly in the sky. Like butterflies. Like Belle.' And she nods, her eyes filled with the light of daring, of adventure.

In that moment, I see all the years of her life, of both our lives, unspool before me. The doctors' words come home to me. Words I finally begin to understand in a way I never have before.

Then, I begin to shake until my teeth chatter. I can't even think of letting her go. I want to hold on to her forever. Never leave this house. Never leave this *room*.

Belle begins to struggle against me at last. And then she's looking up at me, smiling. 'Fairies, Mama,' she says, one small hand stroking my hair. 'Belle and Tinkerbell. We fairies.'

*

Later, I learned that Paddy had spotted her on the windowsill as he completed his milk round. Several houses down the road from ours, as he stooped to leave bottles of milk on the tiled surface of a neighbour's porch, he became aware, out of the corner of one eye, of a flash of pink in the distance. He'd straightened up, puzzled.

When he looked properly in the direction of the strange pink blur, he at first had no idea what he was seeing. Then it hit him. He said his first instinct had been to shout and wave his arms around to get Belle's attention, but he didn't. A father of young children himself, he realised that the last thing he wanted to do was to startle this slight, pyjamaed child into falling.

He abandoned his bottles of milk and ran back to our house, ringing urgently at the doorbell. 'That took some doin', Missis,' he said later, shaking his head, running one trembling hand through his dark hair, its tips glinting with grey light. 'Jaysus, but I was terrified.'

Later, I learned that Eileen and Paddy had stood, unmoving, directly underneath the window of the upstairs bedroom, waiting to catch my small daughter as she fell.

*

When Belle was just over two years old, the specialist told me there was no doubt. 'Hypoxia,' he said.

I looked at him, not understanding.

'It means there was significant oxygen deprivation at birth.'

I heard the words as they came out of his mouth. Or rather, I think I saw them, or imagined them float somewhere above our heads.

'It can happen as the result of a difficult delivery.' He paused. 'How long were you in labour?' His tone was gentle.

It was Georgina who'd told me. 'About thirty hours, I think. But I can't be sure. It's all a bit of a blur, to be honest.'

He looked down at the desk for a moment. I had the sense that he didn't want to say what he said next. 'What butcher left you that long?'

I looked at him in surprise. 'I . . .' and stopped. I couldn't find the words in the present. They hovered somewhere above that other me, in the past.

'You don't have to tell me, if it's too painful,' he said.

I watched his hand clench around a pen. A beautiful black and silver fountain pen. I tried to stay focused on it and then I knew I needed to look him in the eye. I was terrified that I would break.

'Don't be kind,' I whispered, burying my head in the space between Belle's shoulder and her neck. 'I can't bear it.'

'I'm sorry,' he said. 'I'm sorry for what you've been through. No woman should labour for that long. It's unnecessary.' He stopped.

'Thank you.' The salt tears began to gather at the corners of my mouth. Then I felt myself slipping into that other place. I stopped and pulled myself back to the now. I couldn't allow myself to go there anymore. I had Belle to look after. I could feel the tender weight of her small, trusting hand in mine.

'What will it mean for her, as she grows?'

I understood the terms well enough. Impaired cognition. Developmental issues. Poor grasp of concepts. Misunderstanding of social cues.

Later, Eileen and I did our research in Dundalk library. We pored over volume after volume of medical textbooks. Every week, something new. Behind the specialist's clinical words were all the learning difficulties that Belle would face. And she might not understand how to keep herself safe. She might trust others too readily. She might not understand consequences.

But that day, it was impossible to believe the specialist's words. My daughter was bright: a beautiful, loving, happy toddler. I took her out of the hospital and headed for home. We stopped off in the local park on the way and I watched her as she followed other children around, her eyes shining. My courage began to fail me as I thought about the years ahead.

Someone yelled 'Maeve!' and I looked up, startled, as their little girl – a miniature Maeve – hurtled down the slide and ran towards her mother.

I sat up straighter. Weakness was for that other me, not the Warrior Queen. I lifted Belle up off the grass and we made our way home together for her favourite Peter Pan video and her Friday ice cream.

When we left St Brigid's together, I told her I'd look after her, protect her, make sure her life would be nothing like mine.

I was going to live up to that promise.

Eileen had closed the shop early that day and was waiting for us. Belle ran to her the moment we stepped into the hallway. 'Mama Leen!' she said, hurling herself into Eileen's arms. Eileen lifted her up for a hug, swung her around, then looked back over one shoulder at me. She saw my face and nodded, saying nothing. She just patted Belle's back, gently.

'How's my beautiful girl? Did that mama of yours remember to get you an ice cream?'

Belle squealed in delight, her arms wrapped around Eileen's neck, pressing their cheeks together with a sticky kiss.

I was reminded of the first day I'd seen her, standing at the fireplace in St Brigid's. I walked towards her now – as I had on that other day – feeling that yet another new part of my life had just begun. Eileen pulled me close. Held both of us, without a word.

It was my eighteenth birthday.

33

Eileen, 1978

I was in Arnotts for the first time in donkeys' years.
I hardly ever came to Dublin – I'd been maybe two or three times since I'd come back from London. Dundalk was home: home and work. In the early years, the mid-sixties, Maria used to come with me on my visits to fabric suppliers in Drogheda, Newry, Belfast, even as far away as Derry and Donegal. And she seemed to know everybody; she introduced me, negotiated discounts, set up webs of friendly connection. I loved the fast-fire banter between her and the fabric merchants – in those days, they were mostly men.

'How's about ye?' they'd say, as soon as we stepped across the threshold. There'd be a lift of the eyebrow, a friendly hand extended across the counter, a lot of nodding and smiling. It took a while for me to learn to love the lilt and the melody, along with the occasional harshness of their accents.

The Material Men, Maria called them – but not to their faces. To my young eyes, these were men who all seemed the same: old, balding, talkative. Men who loved the cut and thrust of the bargain. Men who stood behind huge gleaming counters, with shiny brass yardsticks set into the wooden surface. They measured out length after length of fabric with a speed and accuracy that used to astonish me.

Afterwards, Maria would always say the same thing: that's another contact. Next time, you fly solo. I went back and forth across the border, until 1968 meant I no longer could. The Troubles saddened me, on every level. On a selfish one, I missed the friends I'd made: the cups of tea, the gossip – the men were great gossips – and the black humour of their endless stories.

Anyway, years and years had passed since I'd bothered with Dublin. There was nothing for me there. But in 1978, for some strange reason, I allowed myself to be lured by the summer sales. I'd just been to Hickey's in Mary Street and filled the car boot with fabric – offcuts, remnants, ends of lines. I hoovered them all up. I'd also bought yards of cotton, silk, crepe, Cheviot, Merino: I loved the names, the texture of the fabric, the scent of all those bales piled high in anticipation.

It was an exhilaration that never waned – that sense of stepping into a space that always felt like mine. And then there was the thrill of making something beautiful out of ordinary stuff. It never lost its magic.

Each time I walked into a fabric supplier, I thought about Betty and Jack from Kilburn, and all their kindnesses to me. I'll never forget the emotion that welled up, as I stepped into my small, functional bedroom on the night they gave me the generous, practical gift of my first sewing machine.

Betty had transformed my room into an Aladdin's cave of treasures: jewel-coloured, studded, beaded, sequinned pieces of fabric, with tiny, mirrored shards reflecting the light. Standing there, that grey London evening, I felt as if I was swimming into a sea of brightness. I couldn't speak. Betty hugged me and said, 'For the start of your new life.'

She and I lost touch after a few years, something I regretted. But at the back of my mind lay the knowledge that I could probably find their address again, if I really wanted to. I think I understood, though, even as that very young woman, that London was a place I wanted to leave behind me for good.

*

Arnotts was thronged that afternoon. The air was heady with the excitement of bargain-hunting. Salesladies everywhere looked hot and hassled and the noise was tremendous. I'd just stepped onto the escalator. I was on my way up to the fashion area on the balcony. Idly, my eye drifted towards the down escalator and that's where I saw them. Frank and Esther, each of them staring straight ahead. They never did have much to say to each other.

I froze. I stumbled as the top step disappeared into the floor of the balcony and the sudden change in levels pitched me forward. I'd have fallen, but for the strong grasp of the woman who'd been standing behind me.

'Careful!' she said. 'Are you okay?'

She had a large face, a bright arc of red lipstick.

'Yes, thank you,' I said. 'I just got a bit distracted.'

'Okay, then. Mind yourself.'

She moved away and I'd already made my decision. I knew I had a choice: I could always do nothing. Carry on as though I hadn't just spotted my brother and his wife for the first time in almost twenty years.

But an energy stirred inside me. A defiance that still raised its head from time to time. Quickly, I walked away from the up escalator and stepped onto the downward one. I scanned the ground floor and spotted Esther. She was wearing a dreadful yellow patterned blouse – the woman never did have any taste – and she stood out from the crowd like a sore thumb. I could see her rummaging through a pile of sale items – the cheapest of the cheap – while Frank stood behind her, bored, looking off into the distance in that aimless way he had.

For a moment, I hesitated – did I really need this? – and then the strength came back. I'm not one for swearing, but at that moment, nothing else would do. Fuck you, Frank Garvey, I thought; fuck you and your nasty wife. One word from you – who could do no wrong in our parents' eyes – and I would never have been banished the way I was. I would still have my son. I would still have Cillian.

'Well, Frank,' I said, as I marched right up to him, 'isn't this a coincidence? After all these years. How are you? And Esther, how lovely to see you.'

I had the pleasure of watching shock ripple across his face. He went grey. And Esther, when she turned around, blushed bright red to the roots of her badly dyed hair. Neither of them spoke.

I didn't fill the silence.

'Come along, Frank,' Esther said, when she'd recovered. 'We're leaving.' She put one hand on his arm and began to push her way towards the door. He followed like a lamb. Maybe it's not fair to think this: maybe we're all responsible for the selves we become in the end, but I've always thought that if Esther had been a better woman, my brother might have been a better man.

I followed them out the main door to Henry Street. I walked quickly so that I overtook them and stopped them in their tracks.

'Have you not even one courteous word for your sister, Frank? Nothing to say after all this time?'

Esther kept tugging at his arm, but in fairness, he faced me. 'Eileen,' he said. Then 'Eileen,' again, and that was all he could manage. Despite myself, I softened, just a bit. There had always been a narrow seam of kindness in his nature, even if it wasn't up to much. A kindness that was just . . . there, except when it mattered.

'I don't want anything, Frank,' I said. 'Just an acknowledgement. If what I did was so wrong, I've been punished enough, believe me. I had to give my son away. But of course you know that, don't you?'

He wouldn't look at me. Esther tugged harder at his sleeve. Some badness inside made me prolong this non-conversation.

'How's Gerard?' Apple of their eye.

No response.

'And Fiona?' I knew their daughter's name. Ireland's a small place.

At the mention of Fiona, Frank looked distressed. He glanced at his wife, who looked stonily ahead. Something about that glance, something about the air that tensed, darkened between husband and wife, made me suspicious.

Without looking at me, Esther dragged him away. I watched them as they marched towards O'Connell Street. Neither of them looked back.

But my gut was on fire. Fiona must be sixteen, maybe seventeen. Something was going on. I would make it my mission to find out.

*

My brother had always been a creature of habit. I suppose most of us are, really – but Frank's habits were more habitual than most. I looked him up in the Dublin phone book. My brother was ridiculously proud of his second name, our grandfather, William's. He'd been some big shot solicitor in his day. Frank's use of the inherited initial made him feel grown-up, important. He'd started using it when he went to university.

I saw, to my surprise, that he and Esther had moved house. I wondered why. I suspected he wouldn't have changed job, and I was right. I drove back to Dublin the following week and I waited for him, outside his office. Maria had helped me find someone to look after the alterations for the occasional half-day. Teresa was bright and hard-working. I could trust her for as long as it took me to confront my brother.

And so I lurked in nearby shops, glancing out every time a door to the street opened or closed. On the second afternoon of my stakeout, I got him. He walked out onto O'Connell Street with a couple of colleagues. The three of them were replicas of each other. Dark suits, sober ties, each carrying a briefcase. I stepped right into their path and stopped dead, beaming.

'Frank,' I said. 'What a lovely surprise.'

The other men melted away.

'What are you doing?' he asked, flushed this time, and angry. 'What do you want?'

'Something very simple,' I said, 'and then I'll leave you alone. The other day, I asked about your children. I still have a nephew and a niece, even though you think I'm not good enough to have anything to do with them. So how is Gerard?'

He looked as though he'd rather be anywhere else than here. 'He's fine,' he said, curtly. 'He's at UCD. He'll be graduating soon.' He couldn't help the touch of pride in his voice. My son, the university student. How history repeats itself. He began to walk away and I stayed with him, right at his side. I was enjoying this.

'And Fiona?'

'She's away. At school.'

I almost laughed, seeing how evasive he was. 'Frank,' I said, 'you're such a shite liar.'

He began to bluster. 'How dare you accuse me . . .' And he stopped walking. I stopped, too, and faced him.

'Oh stop it, will you. Look, I'll go away and leave you alone. I will never let Esther know that we spoke. But you must tell me where Fiona is. I'm not moving until you do.'

I watched the expression on his face change. It was like watching clouds form and disperse. He moved from frustration to fear to indecision.

'Frank – you owe me this. I'm warning you: I'll come to your house. I'll make a scene so the neighbours will know. Just *tell* me.'

Finally, he managed to say it. He told me where Fiona was.

I didn't know the name, but I guessed. 'Why?'

'You should know,' he shot back. 'She got herself into trouble, just like you did.'

'Really?' I said. 'All on her own? We both managed it all on our own, did we?'

He looked anywhere but at me.

'Give me the address.' I tried to hide my contempt, at least until I'd got what I wanted. I rummaged in my bag for a bit of paper and a pen. 'Here,' I said. 'Just write it down.'

He scribbled for a minute or two and handed the paper and pen back to me. 'Don't . . .' he began.

'You needn't worry, Frank. I won't land you in it.' I closed the clasp on my shoulder bag and looked up at him. 'You never did understand, did you, you or Esther?'

He looked puzzled. 'What? Understand what?'

'That I'm far more ashamed of you than you could ever be of me. Don't worry, Frank. Your secret is safe.'

I had the immense satisfaction of walking away, leaving him standing at the corner of Henry Street and O'Connell Street, an astonished look on his face and his mouth hanging open.

It's still one of my most treasured memories.

34

Joanie, 1980

It was Sr Lucia who got her the job in the kitchen. She came across Joanie, a few days after Maeve had disappeared, lying on the bed – Maeve's bed – face down, and sobbing.

Joanie became dimly aware of a cool hand on hers and she knew she should sit up, wipe away her tears and get back to work before she got into trouble. But she felt so desolate she no longer cared about trouble. It didn't matter who was standing over her, waiting. Let them wait. Things couldn't be any worse.

'What is it, dear? What's the matter?'

Joanie started. She recognised that voice. She wiped her eyes as best she could and struggled into sitting. Sr Lucia was looking at her.

Joanie didn't know what to say. She missed Eddie, and now she missed Maeve and her wee babby, but most of all, she missed Charlie. But she wasn't allowed to say any of those things, so she stood up and shook her head, shaking off the sadness at the same time. She turned towards the door, but Sr Lucia stopped her.

'Just a moment,' she said. 'Before you go.'

Joanie waited.

'There is an opening in the kitchen. A permanent one, I believe. I need someone to help Cook, and I was wondering if you would be able for the duties?'

Joanie looked at her. What? Able for scrapin' and choppin'? Sure, wasn't everybody able for that? Was this another class of a trick?

Cautiously, she said: 'Yes, Sister. I've already worked in the kitchen.'

Then she remembered the vegetable gardens outside, the beckoning freedom of the fields. This, suddenly, was something she wanted.

'I've four younger sisters at home, as well as one older brother. Mam isn't well, and I cooked for all of them, before . . .' She couldn't stop herself babbling.

Sr Lucia nodded. 'Let me see what I can do.'

Joanie's heart lifted at the thought. But she couldn't trust it. Could she?

'I have to go.'

'Yes.' Sr Lucia's smile was quiet, but lovely, Joanie thought. 'Away with you. And not a word to anyone.'

Joanie fled.

*

Billy was standing just outside the open kitchen door. He touched the peak of his tartan cap as he handed a box of carrots and turnips to Joanie. 'Mornin', miss,' he said.

He always made her feel shy. He was the only one to call her 'miss', and to look at her kindly. None of the other men would meet her eye.

'Thank you.' Joanie blushed. As he turned away, she was reminded of the night she'd hidden herself in the sluice room. The night she'd spotted Billy from the window, as he stood in a pool of yellowish light, reaching out for something they handed him from the back door.

A box just like this one. Once, during her early days in the kitchen, she'd risked asking Cook about that late-night visit. She kept her question vague: Joanie knew there were times when it paid to pretend to be slower, clumsier, than she really was.

Like the time when Cook gave her the job of serving afternoon tea to Father Farrell and the nuns, all of them fussing and flapping around him. Joanie didn't like Father Farrell, mostly because she remembered that Maeve hadn't liked him, either, but Joanie had her own reasons, too.

She didn't like it when he looked down his long, shiny nose at her. Or the times when he'd correct the way she said things. But that day, she couldn't think of how to get out of serving tea to all of them in the big front parlour, because Cook was determined that Joanie wouldn't be idle, and there wasn't any other job in the kitchen that she was capable of doing, just then.

Cook was already bad-tempered enough and she snapped at her for the way she was setting the tray. All at once, a solution came to Joanie: a bright flash of inspiration. She lifted the tray, already crowded with scones and cakes – the kinds that made her mouth water – and little dishes of jam and butter and then she tripped over her own booted feet, measuring her length on the tiled kitchen floor.

The tray sailed off on a journey of its own, sending scones and cakes, jam and butter, cups and saucers flying everywhere. Cake stands and plates and dishes all clattered to the floor with a racket that was almost shocking, even though Joanie knew the noise had to be coming.

Cook shouted JesusMaryandholySaintJoseph so many times Joanie lost count. Then youstupidclumsygirl over and over, until Joanie thought it might be a good idea to cry. Cook would always keep it going until she made the girls cry. Then she'd stop. Sometimes she looked satisfied, sometimes ashamed. That day, she just looked enraged.

Joanie kept her head down and cleaned up the mess. She didn't say a word for the rest of the day, just meekly went ahead with her evening chores. When Sister Lucia came into the kitchen later, she overheard Cook say stupidclumsygirl all over again. But she didn't care. Inside, she felt little pulses of delight at the success of her plan. Serving afternoon tea was the one job she'd never be asked to do again.

Cook didn't speak to her for days after. Her face closed over, just like it had the time Joanie had dared to ask the question about why Billy had been in the vegetable garden so late at night. Once the words were out of her mouth, she saw a flash of fear in Cook's eyes – just for an instant, but it was there. It was definitely there.

Cook reached out and clamped one hand on Joanie's forearm. She shook her head at her and finally, her voice low enough so that only Joanie could hear, she said to her to remember that curiosity killed the cat, my girl.

You just remember that. Curiosity killed the cat.

35

Tess, Summer 2019

S oon, is all Matthew will say. Luke's formal interview will be soon. There are no details yet. The legal process, he says, is one that moves slowly.

His words stir something in Tess's memory. She sees her father, Jack, sitting in his chair beside the fire. They've been watching the TV evening news, the whole family. The crammed living room is strangely silent as the six children crowd together on the sofa, with Betty in the middle. She is gathering them more closely to her as image after image unfolds on the small screen. Eleanor is on her lap.

Tess is fourteen at the time. She can still feel the confusion that stalked her that day – just an ordinary evening in May – as she watched the Dublin streets she knew so well: Talbot Street, Parnell Street, South Leinster Street, fill up with mangled cars and body parts and rubble and horror. Three bombs, each of them two minutes apart.

Within six minutes, the city – her city – was unrecognisable. Later that same evening, another bomb exploded on the North Road, in Monaghan. Tens of people dead between the different locations; hundreds wounded; thousands of lives changed forever.

'Who would do such a thing?' Betty asks, her voice filled with wonder. Eleanor turns away from the screen and burrows further into her mother's solid, cardiganed presence.

Nine-year-old Sheila stares at the screen, her eyes wide.

'They'll catch them, Dad, won't they?' Eoghan asks.

'Some day,' their father's tone is grim. His face has darkened. 'It will take time. The mills of God grind slowly but they grind exceeding small.'

Tess hears her father's words again as she steps outside onto the garden path. She needs fresh air. The house has been full of tension, the atmosphere dark and fractured with whatever is awaiting Luke. With whatever awaits all of them. This is not just about Luke.

Is he guilty? Will the mills of law grind slowly and grind exceeding small for him, too? And what will that mean for her, for Mike, for Aengus? And for Betty.

Tess pulls her jacket around her and begins to quicken her step. It's chilly out today, but the sky is bright blue. In the distance, clouds hover, but she's safe for the next hour or so.

As she approaches the corner of the park, she sees Mary from next door. The elderly woman is carrying two full bags of shopping. She is in animated conversation with another neighbour, Deirdre, from number four.

As Tess gets closer, she sees the two women look in her direction. They stop speaking as she approaches. They look uneasy, as though caught in some guilty act. Tess feels the flush begin at the base of her throat. They will have seen the Garda car, with Luke sitting stonily in the back. God only knows what news has been spreading around the neighbourhood since that evening.

She keeps her head up as she passes. 'Good morning, Mary, Deirdre.' And she walks on.

There is no response. As she turns out onto the main road, she begins to tremble.

Is this how it's going to be? Her entire life has been lived on this street, apart from a few years in a tiny, draughty flat in Drumcondra. People know her here, trust her; some of them have even known her since she was a child.

It feels as though the seams of her life are being pulled apart, no matter which way she looks. Stitch by stitch, the world that she and Mike have crafted together is coming undone.

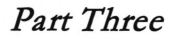

Part Three

SUMMER *2019*

I ignore the tapping on my bedroom door. She'll go away, eventually. I'm not
ready yet for anyone's sympathy, anyone's concern. Right now, I'm just angry.
No, 'angry' doesn't cut it: it's rage. This morning, I'm filled with rage.

I haven't slept. I can see the dark shadows under my eyes. Before I can
change my mind, I pick up the dressmaking shears. The tapping on my door
becomes louder, more insistent.

Go away, I say. I try not to shout. I don't want the others downstairs to
hear. Leave me alone.

You can't stay in there forever, she says. Please, just talk to me.

I hear the way her voice breaks at the end. When I'm ready, I say. Just not
now.

I hear her footstep on the landing, and on the first creaky tread of the stairs.
Then silence.

I look at my reflection in the mirror. Then I grab a handful of hair in my
left hand. With the shears in my right, I make one quick cut, straight across.
The swath of blond falls onto the dressing table. For a moment, I think it looks
surprised: it lies there, curling back on itself. Adrift from its moorings. I cut
again, and again and again.

When I finish, my head looks smaller, vulnerable. I like the feeling of
having shed something. I feel lighter now, freer. I run one hand over the spikiness,
snipping here and there at the bits that I've missed.

I lift the plastic liner out of the wastepaper basket and sweep one hand over
the surface of the dressing table. The hair falls gracefully, obediently, into its
depths.

I tie the handles of the liner together, a double knot, so that nothing can
escape. In the morning, on my way to the park, I'll dump it into somebody's bin.

I pull off my tee-shirt and leggings and stuff them into the holdall that already contains my clothes from Friday night.

I make my way into my tiny shower-room and turn on the water. I move the dial to the hottest temperature I can bear. Then I step inside, pulling the folding door shut. I stand there, letting everything wash off the surface of my skin.

I stand without moving until my flesh stings.

36

November 2019

Tess makes her way up Grafton Street. The Christmas lights add a kind of cold cheer to the late November afternoon. Their glitter feels out of place. Or she feels out of place.

She steps to one side, avoiding a swell of shoppers. As she does so, she almost trips over someone lying in a doorway. Someone all but invisible: just the crown of a dark beanie poking out. A huddled form, moulded by the hills and valleys of a tattered sleeping bag.

Should she stop, make sure the person is still alive? She hesitates, the sleeping bag coughs, shifts a little on the thick layer of dampening cardboard. She moves on, guiltily, reminded of what her mother calls the Birth Lottery. Betty likes to tell Tess how lucky she is to have been born when she was. From factory floor to department store in one generation, she says.

But Tess is not feeling lucky now. She pushes open the door of Bewley's and glances at the exhibition that fills the windows: *Time for Joy.*

Joy. Jesus.

She remembers Luke as he was this morning, sitting at the breakfast table. Even the collar of his shirt looked too big for him, standing stiffly away from his neck. Pale and still, he seemed smaller than he did yesterday.

She had tried to get a conversation going over breakfast, but Luke has been more or less silent for months. This morning, Mike was no help. He just looked down at his hands. Once, he leaned over and patted Luke's forearm, about to say something, but Luke pulled away from him. These days, defeat is etched into the deep, greyish lines of her husband's face. He'd looked blankly in Tess's direction when she asked if he wanted more coffee.

'Mike? A refill?' she repeated.

But he didn't seem to hear her.

She had to turn away herself as exhaustion washed over her in a fierce, gritty-eyed wave. All this fighting; so many sleepless nights.

She has agreed to meet in Bewley's café, under the three Harry Clarke windows. It's five o'clock, so they will have an hour or so in each other's company. Tess spots her right away; the anonymous woman fits her own description perfectly. She is sitting upright, her hands resting on the cool surface of the table. She is looking straight ahead.

For an instant, Tess wants to turn on her heel and walk away. But she needs to know. She's already had her doubts, hasn't she, in those small treacherous hours between midnight and four in the morning.

As if she has sensed Tess's eyes on her, the woman's head shifts a fraction to the right. For an instant, Tess thinks she catches something familiar in that delicate movement. There are ripples in the pool of her memory, spreading outwards, almost reaching the shore where remembering lies. But as soon as she grasps at the might-be-memory, it disappears, sliding back under the surface again, down into the murk.

She forces herself to keep walking towards the stained-glass windows. In this light, their beauty glows red, blue, green, amber. The woman is looking at her now. She has things to tell her about Luke.

'Ms Killeen?' she says. 'I'm Tess McGrath.'

The woman extends her hand. 'Thank you for coming,' she says. 'I've ordered us some tea.'

*

I recognise her as soon as she starts walking towards me. It's a strange sensation, the way the decades can peel themselves away from a face as soon as you know who you're looking at. I watch her making her confident way towards my table. Some things never change.

I think about my wee girl. She's the reason I'm here: I need to keep remembering that. She has been drifting away from me recently, a deliberate act, one I have to respect.

On the nights that I manage to sleep, I have the same dream over and over again. My girl is only wee, no more than five or six years old, and she's pestering me to teach her how to knit. I've no wool in the house. And so I start to undo a sweater I once made for her, one that is now much too small. She's always been tall for her age, even as a child.

In the dream, I take a pair of scissors and nick at the cuff of one of the sleeves. I begin tugging gently at the scarlet yarn. I don't want it to fray and break under pressure. As I pull, the knitting begins to unravel more and more quickly, great lengths of rippling wool, filling the room around us. We become tangled in the crimson tide of yarn until she begins to cry. I reach out to comfort her and I see the anger: the way it shines up at me from the green depths of her eyes.

I'll wake in a sweat, and there's no chance of getting back to sleep. I get up, make tea, clean the kitchen surfaces, anything to distract myself.

I breathe deeply now, slowly. It helps, a little.

I wonder, and not for the first time, if what I am doing is the right thing after all. I do worry about that. 'It's not your life, it's mine,' she shot back at me once, months ago, in a whole other universe. Her eyes had been lit by an anger I'd never seen before, not in the real world. That cut me to the quick.

And now I watch as this stranger, who is not a stranger at all, reaches my table. She holds out one hand, tells me she's Tess McGrath. As if I didn't know. Years telescope, the past flows into the present, the present sinks into the past.

But there is no such thing as the past, not really. The past is never over.

We shake hands. Hers is warm, firm. Mine is trembling. She pulls out a chair and sits, facing me. I meet her eye, woman to woman.

'Thank you for coming,' I say. 'I've ordered us some tea.'

Suddenly, I know what to tell her. My anxiety falls away.

And I begin.

37

Maeve, 1990

I place the rectangles of material on the kitchen table and smooth them flat, one by one. Watching my hands move in that way across fabric has always helped to soothe Belle's agitation. I've gathered together all of her favourite colours today: the brighter the better. Cobalt blue; vermilion; canary yellow; jade green.

Her smile is uncertain. But the storm of screaming has passed and she's ready to listen.

'We can use these instead,' I tell her. 'These can be your pages.'

She wipes her cheek with the back of one small hand, sits forward, touches the first of the panels. She has always been drawn to blue.

'What do you mean, Mama?'

'We can use these to tell your story. You won't have to write anything down. You can use your needle instead.'

I have her attention. As simply as I can, I remind her of Aafreen. 'Remember our friend, all the way from California? Remember the story-quilt she told us about?'

Her face lights up. 'Yeah! I like Aafreen. I miss her.'

'I miss her, too.'

'Can we go see her?'

231

'Some day. She lives very far away, remember, in America? But maybe one day we'll be able to go.'

Aafreen. Each time she and I were together, I would feel my world opening up, changing, filling with a sudden thirst for *knowing*: about other lives and places and people.

I don't tell Belle this, of course, that in my late twenties, I've started to chafe against the familiar. My life has begun to feel too tight for me. I'm grateful for everything I have, for my home, my work, above all for Eileen and my beautiful eleven-year-old daughter.

But I've learned that it's possible to feel all kinds of gratitude and still long for more. For wider, broader horizons than our own kitchen and the familiar streets of Dundalk.

*

The truth is, Aafreen and I stumbled across each other. She'd come into the shop, one slow Saturday afternoon in early November.

'Hi,' she said, her accent unmistakeable, even in that one word. She stood for a minute at the threshold, her umbrella dripping. I was struck by more than her accent. She had the most beautiful face. And she was tall and confident and commanding in all the ways I'd never be.

'Come in. Let me take that for you.' I hurried to meet her. I took her umbrella and shook the rain off, leaving it to one side to dry. 'Come and sit down – there's a stool over here by the counter.'

'Thank you. I will.' As she sat, she pointed to something behind me. 'I just love the colour of that fabric – do you think I could take a look?'

'This one? Yes, of course.'

I pulled the roll of turquoise off the shelf and spread a few lengths across the counter. Flecked wild silk: this woman had a good eye. The shade was somewhere between blue and green and gleaming, the texture slightly raised and varied.

'That's just what I'm looking for. The colour of hope and renewal.'

I was taken aback. I was used to: Will it wash well? Does it crease? Can you do anythin' on the price?

Without any warning, I knew what I needed. I needed this woman to stay. To sit right there, across the counter from me. I didn't want her to leave.

'It's horrible outside,' I said. 'Why don't you take off your coat and have a cup of tea while you decide? I've a few more shades you might like.'

It was her turn to be taken aback. 'Why, sure!' she said. 'That would be wonderful.'

We sat for the rest of the afternoon. The shop morphed into another world, a whole new everywhere. As if the walls had crumbled away without a sound. I kept hoping that no random customer would wander in and break the dream.

Aafreen had come to Ireland to find the parents of her best friend. They lived in Blackrock, she told me, just south of Dundalk. I knew it well: a small seaside town, with a beach and ice cream and all the things that brightened Belle's life for one week of every summer.

She told me her friend had died of AIDS. I'd heard of it, had read some articles about it, but it felt like one of those things that were always happening far away from my life. But now, here it was:

real knowledge, present in a form I could recognise, sitting across from me on a sleety winter afternoon.

'Tom's parents refused to travel to San Francisco for his funeral,' she said. 'I need to meet them.'

Hearing her tone, I felt a gentle nudge of sympathy for the parents, people I didn't even know.

'Because they're not getting away that lightly,' she said. 'They might have abandoned Tom in life, but I have his ashes.'

She looked down for a moment and I waited. I said nothing. Belle had taught me the necessity of silence.

When Aafreen gathered herself, she told me about the AIDS memorial quilt. A group of people in San Francisco had come together, she said, to create a giant patchwork quilt: a tangible memory of every unique and individual life lost. It would be something beautiful to counter the ravages of all that illness.

When she finished, I began talking. I couldn't stop myself. Everything came tumbling out, as if I had been waiting for her. I told her about St Brigid's; about Eileen; about the shimmering quilt that had greeted me on my first evening in Dundalk.

And I told her all about Belle. Aafreen understood more about my life in a single afternoon than all the people I'd grown to know in Dundalk in over a decade.

Perhaps it was because she was a stranger; because she came from a bigger, more complex life; maybe even from a more forgiving place. Maybe, above all, because she had no expectations of me.

'That's hard,' she said. 'I'm sorry you had to go through all that. You were only a child yourself.'

I was struck by the simplicity of what she'd just said, and by its impact.

*

Aafreen and I saw each other several times during the three weeks she stayed in Dundalk. We talked; we took Belle on day trips together at the weekend; we spent time with Eileen. They liked each other.

Once, I told Aafreen how trapped I felt. It was something I had never spoken out loud before. How could I ever have confessed something like that to Eileen?

'Sometimes, I feel like I can't breathe,' I said. 'Is this it? I mean, is this all I'll see for the rest of my life?'

'You're still very young,' she said, quietly. 'You'll get your chance.'

'Will I? Belle will never be able to live independently, at least, not completely.' And then I cried, filled with shame at such a betrayal of my own daughter.

After Aafreen left, I pored over images of San Francisco. Fantasised about how I might get there some day. I even opened a special savings account for the future.

I saw the way Eileen looked at me, those evenings I spent with a new map spread out in front of me on the kitchen table. She never spoke of it.

Maybe when Belle was sixteen, I thought, just that few years older, that bit more stable, then we could make the trip together.

*

Now, as Belle and I sit across the table from each other, I say: just because Teacher has asked her to write her own story, that doesn't mean we have to use words and pages and pencils like everyone else. Instead, I ask her, 'How would *you* like to tell your story?'

She looks down at the various pieces of fabric on the kitchen table, then up at me again, curious. 'With my needle, like you said?'

'Exactly. Why don't we sew a fabric-story?'

'What's a fabric-story? Will Teacher like it?'

'She will love it, I promise. And we can make it look just like a book when it's finished, with its own covers. Will I show you?'

And so we trace pictures of a Moses basket and the house in Willow Grove and butterflies and flowers and trees and the sea and all the things that are important to Belle. We cut out patterns for each fabric page, and Belle gets excited as she gazes at the rainbow of embroidery threads in her sewing basket.

'Can the sky be pink?' She's concentrating hard; a little furrow appears between the darkness of her eyebrows. For an instant, she bears a startling resemblance to David.

'Absolutely. The sky can be any colour you like. This is your book.'

I watch as she threads the needle. She chooses blue chenille to outline the house against the sky. It's strong, tufted, perfect for defining boundaries. I feel proud that she has mastered the slight tremor in her left hand, that she is growing in confidence every day.

'Well done,' I say. 'You're a wonder.'

She laughs in delight. 'I'm a wonder. I'm going to start with the sky above our house.'

'Off you go.'

She begins to sew. I never mention St Brigid's. She never asks about her father. She has long accepted that we have a different family from other children. She has two mamas, she tells me. Mama Maeve and Mama Leen. She told me once, with great solemnity, that we had no place in our lives for a father. That we had only three bedrooms.

I cut out small shapes for her to appliqué.

I am grateful, once again, that in all the exercises we've done together to develop her hand-eye coordination, my little girl has learned to use a needle in a way that surprises me.

Every time she sews, she becomes quiet, still, intent on her task. Sewing is something that cannot be rushed. She is neat, careful, with an eye for colour that is all her own.

I have no idea back then – nobody ever can – of what lies ahead. Maybe life is better that way.

38

Joanie, 1987

When Joanie's brother, Eddie, asked her if she'd like to come with him to England, where there was a lot more work than in Ireland, she jumped at the chance. She was glad to shake the dust of Cork off her feet.

Even though Sister Lucia had told Joanie that the family in Cork were kind people, they weren't, not really. She'd overheard the mother talk about her to one of her posh friends – calling Joanie an 'institution girl'. Saying things about her rough edges and her unfortunate past. Three years was more than enough of that. Joanie was tired of always feeling not good enough.

By the time she and Eddie had managed to meet up, she'd had her fill of looking after other people's children. Eddie took the train to meet her and when he stepped onto the platform in Kent Station, Joanie had never been so glad to see anyone in her life.

Over pots of tea, in the café in Patrick Street, that the nice woman kept refilling and didn't charge for, Joanie told her brother that she couldn't stand her life any longer. She had to get away to somewhere else, anywhere else.

*

For the first couple of years, Joanie didn't like Nottingham much. But Eddie said he had to follow the work, and that's where the work was taking him. Besides, it wasn't as scary a city as London: she'd never felt easy in London. Couldn't wait to get out of it after the six months they'd spent there.

And this new hotel in Nottingham wasn't so bad. She'd worked in worse places in Kilburn. It was busy enough, being so close to the railway station. Eddie had found them a wee house nearby; not too expensive, a bit shabby, but it would do grand.

It was somewhere to stay, to stop moving for a while. Not that they'd be putting down roots, real roots, anytime soon. She'd never do that, not in any place on God's green earth where Charlie wasn't. But this two-up two-down on a street behind Nottingham train station would do her rightly for now.

And Sister Lucia had promised to help Joanie keep looking for her boy. But she wasn't 'Sister' anymore, she'd said in her last letter. Joanie had wondered about that. Once a nun, weren't you supposed to be a nun forever? When she told Eddie, he just grinned.

She decided not to puzzle about it any longer. If Sr Lucia was out, she was out, and it was none of Joanie's business. She was just glad that before she walked away from St Brigid's, Sister Lucia had found out that it was 'highly likely' Charlie had been adopted in England – not Ireland, not America. So at least Joanie was in the right place, no matter how big it was, and there were special offices that she could go along to and ask for help in tracing her son. Agencies, they were called.

Joanie was learning fast. She knew to scrub the kitchen off herself, and dress in her best clothes before making each visit. She tamed the Monaghan out of some of her words, too, the ones that Father Farrell used to correct her on. And she'd go with all of her information about Charlie written in a slow, careful hand on a clean sheet of Basildon Bond writing paper.

She was puzzled at first when the ladies in the Agencies talked about the forms that Joanie must have signed back then. Joanie had no memory of any forms and besides, she'd never been all that good at the reading. No matter how nice Miss Brady at school had been, the words on every page kept playing hide and seek.

Letters would slip slyly away from her, tumbling down towards the bottom of the page, or scramble their way upwards, mocking her. Sometimes, they'd confuse her even more by leaning to one side or the other. No matter how she tried, Joanie had never been able to win that game: the words always managed to get away from her.

Eddie had helped her write down what was needed. He kept telling her how far she'd come, how brave she was, how proud he was of her. Sometimes, Joanie would look back on those St Brigid days and hardly recognise herself. She was no longer afraid all the time; and if she was sometimes, she'd learned to hide it and get on with things, so that nobody else noticed.

Eddie had warned her not to answer if people said mean things, as they sometimes did, about the Irish all being bombers and murderers. Things like why didn't they go back to the bogs where they came from?

*

Today is Sunday, and Joanie has the afternoon off. Her shift finished at two and her feet are hot and sore. She plans to take the bus to Highfields Park for the rest of the day. There is a lake there and wee boats and all the trees make the air feel cool and fresh, like the orchard at home. She can sit on a bench and look at all the busyness going on around her.

Last time, two teams of wee fellas played football with their families shouting on the sidelines. Joanie guessed the children were about eight – Charlie's age. She sat and watched them for the whole match. Afterwards, mothers and fathers spread blankets on the grass and the wee ones had a rowdy picnic.

It hurts to see them. And it hurts not seeing them. Joanie has decided that the first kind of hurting is a better one: it makes her feel that Charlie is right there with her. She can choose to watch the wee boy with the darkest hair; the one who is taller and skinnier than all the others; the one with the Irish name.

She packs her sandwiches and her flask into the backpack that Eddie abandoned. Someone had said it was girly. He told Joanie it was too small for him.

She hefts it up onto her shoulders now, flattening the straps until they sit comfortably against her chest. Then she counts out the exact change for the fare into the palm of one hand and heads for the bus stop.

39

Eileen, 1997

I got home at eight o'clock that evening. The minute I opened the front door I knew something was up. The silence felt all wrong.

Quickly, I checked that Belle's school coat was there. That her backpack was in its usual place in the hall. Everything looked the same. When I opened the door into the kitchen, I saw Maeve, sitting at the table. She looked dishevelled. Her coat was half-draped over the back of one chair and her slumped shoulders told their own story. There was no sign of Belle.

I closed the door behind me. I went over to Maeve at once. I placed one hand at the centre of her back. At my touch, she started and lifted her head. She mustn't have heard me come in.

'What is it, Maeve? What's happened?'

She began to tremble. After a few moments, she sat upright. I was relieved to see that there was no blankness in her eyes. So whatever was happening to her now was different from the other times. This must be about the present, not the past.

'It's Belle,' she said, at last.

'Tell me.' I sat down across the table from her.

'She was late back from school. By six, I was really worried. She knows to come straight home. I thought maybe she'd missed the bus, so I drove around for a bit, looking for her.'

I risked resting my hand on hers. Sometimes, Maeve did not want to be touched, skin to skin. She looked up.

'She wasn't at the school, nobody had seen her since classes ended, she hadn't got off at the wrong stop – I went looking for her in all the usual places. So I decided to come back here, because she knows, no matter what happens, that home is where she's safe.'

The appeal in her eyes disturbed me. 'And she is safe, yes? She's home?'

'She's home now. Upstairs. She won't talk to me.'

I didn't say: 'We've been here before' or 'Give her time to cool off' or 'I'll talk to her later, it'll be fine.' All of those things were true: and Belle's tantrums as a teenager were very similar to her tantrums as a two-year-old. Full of sound and fury, but over quickly enough. Hiding out, or sulking in her bedroom, had never been her style.

I had to remind myself from time to time that, despite appearances, despite her eighteen years, Belle was still a child in all the ways that mattered.

I changed tack. 'So where did she go after school, then?'

'She said she went with some friends, back to their house. I've told her so many times that she mustn't do that. She's to come straight home to me, even just to ask permission to go out again. She *knows* that's how it has to be.'

There was a catch in her voice and she still wouldn't look at me. I kept a tight rein on my impatience. Maeve always did things in her own time. I let the silence linger for a bit, and then asked what I hoped was a neutral question. 'Did she go to Clare's?'

'She won't tell me whose house she went back to. I've rung Clare's mother and she hasn't seen Belle since last Saturday.'

Now I felt myself grow cold. I began to understand Maeve's studied calmness.

'I'm not sure exactly what's happened, but it's clear she's spent the afternoon unsupervised.'

'What has she told you?'

'She got angry when I kept asking her where she'd been, who she'd been with. I tried to stay calm, but I couldn't.'

'And then?' I prompted.

'I can't be sure . . . and I hope I'm wrong.' Maeve looked straight at me now. 'One of the boys she was with told Belle she was beautiful, special. That he had fallen in love with her. She was thrilled. She went off with him somewhere. On her own.'

Everything inside me grew still.

'All she'll say is that she has a secret now, and it's her secret. Because she's a grown-up and it's none of my business.'

'Let's not get ahead of ourselves.'

It was the only thing I could think of. I didn't know what else to say. I took both of Maeve's hands in mine. 'Look at me, Maeve. Whatever it is, we'll deal with it together.'

*

Belle refused to talk to us over the next few days. She went to school as usual, came home on time, did her chores around the house. On the surface, nothing had changed.

Maeve drove herself like a demon. She never stopped. She must have visited the houses of everyone we'd ever met, all over that city and county. She told me she'd find out who the boy was, or she'd die in the attempt.

Finally, I had to tell her to stop. I could see what it was doing to her. Sometimes, the absence behind her eyes frightened me.

'Maeve,' I said. 'You'll make yourself ill. Let's just take this one day at a time.'

But she couldn't. 'She's my daughter, not yours,' she flung at me once, in the middle of a particularly tense and difficult day.

'Yes, you're right,' I said. 'But I don't think this is helping either of you: you or your daughter.' And then I left the room.

We struggled on for the next couple of weeks. Maeve was gone for hours every evening. I never asked where she'd been, she never told me.

All I could do was wait. Stand on the sidelines. Pick up the pieces where they fell.

40

Tess, November 2019

Tess waits until the teapot has been left in the centre of the table, the cake stand placed carefully over to one side. The young waiter disappears, his cheerful, friendly words having fallen into the space between her and this stranger sitting across from her.

The woman is smiling now. 'Can't resist Bewley's almond buns.'

Tess doesn't know what to say to that.

'You don't recognise me, do you?'

The woman tilts her head to one side, as though considering something.

And then it happens. First, in a confused rush, and then more slowly, astonishingly. The face across the table begins to rearrange its features.

'Fiona?' she says, slowly. Disbelieving.

'Hello, Tess.'

'Jesus Christ. Really? Fiona? Fiona Garvey?'

'That's me.'

'God, Fiona, I went looking for you so many times.' Tess sees herself on the summer streets of forty years earlier, searching for her best friend.

'I'm sure you did.'

There is a dry edge to what she says. It makes Tess feel guilty. 'I tried, but you'd disappeared, and your mother wouldn't tell me where you'd gone. She spun me some yarn about you having gone to stay with an aunt in Donegal.' She stops.

'It's a long story.'

'I want to hear it. I looked everywhere for you, after Conor's accident. Nobody could tell me anything about you.' And then, remembering why they are meeting like this, she says 'Why are you calling yourself Maeve? What have you got to do with my son Luke?'

'That's an even longer story.'

Tess begins to feel defensive. It's as though this woman is judging her for something she did – or failed to do – almost four decades ago. But the only thing that matters now is Luke and finding out whatever it is that Fiona knows.

She makes a show of looking down at her watch. 'Well, we'd better get started.' Her tone is sharper than she's intended. 'This place closes in an hour.'

41

Maeve, 1997

Eileen has stayed quietly on the sidelines for several weeks now and I'm grateful to her. I know she's feeling it, too. I can see it in her eyes. But I've only recently begun to find the words to talk to her about it. Even when I do, something hot and raw swells up inside me and I have to turn away. I know she's there, waiting. I know she'll do anything she can for me, for Belle. I know that.

I hate myself sometimes, for resenting the gratitude I feel. Hate myself for the horrible person I seem to have become.

Belle and I have had a tumultuous time. I've swung from rage to despair so many times I've lost count. I've spoken with doctors and teachers, nurses and social workers, and I'm tired of the whole lot of them.

Fed up hearing all the holy platitudes about motherhood. Fed up hearing, in the same breath, about limited supports for pregnant teenagers, about the overloaded health service, about my daughter's being 'an unusual case'.

Mother Ireland my arse.

She's not 'a case' at all, I've shouted, she's my child and she's pregnant and we need help. And yes, there have been kind people, too, well-intentioned people, sympathetic people – but good intentions are no longer good enough.

We need solid, practical support: *I* need solid, practical support, something to keep me afloat as I steer my daughter through the kind of waters that are both familiar and terrifying.

Telling me how *difficult* this must be, how *challenging*, is the kind of patronising shit that makes me see red. Then I lose my temper. Then nobody wins.

Belle will stay on at school, though, right until she can't. That is one battle I was determined to win. In the end, it wasn't a battle at all. The headmistress was brisk, down to earth. I hadn't expected that, not after the reaction of the teacher I'd first told.

'We'll offer Belle every support we can,' she said. 'I regard it as our responsibility, no matter what anyone else might have told you.' There was a brief silence. 'Please accept my apology. That should not have happened.'

When I told Eileen afterwards, she said: 'Well, maybe some things are beginning to change for the better, in this country. Not before time.'

She and I have exhausted ourselves recently, going over and over all the options. We've discussed taking Belle to England and dismissed it almost at once. As soon as Belle understood what was happening to her – and she did understand, I'm certain: not the future implications, of course, but the *fact* of her pregnancy – her response was immediate.

'I want my baby.'

It has become her mantra. She's repeated it endlessly, whenever I try to probe about who the father is, the location of the house she went back to, who might be responsible for this: *I want my baby* is the only answer.

I have to respect that, even though it devastates me. The enormity of it for my vulnerable daughter. And for me: still in my thirties and about to be a grandmother.

There goes my life.

I have found myself outside the Garda station on several occasions, weeping, clutching the steering wheel to prevent myself from going in.

Because what crime could I report? Who could I identify? My beautiful daughter is eighteen years of age – an adult. To the outside observer, she looks composed, mature, capable of deciding things for herself. Besides, I've watched this community close ranks before, protecting the indefensible. I don't have the energy for that fight, as well as all the other ones that lie ahead.

And so, I've just driven away each time, feeling cheated.

'Anyway, do we want someone like that in Belle's life, in all our lives?' Eileen asks as I rage. We both know the answer to that and so I've decided to stop looking.

'We've done this before,' she reminds me. 'We can do it again.'

But I want to tell her that I'm tired. That I feel defeated. Cheated. That my life is slipping away from me, that I'll never get to be with Aafreen.

I don't say any of those things. I let the dream go.

*

'This is what's happening this week, sweetheart,' I tell her. I open the page for week fourteen. Belle stares at the photograph in wonder.

'Inside me, in my tummy?'

'Yes,' I say.

She runs one finger over the image of the tiny foetus. Coloured pictures make the best explanations. They fill Belle with amazement. They make me feel calmer; I can reach her in a way that avoids misunderstandings, tears, shouting, slamming doors: all the stages we've been moving through together for the past three months.

Now as we sit together at this familiar kitchen table, Belle smiles at me. 'Can we go into town and buy the wool?' she asks.

'Yes,' I say, closing the book of photographs. She's had enough for today. 'And have you decided on the colour yet?'

She is all eagerness. 'Yellow,' she says. 'Clare says yellow is for boy babies *and* girl babies.'

'Okay, then, yellow it is. Have you got the pattern? Or the pictures you liked?'

'Upstairs in my bedroom.'

I watch her as she runs down the hall. My heart turns over.

It is what it is.

Eileen's phrase is always with me. And she's right. I know she's right. Listening to Belle's feet on the stairs I am reminded of the day we opened the new shop. Of the way Belle put one trusting hand in Eileen's and they climbed the stairs together, my little girl carefully placing both feet on each step, pausing before tackling the next one. One thing at a time.

Inexplicably, my heart grows lighter. I pull on my coat and wait at the front door. When Belle reaches me, she throws both arms around me. Her sudden displays of affection have been happening more and more, recently.

'Love you, Mama,' she whispers, 'and Mama Leen.'

I hug her back. 'And we love you, too. Up to the moon and back. Let's go.'

She takes my hand as we walk down the driveway to the car. It's a beautiful autumn afternoon: mellow and golden. It is the colour of optimism.

I allow it to fill me.

42

Joanie, 2015

It's sleeting when Joanie steps off the bus. The icy needles make their way under the collar of her winter coat. The wool smells damp, like old dog. But there's nothing she can do: each of her hands is occupied by a plastic bag, bulging with weekend groceries. She shivers.

Typical November. She hates November. It's the month when things began to go wrong at home in Monaghan; the month when her da's friend first started to look at her like that. It doesn't matter that nearly four decades have passed.

And the few years in Nottingham have now turned into more than twenty-five. How has that happened? Eddie held a surprise birthday party for her back in early August, when she turned fifty. It warms her for an instant, that vision of her brother waiting for her at his front door.

Come for a barbecue with us, he'd said. On Saturday. The kids are only dyin' to see you.

Hardly kids any longer, she'd thought – Janet, the eldest, is twenty-two, with a baby of her own. But Eddie had looked so earnest when he asked, Joanie didn't have the heart to say no.

She'd already booked the day off, once Clodagh had promised to cover for her. Clodagh was reliable, not like so many of the other young ones, and Joanie had been looking forward to her first free Saturday in ages, to putting her feet up in her own garden. The hotel kitchen had just had the busiest July ever and she was exhausted. But it was impossible to disappoint Eddie. He was still a wee boy in so many ways.

When she arrived at his front door that hot summer evening, she saw that Eddie had scrubbed up. A bold Hawaiian shirt and blue jeans replaced his usual overalls. Irene had had a hand in that. Eddie's face was shiny, and Joanie thought he'd already had a few. He had that look about him.

'Gimme your jacket,' he said, after his usual bear hug. He pointed at the shopping bag Joanie had brought with her, filled with a dozen cans of the beer he liked, a bottle of the white wine Irene liked, and a cake Joanie had baked earlier. 'Leave all that for now,' he said.

'C'mon,' and he took her by the hand, almost pulling her down the hallway that led to the huge kitchen-diner. 'We're outside in the garden.'

Eddie had done well for himself. He'd worked hard throughout the eighties and nineties on building sites all over Nottingham. But the best bit, he always insisted, was the luck he'd had, being in the right place at the right time. He'd made his way up from casual worker to subbie to foreman.

And for the last ten years, he had his own firm, McCabe and Sons. Seamus and Bartley worked alongside him, although Joanie was of the view that those two handsome lads were a lot better at spending their father's money than earning it.

She got ready to smile as Eddie pushed open the kitchen door, and then she had the fright of her life. She walked right into a human wall of noise. The force of it made her take a step back. Her hand flew to her throat, to calm the leaping beat of her heart.

'SURPRISE!'

She shook her head now at the memory. They were all there – Eddie and Irene; Janet and her husband, Pete; Seamus and Bartley; and the twins, Jamie and Carol. Although they weren't that wee anymore: teenagers, even young teenagers, were so grown up these days, not at all what Joanie had been like at fourteen.

*

She turns the corner now into her own street and the sight of her house fills her with a rush of affection. Two-up, two-down, with a lovely kitchen extension that Eddie had built for her at weekends, calling in all sorts and sizes of favours from his Irish mates. And then there was the delight of her very own back garden. She still finds it hard to believe that this . . . this is all hers. She loves coming home.

She hangs up her coat in the hall, brushing off the worst of the sleet. It'll dry, once she turns the heating on. Then she goes down to the kitchen and places the bags of shopping on the counter. She turns on the television for the evening news. She rarely pays it much attention: she just likes the company of the voices in the background. Tonight, there's a warning about Storm Abigail arriving in Britain in the next twenty-four hours. Probably the fiercest storm we've seen in 2015, the weatherman said. But it doesn't matter. Joanie has her own cosy fireside.

She's about to take the roasting tin out of the oven when she hears something being shoved through her letterbox. Another one of those bloody local newspapers: nobody pays any attention to the No Junk Mail sign on her front door.

She marches down the hall and pulls the soggy paper through the flap. As she makes her way back to the kitchen bin, she sees that there is an envelope: white, official-looking, clinging to the underside of the newspaper. The postman mustn't have pushed it right the way through this morning, and that irritates her all over again. Now it's creased and damp and smudgy.

She opens it, takes out a single sheet of paper. At first, the words won't settle. But little by little, as she has practised, she makes them out, taking them apart bit by bit, as she has been taught. She sees her own name, the word 'Agency', the word 'son', the word 'contact'.

Slowly, Joanie sits down at the kitchen counter. She gazes at the page for a long time. She traces the words again and again with her finger until she's sure she's understood.

Her boy wants to get in touch. Her own Charlie has come looking for her at last.

Joy fills her, slowly at first. Then it spills over, making the whole room light.

43

Eileen, 1997

Maybe three weeks to the day after Belle had gone missing, I knew. The minute I saw her in the kitchen, early one morning, I was certain.

I was instantly reminded of Majella. Maeve and I had once laughed together about Majella's diagnosis of early pregnancy. The slight flattening out of the nose would give it away, she used to say, along with the look of terror in the eye. Except there was no terror in Belle's eye. Just confusion.

'I feel sick, Mama Leen,' she whispered. She took my hand.

Maeve came into the kitchen then. I knew by her face that she'd been crying. I tried to smile at her, to reassure her, but she wouldn't look at me. Instead, I rubbed Belle's back gently with my other hand.

'Let's have some toast, sweetheart, and a cup of tea. That should make you feel better.'

Then Maeve looked over at us. I saw the despair in her eyes. I knew she'd been feeling hemmed in these past few years. I knew what meeting Aafreen had made her long for. And I was sorry. But this was what it was and we needed to deal with it.

At the same time, I couldn't but be struck by the irony, the strangeness of it all. The three of us: as though we shared some kind of circular fate, destined to repeat each other's lives. Each of us pregnant as teenagers. Each of us being left to get through our futures as best we could.

But Maeve had always had me. As well as her daughter.

And now, Belle had both of us.

I didn't want to feel bitter, not after all these years. But they'd each had more than I ever did. Watching Belle was a living memory of my own young life: a reminder of the baby I had to give up.

I turned away from her, from both of them, just for a moment. Then I busied myself with toaster and kettle. And another day began.

44

Tess, 1978

In the week that followed her little brother's accident, Tess called to Fiona's house, only to be told that Fiona had gone away to County Donegal, to visit her aunt.

'When will she be back?' she couldn't keep the note of disbelief out of her voice. Donegal: the other end of the country? Just like that? Without telling her?

But Fiona's mother seemed to be in a hurry to close the front door. 'She's helping out . . . her aunt isn't too well, you see. She'll let you know as soon as she's back.'

Tess was puzzled. 'So can I have her address, then? I'd like to write to her.'

'Maybe another time. I have to go now,' Fiona's mother said. 'There's something on the stove.' And she closed the door.

Tess walked away, more confused than ever. She wished she could have Friday night back again. Was this what Fiona was trying to tell her – that she'd be leaving Dublin?

If it was, why couldn't she have said it out straight? There were no secrets between her and Fiona, never had been.

Slowly, she closed the garden gate behind her. But not before she saw a face peeping out from behind the downstairs net curtain. With a shock, Tess realised it was Fiona. She was sure of it.

But when she looked again, the face had disappeared, the curtain was back in place, and it was as though nothing at all had happened. She couldn't have imagined it, could she?

And if it wasn't Fiona, then who was it? Not her older brother, that was for sure. The house went up for sale a few months afterwards. Tess never saw Fiona again.

45

Eileen, 1997

These days are filled to overflowing. With Belle's needs, with our plans for the future, with the potent presence of memory. Time has softened all of us: the storms of the first three months have calmed at last and our household is becoming an extraordinarily contented one.

There are times I want to stop the clock: I want to hold fast to the moment, prolong it, or at least store it away somewhere so that I can call upon it at some future date, when life doesn't feel so blessed.

Belle has told us she's having a little girl. She said it, abruptly, a couple of weeks back, when we were all in the kitchen, washing up after dinner.

Maeve looked at her in surprise. 'But when you had your scan, you said you didn't want to know. I was there with you, remember?'

Belle concentrated on drying a plate. Her face was suddenly full of mischief. It made me laugh.

'Belle?'

Then she turned to Maeve and lifted both shoulders in a huge shrug. 'I just *know*.' She patted her stomach. 'She tells me.'

'Okay,' Maeve glanced over at me. Her reply was measured, careful, 'and you're probably right, but we won't know for sure until the baby arrives. So—'

Belle didn't let her finish. 'Mama, *I* know for sure. I *do*.'

'Okay, well, we'll still write down lots of names of boys and girls, just in case – we agreed, remember?'

'Yeah.'

Then the doorbell rang, and Maeve left the kitchen.

'The money for Paddy is on the hall table,' I called after her.

Belle turned to me, one finger on her lip.

'What is it?' I whispered.

'I know her name. I asked Teacher how do you say 'love' in French, 'cos Belle is French, too. It's the word for beautiful.'

'You're right. It is.'

She pulled a folded piece of paper out of her pocket. 'Look.' The teacher had written '*aimer, aimé*' and underneath '*Aimée*'. Belle pointed to it now. 'She said the last word, that one there, is a girl's name.'

'It is indeed. And it's a lovely name.'

'It's a secret.'

'Okay,' I agreed. 'I won't say a thing.'

I'll keep her secret for now because I believe Belle is right. I knew Cillian was a boy long before he was born. And with just six weeks to go, we'll find out soon enough if our girl's instinct is correct.

We've prepared her as best we can. The hospital has risen to the occasion; a midwife has already been assigned to Belle; she's a lovely young woman called Katie. She's calm, reassuring, sometimes startlingly humorous. Belle thinks she's great.

We all seem to have moved into a different place in our selves. I am excited at the thought of new life coming into this house. I am grateful for the sense of looking forward that it has given me. I've been knitting and sewing things for the baby for several weeks now – we've been busy bees, all of us.

Sometimes, when I look around at the three of us in the evenings, I have a powerful sense of being bound to a great circle of other women, other times. Our tasks feel ancient, full of history, the threads of connection pulling us tightly together as we work.

And Maeve is more content than she was. She and Belle have grown closer. I'm glad because it's been hard for her: past, present and future. I know she's had to let go of her hopes, and one dream above all. She mentioned Aafreen just once, recently. The words she spoke were shy, halting, filled with loss.

Sometimes, when I look at Maeve, I remember the terrified teenager who stepped into the parlour of St Brigid's, clutching her new baby. I had to move away, to stand with my back to the fireplace, so that I could convince her I wasn't going to steal her child.

We've weathered a lot together, in the last eighteen years. And I've no doubt hard days lie ahead. But we'll manage.

We're family.

46

Maeve, 1998

'She's so beautiful, Mama, isn't she?' Belle is glowing.

'She is a picture. She's just like you when you were a baby.'

I stroke the tiny cheek, feeling its softness under my finger. I am reminded of Sister Lucia, almost two decades ago. I remember how I snapped at her to move away, not to do that to my child.

I am so grateful to be in this room, now, this evening, with my proud and peaceful daughter, a smiling midwife and a grandchild who has already stolen my heart.

*

Earlier, Katie had taken me to one side. 'I can see you're really worried, Maeve. How can I reassure you?'

I could see the compassion in her eyes. It almost undid me.

'Belle is strong, healthy, and she understands enough, I promise you.'

I'm not worried, I told her. I'm petrified.

As gently as she could, she let me know that Belle was picking up on my fear. I wasn't helping. As soon as she said that, I broke. I told her about thirty hours of labour, no kindness, no real

264

understanding of what was happening to me. All I heard was how *this* was the natural result of my sin.

Katie touched my hand at that. 'I can promise you Belle will have everything she needs. Her labour will be managed properly, and I will be with her the whole time.' She paused. 'But above all, what she really needs is her mother.'

'I hear you,' I said. I went to the bathroom down the hospital corridor, combed my hair, applied blusher and lipstick and took my new smile back with me to the labour ward.

*

'Don't leave me, Mama,' Belle says.

She's gripping my hand so hard I wince. 'I'm not going anywhere, sweetheart. I'll be with you all the time, I promise. You can do this.'

Katie smiles over at us. 'Just one more big push when I tell you, Belle. Just little, short breaths for now. You're nearly there.'

I cannot describe the tsunami of emotion that engulfs me when my granddaughter slips into the world. Her eyes are open. She's already curious. Her cry of protest is over almost at once. She's happy to be home.

Katie places her on Belle's tummy. 'Here she is,' she says, all smiles. 'Here's your own gorgeous girl. Well done – you were terrific.'

Hesitantly at first, Belle touches her new daughter's face. Instantly, the baby begins rooting for the breast and Belle laughs out loud in delight.

'Welcome, little one,' I say. I take the baby's tiny hand in mine. 'You are so welcome.' I don't even try to stop the tears running down my face.

Then I hug my girl as best I can. 'You were wonderful,' I say to Belle. 'I can't tell you how proud of you I am.'

Belle smiles up at me. 'Her name is Aimée,' she says.

I pretend I don't already know. I kiss Belle's forehead. 'That's a perfect name,' I say. 'I love her to bits already.'

*

There is a knock at the door and Eileen puts her head around it. 'May I come in?'

'Mama Leen!' Belle calls, excited. 'She's here! Aimée's here!'

Eileen puts a gift-wrapped box on the floor. It is pink, with ribbons of rose, lavender, coral, rouge, all tied together in the biggest bow I have ever seen. She moves at once to Belle's bedside.

'Oh,' is all she says. And 'oh' again, as she looks down. She goes completely still. Out of the corner of my eye, I see Katie leave, closing the door quietly behind her.

All three of us fall silent, until Belle says: 'Sit down, Mama Leen, and you can hold her.'

Silently, I thank her for knowing *exactly* the right thing to say. Eileen's expression is tenderness itself.

Belle looks at Eileen, then at me, then at Eileen again. She is puzzled.

'It's okay,' she says. 'Mama Leen, it's okay to happy-cry.'

*

Together, Eileen and I make our way back to the car. We can take Belle and Aimée home tomorrow.

'Wait,' I say, as she opens the driver's door.

She looks up at me. I pull her towards me, put my arms around her. She rests her head against my shoulder.

'I don't say this often enough, Eileen. And I know I haven't been easy to live with for the past nine months. I'm sorry. And I'm more grateful to you than you will ever know.' I stop, trying to keep my voice level. 'You saved my life; mine and Belle's.'

She kisses my cheek. 'Then we all saved each other,' she says.

We stand in the freezing underground carpark for another couple of minutes, not saying much. Finally, I pull away. 'When was the last time you had champagne?'

She looks at me in surprise. 'Champagne? God knows!'

'Right. That's tonight's plan, then. I'll drive us home. You order a taxi for an hour's time, look up where you want us to have dinner. You and I are going out on the town.'

*

Much later that night, I email Aafreen. I tell her the good news. I write of our joy, our relief. Our new family. And I write, too, of Eileen's sadness. I tell her that I should have realised before now, but I didn't, despite all the years we've spent together.

It has taken Aimée's arrival to shake me out of my complacency. Seeing Eileen hold my granddaughter has shamed me. I have understood so little. I will do better now.

This is where I need to be: on this island, in this city, in this house. Now, Eileen needs me, needs us.

It's my turn to stand with my back to an unseen fireplace, to open my arms and say I will take care of you.

It is what it is. I am, at last, content.

Part Four

*A*bove all, I don't want my mother to know. Or Eileen, if it comes to that. Or even Maeve: but I've never been able to keep secrets from my grandmother. I've never learned the knack. Her practical kindness has saved me so many times in the past. I already know what she'd say: everything will be all right. It's not your fault. We're family and we'll get through it together. She'd be loving and capable and resolute.

But I don't want that: I want it all to go away.

I'm tired. Tired of running; tired of feeling ashamed; tired of feeling I'll never be good enough ever again. Damaged goods, I once heard someone snigger – not about me, not then. But I've never forgotten the ugliness of that judgement. Damaged goods.

I keep imagining Belle's face if she found out. She'd become agitated, fretful. I'd see the fear in her huge blue eyes, and my courage – if I ever had any – would fail me. I see her when I'm dreaming and when I'm awake and above all when I'm lost somewhere in between. My mother is strong in ways that often surprise me, but fragile in others: particularly those that relate to me.

Belle is a real home-bird, Maeve used to whisper to the child-me, whenever I puzzled over my mother's reluctance to step outside into the world on her own. She always had Maeve by her side, and if not Maeve, then Eileen. Even as a child, I knew how stitched together we all were. More so than others – I remember how fiercely I'd defend our family's shape when the schoolyard taunts began. You don't have a daddy, went the chant.

I have what's better, I'd shout, small fists clenched in fury. I have two mums and my own Grammaleen.

I have vivid memories of my hands being held, one by Maeve, and the other by Belle: they'd swing me high up into the air and down again, with me squealing with laughter as we made our way to the school, or the park, or the shop.

I loved that shop. It was woven into every single day of my childhood. A busy, buzzy place. But underneath the buzz, there was a solid layer of peace, of belonging. I think it's where Belle was always at her happiest. Her skill with the needle used to fascinate me then – it fascinates me still. I did not inherit that talent.

I was probably only four or so when I realised that Belle was different. Not to look at: she's always been beautiful, and her beauty hasn't aged. These days, we're often mistaken for sisters.

But I learned to recognise the absence in her eyes when something happened that she didn't get. Maeve would step in then, her hand gentling Belle's, her voice calm and low. She'd disentangle Belle's confusion, separating the threads so that my mother could grasp them, one by one.

I learned to do that, too. I learned to protect my mother, to be careful of her, to accept that her feelings were more fragile than others'.

But this. This is something I can't unravel. There are no bright, careful threads here that she can stitch together into the fabric of her understanding.

47

Tess, November 2019

'Wait. Stop. Rewind.'

It's been almost an hour and Tess's head feels hot. The café noises are all around her. They make her wonder if she's heard Fiona properly.

'Tell me again, please. I'm sorry, I'm just finding this really hard to take in.'

Fiona starts over. 'You remember our summer outings to Dollymount strand?'

'Yes, of course I do. I've got that bit. You and David somebody or other. I never met him, did I?'

Fiona shakes her head. 'No. You weren't there the night we met. Maggie was. And she was furious that he fancied me.'

Tess tries to smile. 'That sounds like Maggie, all right.'

'The thing is,' Fiona wraps her hands around her cup again, although the tea must be stone cold by now. And she hasn't touched her almond bun. 'The thing is, I don't think it was a case of him "fancying" anybody. David was a few years older; he saw my vulnerability and he went in for the kill.'

'Is that what it felt like, even then?' Tess is doubtful.

'No, of *course* not. I just thought I was a very lucky girl. To have this gorgeous fella feel the same way about me as I felt about him.' She pauses. Fiona has always done things in her own time. Tess is trying to be patient.

'I didn't know how to say no.' Fiona tilts her head to one side again. 'As incredible as that sounds now, I didn't know how. Didn't know I had the right.'

Something shadows her face, something that Tess can't read.

'What did we know about consent, as teenagers? What did we know about *anything?*'

'Nothing,' Tess says. 'We knew nothing.'

'I did believe, or at least half-believe,' and here Fiona almost smiles, 'in the old wives' tale. That you can't get caught the first time.' Her laugh is rueful. 'When they found out I was pregnant,' she went on, 'my parents sent me to Saint Brigid's.'

Tess looks at her in alarm. 'That awful mother and baby home?'

'Yes. I believe some of the homes might have been kinder than others, especially by then. But this wasn't one of them.'

'I am so sorry. I didn't know.'

'Of course you didn't. That was the whole point. Secrecy and shame, hand in hand. They even stripped us of our names when we got there. They decided who we were.' She lifts her chin a little. 'But I managed to choose my own name. That's when I became Maeve.'

Tess is with her so far. 'Okay, I'm getting my head around all of that.'

She stops, searching for the best way to ask the question. 'So, what name would you prefer now? I mean, you've been Maeve for a lot longer than you were Fiona. I can get used to it, if that's your choice?'

She thinks about it for a moment. 'Yes, you're right. It's best we keep to Maeve. Fiona disappeared a long time ago.'

'I'm sorry.' Tess doesn't know what else to say. But she's beginning to feel the years slot into place. 'Tell me what happened next. Tell me about your baby.'

For one terrible moment, she wonders if Maeve's baby survived. All those women. All those thousands of babies who never made it.

'My daughter, Belle, suffered oxygen deprivation at birth. She's had learning difficulties all her life. She manages, but not independently.' Maeve looks down at her cup. When she speaks again, her voice is softer. 'She is, though, a very good mother.'

Tess is surprised. She does a rapid, silent calculation but Maeve answers anyway.

'I was almost seventeen when she was born. She had her own daughter when she was eighteen – but Belle wouldn't have had the street-smarts of other girls her age. She's always been much too trusting.'

'And how is Belle's daughter?' Tess feels that it's safe to ask.

Maeve leans forward. Both her arms are resting on the table now.

'That's why I'm here. You have children. Sons.' It is not a question.

Tess waits for the impact that she somehow knows is coming.

'My granddaughter's name is Aimée. She is a student at UCD. Someone there told her that her name was pretentious, so she usually writes it the English way, Amy.'

The café begins to swim.

'We're closing in ten minutes, ladies and gentlemen. Ten minutes.' The young waiter smiles at them, picks up the cups, saucers, teapot.

'Just give us a minute, please. I'll come up to the till.' Maeve holds out one hand, stops his clearing of the table.

'Of course, of course,' he says to her, embarrassed. He has blushed bright red. He turns and walks stiffly away.

'What are you telling me?' Tess's voice splinters.

She can no longer feel her legs. Everything around her has frozen. She's a prisoner of this woman and her astonishing story.

'Amy and Luke know each other. They were at a party together, almost six months ago.' She grimaces. 'You know the one I mean. Ireland is a small place.'

Now, Tess begins to shake. She forms the words with difficulty. 'Your granddaughter . . . Amy . . . is she the girl who reported Luke to the guards?'

Maeve nods. She doesn't speak, just waits for Tess to say what she must.

'Are you telling me he . . . hurt her?' The other word sticks in her throat. 'That he's guilty?'

'I am.' Maeve sits back. She takes her hands off the table, clasps them in her lap.

Tess can't breathe. There is no longer any air in the room. 'No,' she says. Then 'No,' again. 'I have to go.' Fear courses through her.

Maeve reaches out quickly, places one hand on Tess's arm. 'Please, don't leave, not just yet.'

Tess shakes her hand off, angrily. 'What do you want?'

But she doesn't wait for an answer. Instead, her vision blurs. The only need she has is to escape.

She pushes herself away from the table. The Bentwood chair clatters to the floor, and she runs, blindly, towards the exit.

48

Maeve, 2008

W e're fast approaching Eileen's seventieth birthday. The house
is awash with preparations these days. Belle is making bunting
of several colours. Aimée is drawing birthday cards, making lurid
crepe paper party chains, painting posters with the number 70 in
huge, shaky brushstrokes. The three of us spend hours choosing
what decorations will best suit which room. Aimée makes lists of the
cakes she wants to bake.

Eileen pretends to be oblivious.

'Just stay out of the kitchen,' I tell her. 'You know what these
two are like. The chaos will wreck your head. Besides, it's supposed
to be a surprise for your special birthday.'

'I don't need to be told twice,' she says. '"Stay out of the
kitchen" sounds just fine to me.'

Eileen has a whole new life now and it gladdens me. In the past
five years or so, she has stepped back from the shop. She's gone
travelling with friends, joined active retirement groups; she
volunteers for more of Dundalk's community organisations than I
can shake a stick at. She galvanizes the others around her to be busy,
engaged, connected.

And there is a man, I'm sure of it. She's mentioned a name, Anthony, a few times. All very casual, but I get her drift. I dared to tease her about it recently and she just arched one eyebrow at me.

'I am of the opinion,' she said, 'that you have more than enough here to be thinking about. Don't be concerned about me.'

But she flashed me a smile nonetheless, on her way out of the kitchen.

*

Jackie has been a godsend, ever since she made her first appearance in our lives.

Since Aimée was five, she's minded her, collected her from school, made her one of the family. Her own daughter, Emily, sticks to Aimée like glue. They are a mischievous pair, full of energy, and they display an astonishing amount of independence for their age.

It's a good thing to see. They are outspoken, fearless in a way I never was. I hope they don't lose that, as they get older. Just now, they feel entitled as ten-year-olds to all the space they take up in the world, no apologies.

You go, girls.

Aimée has not inherited our skill with the needle, mine or Belle's. When she was about five, she pestered me to teach her how to knit. I tried my best, but there were too many tears, too many dropped stitches.

Then she discovered baking. It quickly became her passion and now she thrusts the recipe book under my nose. 'This one, Maeve,' she says. 'This is what I want to make for Grammaleen.'

Like her mother before her, she, too, has accepted our little family's unusual shape. She must have been four or five when she asked me how come there was no daddy in our house. I'd been waiting for this, and I had a long, careful answer prepared. I took her on my knee. After two or three minutes, she slid away from me, planted both feet on the floor, and looked at me with the sort of impatience I recognised in myself.

'Can I have ice cream now?'

I'd given her little bits and pieces of information, over the years, every time she asked. She took it all in her stride. No big deal, she'd said to me once, with a shrug that made me laugh. Not too long ago, she told me she'd had a fight in the school playground. She was indignant afterwards.

'So I told her,' Aimée said, as she licked icing from the bowl of the wooden spoon. Something I'd often told her not to do, but no matter. 'I said that I was luckier than she was, because I have two mums *and* my own Grammaleen lives with me as well. I can have cake whenever I want.'

'Well, not *every time* you want,' I said, nudging her with my elbow. 'But' – and I made her look up at me – 'good answer, kid.'

I study the photograph of the birthday cake now, the one that already has Aimée's fingerprints all over its glossy surface. The cake is three tiers high: chocolate sponge, buttercream icing, the top layer crammed with summer fruits and whipped cream. It will take time and care, but it's not as complicated a choice as it might have been. Which is just as well. Our Aimée has very fixed opinions.

'Okay,' I say. 'If that's the one, then that's the one. We'd better make a shopping list.'

I watch her face. I think she's been expecting me to say no. That's far too much work for a ten-year-old. But I've learned.

Nothing is too much for Aimée if she puts her mind to it. She's taught me that, over the years. And so has Belle, in a different way.

Aimée's green eyes shine. 'Really?' and she jumps up and down.

'Yes, but you'll have to be the one to make the list and do all the work. I'll just supervise, and your mum can do the decorating.'

She looks over at Belle. 'That okay, Mum?'

'Grand,' Belle says. 'I'll do a lovely job.'

She's altering a dress for me. She comes to the shop almost every day now, and on the days that she doesn't, I've learned to be fine about that. We've put some things in place over the years. She's more cautious now, less trusting of others.

But motherhood has made her blossom and she and Aimée are close. The little girl has an instinctive understanding of her mother: of what she can and can't do. She's protective of Belle, in a way that moves me.

We're doing okay. All of us. We are.

It's a quiet life. But a good enough one.

49

Joanie, 2016

Joanie finishes in the hotel kitchen at seven and takes the bus to Highfields Park.

They've agreed to meet by the lake. She's nervous; thought her afternoon shift would never end.

She hasn't told anybody yet, not even Eddie. There have been times when she thought the knowledge would just take over and burst its way out of her, but she's managed to keep a tight grip on it.

She's waited nearly thirty-seven years. Her brother can wait a bit longer.

Ever since the letter, nine months ago, Joanie has hardly slept one full night. She moves from excitement to fear in a heartbeat. What if it's all a big mistake? What if it's not Charlie, but some other mother's son? What will she do then?

*

The Agency ladies have been kind. They've helped her with everything that needed to be done. They read her the letters where Charlie introduced himself, said why he wanted to meet, told Joanie he'd understand if she didn't want to take such a big step just yet.

Charlie's letters have given her to understand that he's had a happy life. A good life, he says, with parents who loved him, treated him exactly the same as their other children. But now, about to be a dad himself, he really wants to meet his natural mother, if she feels ready.

Ready? She's been ready since she was fourteen.

But the Agency ladies make her take things slowly. After months of letters back and forth, they arrange one call with Charlie, from the Agency phone, during which Joanie is hardly able to speak.

He is called Philip, now, he tells her. She doesn't care what his new name is. She just wants him to keep talking so that she can hold on to the sound of his voice and play it back to herself again afterwards. So she manages to ask him about his wife, about their new baby. And then he says how much he's looking forward to getting to know her, Joanie.

At the end of the call, Joanie says yes, she still wants to meet; Charlie says yes, he still wants to meet and at last the Agency ladies agree that both of them are ready.

*

But Joanie is now late. A car accident in Nottingham city centre has turned the Friday evening traffic into a hot snarl of beeping horns and furious, trapped faces. The police have closed the road and forced the bus to detour, so the last bit of the journey is now taking forever. Joanie is too impatient to wait. She gets off one stop early and half-walks, half-runs towards the park entrance.

What if Charlie's got tired of waiting for her? Or he thinks she's changed her mind? Or maybe he's changed *his* mind, and he won't even be there and this is all for nothing?

Joanie tries to push the panic down hard inside her as she makes her way to the lake. The sound of her own heartbeat is deafening.

As she crosses the grass, the rain begins – great, big thundery drops that fall without warning. But she can see that there is a man sitting on the bench, her bench. She gathers all the strength she has left and breaks into a halting, awkward run. The man looks in her direction. He hesitates for a moment. Then he gets to his feet, slowly. His whole body is a question.

And then she stops, just a few feet away from him. He's as tall as she's imagined, dark-haired, dark-eyed. She can't stop looking at him.

'Charlie?' she whispers.

He clears his throat. 'Are you . . . I mean . . . Elizabeth McCabe?' He moves towards her, his arms already beginning to open.

Afterwards, Joanie will remember how, in the slanting light of an August evening, the rain falls in sparkling threads – like a loosened spiderweb, shaken by the wind; or shiny filaments of spun sugar.

The tears run down her face, and she makes no attempt to stop them.

'I'm "Charlie",' he says. 'I'm your son.'

'Charlie, my own wee Charlie,' she says, sobbing so much now it's hard to breathe. She pulls him into her arms, into her life, and he doesn't resist. They stand there, hugging, while everybody else in the park runs for cover, kids shrieking, teenagers calling out to each other, their voices high and joyful, skimming along on the heady evening air.

He laughs. 'We're getting drenched!' he says, but still he doesn't pull away.

She feels the cold of his wet hair against her cheek. Just like the first time she held him: the sleek babywetness of him.

He rests his head on her shoulder now and almost forty years fall away. Inside Joanie, everything becomes quiet at last.

Her flesh, her bone, her heartbeat.

Charlie has come home.

50

Aengus, Summer 2019

It's around midday when I get the WhatsApp from Luke.
You free?

I hesitate. Luke hardly ever contacts me. So I figure that this message out of the blue means something is wrong. Either that, or he's looking to borrow my clothes again. I take my time getting back to him.

What's up?

Cn u meet me @ home @ 5?

I look at the message for a minute. He isn't asking to meet up straight away, so it can't be anything too urgent, and five suits me. I'll be seeing Emily later on, and that thought makes me feel lighter.

I can do that. U ok?

I get a reply instantly.

Talk then.

*

Luke arrives home shortly after four. I've already made my way down to the living room. I hear him go upstairs and I decide to wait where I am, to let him come looking for me. Whatever is going on, I've no intention of making it easy for him. About ten minutes later, I hear his footsteps. Then the living-room door opens and there he is.

My brother is vain. He's tall and good-looking, with his carefully gelled hair, clothes bang up to date, expensive trainers. He puts a lot of work into Luke Public. So when I see him standing there, I'm taken aback. He looks sloppy. Laces undone, a stain on his shirt and he reeks of cigarettes. He looks as if he hasn't slept, but I know he wasn't out partying last night. I know because I heard him in his room. His mobile beeped so many times that I messaged him to put it on silent. It was driving me crazy.

'You okay?' I feel I'd better ask, since he isn't saying anything.

He sits down in the armchair opposite me. He starts to get agitated. I've never seen him like this before.

'I'm here, Luke, just as you asked. What's up?'

'I might be in a bit of trouble.'

'Go on.'

'I was at a party last Friday night.'

I remember.

'The thing is,' he says, 'now there's a girl throwing accusations around.'

'What kind of accusations?'

'She says . . . I . . . assaulted her. But it isn't true.' He says the last bit in a rush, as though I've already challenged him.

'Hang on a second – assaulted her how? And before you go any further, who is she?'

His words begin to tumble out, falling over one another. I can hardly keep up. A story about a girl he's seen around, a girl he doesn't really know. She's a year or so ahead of him in UCD, but they chatted a few times, sat together in the pub the night of the party. He kind of knew she'd fancied him for a while. She had gone upstairs with him during the party, he says, shrugging. She was more than willing.

'So what's the problem?'

'She's obviously changed her mind. She's been to the guards. Made a complaint about me and landed me in the shit.' He runs one careful hand through his hair. 'The guards are probably on their way here now. Some of the others at the party were questioned this morning.' He stops. 'But I didn't do anything wrong, I swear.'

I don't know what to say.

'I wanted you here to tell Mum.'

'Gee, thanks.' That makes me furious. 'Why don't you tell her yourself?'

'Because they might take me to the station before she gets home.'

'Jesus, Luke.' One part of me doesn't want to hear him. The other part of me doesn't know if I can believe a word out of his mouth. *I didn't do anything wrong.*

He hasn't been exactly truthful on other occasions. I need to get out of here for a minute. I need time to think.

'I'm going to get a glass of water,' I say. 'Do you want one?'

'Yeah,' he says, and looks down at his hands.

I go out into the hall and down into the kitchen, taking my time. I almost drop the glasses twice – once when I take them out of the cupboard, and once when I'm standing by the sink, filling them. What the fuck am I supposed to do now?

I pull my mobile out of my jeans pocket and call up Mum's number. She needs to know. I can't let her arrive home without warning her. But it goes straight to voicemail. 'Fuck!' I try again. Same result. I push the phone back into my pocket and pick up the glasses. My hands are shaking.

I make my way back to the living room. Luke is standing by the window, looking out onto the green. I glance out myself, suddenly terrified that I'm going to see flashing blue lights. 'Here,' I say, handing him the glass of water. My tone is rougher than I intend.

He looks down at the glass. 'Why don't you ever believe me?' His voice is quiet.

Why? Jesus Christ, let me count the ways. 'It's a bit of a shock, Luke. Whatever I expected when you asked to meet me here this afternoon, it wasn't that.'

He moves away from me, sits in the armchair again.

'You don't need me to tell you how serious this is.'

'But I didn't do anything wrong.' He keeps his head lowered, still not looking at me.

'Okay. Well, that's kinda hard to prove, isn't it? It's your word against hers.'

He looks up, but not at me. I watch as his gaze is drawn up and outwards. I stand, feeling everything inside me go into sudden, sickening freefall. There is a squad car pulling up outside. The doors open and two men step out. One is huge – really tall, powerfully built. The other is shorter. Even from that distance, I can see which one of them holds all the authority.

'Go upstairs,' I say, urgently. 'Change your shirt. And tie your shoelaces.'

But he doesn't move. 'I haven't time,' he says. He sounds almost matter of fact. Then he turns and looks at me. 'You need to help me out here. Mum's just turned the corner.'

I pull my phone out – a last-ditch attempt at trying to warn her. Voicemail. 'You stay here,' I tell him. 'I'll answer the door.'

I step out into the hall. I can see the figures through the glass of the porch. My heart is pounding so hard it feels as though it's knocking against my ribs. I open the front door.

As I do, I watch my mother approach. She's seen the squad car – half the park has seen the squad car – and it strikes me that her face looks strangely calm. Somewhere in the back of my head, a suspicion stirs. Has she been waiting for this? Is there something I don't know, something I *should* know?

The only thing I do know is how angry I feel that she didn't answer her mobile.

She takes over at once, in that way she has. I step back. Everything is getting a bit blurry. So I take a few deep breaths and wait.

I watch as they take Luke away. He doesn't look back, not even once. The next thing I remember properly is standing in the kitchen, with my back against the counter, trying to answer my mother's questions.

51

Tess, November 2019

By the time she reaches the bottom of Grafton Street, Tess is shaking so much she has to get a taxi home. She's already missed her footing at the kerb. Some random man grabs hold of her elbow.

'Careful!' he says.

She shakes him off.

He shouts something after her, but she doesn't look back. She doesn't care what he thinks of her. Doesn't care about anything except the words of that familiar stranger across the table, words that will make her stumble through the rest of her life.

*

When she steps out of the taxi, the house is in darkness.

Mike has a meeting tonight. God knows where Luke is, and right now it's just as well he's not home. Tess doesn't know what she would say to him if he appeared in front of her. Everything about him feels falser than ever: his wide blue eyes, his beautiful face.

For more than six months now, Luke has refused to budge from his story. He's word perfect. She doesn't want to hear him insist, over and over again, that he's innocent.

Maeve has made real the fears that Tess has had since the summer. It's hard: when everything she wants to believe about Luke has been undercut by raw, brutal truth. She can't even begin to untangle all the strands that have choked her ever since Maeve began to speak.

It's Aengus Tess wants to talk to now. He's hiding something, she's sure of it, and she's angry that he's not here. But it's the weekend: what does she expect? He has a life, and a girlfriend too, someone called Emily. He'd let her name slip, a few weeks back. And that's the only thing Tess knows about her. As always, Aengus is keeping his cards close to his chest.

Tess steps into the hallway and switches on the light. Before she takes off her coat, she pulls her mobile from her handbag. She brings up Aengus's name and presses the call button. It goes straight to voicemail. She's about to leave a message, then thinks better of it. It's not his fault. He's not the guilty one. Her anger shifts and she feels deflated, exhausted. He'll see the missed call and ring her back, eventually.

In the meantime, she needs to think.

*

The message had arrived as an attachment to Tess's work email, from someone called Maeve Killeen. The subject line read: CONFIDENTIAL.

Tess had opened it up without thinking. The entire day stilled around her. Her eyes raced down the screen.

This is not an easy letter for me to write. I would not contact you if it weren't essential. I have information about your son, Luke, and I would like to speak to you about him in person. You and I once knew each other, a long time ago. I won't take up too much of your time, but I think you need to hear what I have to say. Sincerely, Maeve Killeen.'

A mobile number followed the message. Tess added it to her contacts.

Over the following days, she couldn't get the message out of her head. Something about it felt real, authentic. Eventually, she texted a cautious reply.

She tried to remember if she'd ever known anyone called Maeve, or anyone with the surname of Killeen. But there was no one, no matter how far back she went.

And people didn't change their names like that, did they? Not their Christian names anyway. They were for life.

She wondered how this Maeve person had tracked her down. And then she remembered what she'd always known. That Dublin was a small place.

*

Tess takes off her coat now and hangs it up. She pulls on a thick cardigan and goes down to the kitchen to switch on the heating. Maeve's face swims before her eyes: as she is now, and as she was then, back when she was Fiona. And the words keep repeating themselves.

Are you telling me he's guilty?

I am.

Maeve's certainty frightens Tess. Her own suspicions have been waiting patiently in the wings until tonight. And now here they are: standing beside her onstage. Perfecting their lines.

She needs a cup of tea. Something to warm her up. As she opens the cupboard door to refill the caddy – she hates teabags, just like Betty – she sees a bag of popcorn kernels.

Tess had taught Aengus how to make popcorn when he was twelve. It made him feel like a grown-up when he had friends to stay over. She remembers the sleeping bags all over the living-room floor, the midnight feasts, the stifled laughter long after they should all have been asleep.

That was something Luke never did; no matter how often she encouraged him. Luke never brought anyone home.

She's reminded, too, of the last time she'd seen Maeve, here in this very kitchen. After she'd disappeared, Tess had begun going out with a boy – Declan, wasn't that his name? They'd been circling each other for a week or so on Dollymount. Her first romance, a summer love that took up all her free time.

A time filled with long blue days on the beach, once Conor was back on his feet; with scrambles up and down the sand dunes; with all the heady freedoms of a teenage summer. She'd fought hard for her independence, until Betty gave in, at last.

But now Tess can't help feeling a wave of remorse. She'd let her friend down. Maybe she couldn't have made a difference, but she'd never even tried. A letter might have helped, a visit. Something, anything. And where did Maeve go afterwards, once she'd left the mother and baby home? Tess hadn't even asked.

All of their lives – hers, Maeve's, Belle's, Aimée's – are now knotted together with what Luke has done. Tess sits with the knowledge – she can call it that now – that her son is guilty. She can't turn away from that, not anymore.

And she can't betray Maeve again. She has no idea how, but she needs to try and make this right.

She calls up Maeve's name from her contact list and types in her message.

I'm just heartbroken – for all of us. Can we meet again?

The reply comes back a couple of minutes later.

Of course. Name the time and place.

52

Aengus, 2019

So, I made myself scarce on that Friday evening. I didn't find out what happened to Luke at the cop shop, because by the time I got home that night, everybody was in bed. I was relieved. Dad's coat was in the hall, so I was off the hook.

I stayed away all weekend in a mate's flat and came home after midnight on Sunday. The following morning, I'd the house to myself when I woke up. Then Luke called me and asked me to go into his room to log him off. He'd left his laptop on, he said, and he'd had to leave in a hurry, so could I just do him this one favour?

'Are you okay after Friday?' I asked.

'Yeah. Look, will you just turn off my laptop?' And then, as an afterthought 'I'll owe you one.'

'Yeah, right. Just this once,' I said.

If he didn't want to talk about it, he didn't want to talk about it. And I was already late. I raced up the stairs, two at a time, and flung open his bedroom door. If I was really quick, I'd make it to the station, with just a couple of breaths to spare.

There was one of those spinning shapes on the screen. One of those multicoloured elliptical ones – I hate that eye-rolling shit – and I reached to one side to grab the mouse.

The screen jumped into life. His laptop was open on WhatsApp. I barely glanced at it – but I was aware of all those squared-off speech bubbles, green for Luke, white for whoever he was messaging.

I didn't intend to look, I really didn't, but something in capital letters leapt out at me just before I shut it all down. 'FFS,' it says, 'JUST KEEP YOUR MOUTH SHUT'.

I stopped then and looked more closely. The message was from someone called Hunter.

I knew who that was. Everyone knew who Hunter was. One of those wealthy, arrogant, entitled fuckers. Anytime I'd caught a glimpse of him, he'd been surrounded by the posh girls, the ones who wore full make-up and designer jackets and handbags at nine o'clock in the morning. He was also a creep. I'd spotted him a couple of times, hanging around the campus with Luke and his friends.

Quickly, I scrolled up. The next few messages didn't make a lot of sense. But it was one hell of a tense conversation.

I logged off, slammed the laptop closed, and charged back down the stairs. I really was going to be late.

But the messages disturbed me. They had to have something to do with the cops turning up at our door. I just couldn't figure how Hunter came into it. Everyone knew that his father was a big shot barrister, his mother some kind of society fund-raising Florence Nightingale. Hunter and his brother Quigley – Quigley! for fuck's sake: where did they all think they were from? – swanned around the place as though they owned it.

There was nothing I could do, and Luke wasn't there to be asked. I legged it to the station, just in time to see the Dart pull away from the deserted platform.

*

I didn't get a chance to ask Luke about it later. The following morning, he left before me again. So that meant another chance had gone by. Then I kind of lost the momentum. But one night, later the following week, I asked Mum if everything was okay.

She just said that things were under control. Luke had a solicitor looking after him. She'd let me know if there were 'any developments'. That was all I needed to hear. Things were looking up for me at last, and I really didn't want to get into whatever my brother had or hadn't done. I wanted to forget about him and get on with my own stuff.

I texted Emily when I got on the Dart – I made it this time with a bit to spare. 'What are you doing tonight?' I typed. 'Home is doing my head in. Fancy meeting up?'

It took a minute before a smiley face appeared on the screen. 'Sure,' she wrote. 'There's live music in Whelan's – Less Than Jake are playing. I've two free passes. That work for you?'

'Sound,' I typed back. 'Nice one.' Then, having thought about it for a couple of seconds, I added 'xx'.

It felt like something big, like I'd made some declaration of intent, or something. I didn't mind. It actually felt good.

And for the whole day, it was as though something had lifted. I didn't think about Luke, not even once.

53

Tess, December 2019

This time, Tess doesn't tell Mike she's meeting Maeve. He'll tell her again what a really bad idea it is. And she knows he's not wrong. But this is something she urgently, desperately, needs to do.

'Are you insane?' he'd shouted, when she told him about the first time. 'Jesus Christ almighty, Tess, that could be used against Luke in court. How do you think it'd look – the accused's mother sympathising with the family of the alleged victim? For fuck's sake!'

'I had no idea who she was until I saw her. She said she had information about Luke, and I wanted to know what it was.' Tess kept her voice even. 'That's all.'

She has already decided what she's going to do. There is no point in fighting with Mike about it tonight. Besides, he's leaving for London again in the morning.

He sighs, grasping at the back of his neck.

'Look,' she says. 'Can we just leave it alone for now? Everything has already stopped for Christmas, all the legal stuff. Matt said so. The courts are closed. Besides, nothing like that is going to happen for at least another year.'

She stops. Even thinking about Luke before a judge and jury makes it difficult to breathe.

'Why don't we go out for a bite to eat before you have to go back?' she says. 'Just a tiny bit of normality, for this one evening?'

Dinner will be a distraction. If it's a good enough distraction, Mike might not notice that she hasn't agreed not to meet Maeve again.

It isn't a lie, not quite.

But it is another one of those evasions and uncertainties and guilty half-truths that Luke continues to cause, even when he isn't around.

54

Aengus, Summer 2019

Emily is waiting for me at the bar. She's on her phone and she's looking worried. I know that sort of look from home, and something begins to sink inside me. She puts her phone away as soon I reach her.

'What's wrong?'

'It's Aimée. I can't get hold of her. I haven't seen her all day. Nobody has.'

I like Aimée, I do. But right then, I'm happy to have Emily to myself. She and I are only really starting. 'Why are you so worried about Aimée?'

'She said she'd text me. But she didn't. And I was working all day Saturday and Sunday, so I messaged her saying I'd see her today. But there's no reply.'

'Do you have a home number for her?'

'Well, yeah, I have Maeve's number, but . . . I don't want to call her and scare everybody in case . . .'

'In case Aimée just got lucky,' I say, and we both laugh.

The band is about to start, and I take her hand. 'Come on. Let's sit down. There's nothing else you can do now.'

But she hesitates.

'I tell you what,' I say, 'let's wait until the interval. If you haven't had a text by that stage, then we'll call . . . Maeve, isn't that her name?'

'Yeah, okay.'

She seems happy enough with that.

The gig is good. Very good. But Emily isn't really there. She keeps glancing at her phone. We're just about to go back to the bar when she clutches my arm. 'It's her,' she says. 'She did go home after all, on the early bus on Saturday morning. She's fine.'

'Okay, great,' I say.

But she just looks at me, then down at the phone again, then back up at me. 'There's something wrong,' she says. 'This isn't like her.' She reads: '*Home since Saturday. All fine*'.

'So?'

'This is *Aimée*. This is "why-use-one-word-when-ten-will-do" Aimée. Something is wrong. I know it is.'

'Okay,' I say. 'What would you like to do, then? You can't go to Dundalk at this hour of the night.'

'I'll maybe go tomorrow, if you'll take lecture notes for me on Monday?'

'Sure. I'll try to make sure they're up to your standard.'

She kisses me and I feel well pleased with myself. I like the way every time we meet, something nudges us forward, together, just a little.

'Pint?' I ask, squeezing her hand.

'Please.'

When we sit down, she takes my hand. 'I've the flat to myself tomorrow night. Will you come over?'

I can't stop smiling. 'Yeah,' I say, 'yeah, I'd love to.' And I lean towards her and kiss her. 'I'm really glad that this is happening, that we're happening.'

She smiles. 'Me too. Let's take our time, let's go slowly. I don't want us to mess it up.'

55

Tess, December 2019

The following day, the interior of the hotel lobby is quiet enough. It's mid-afternoon on a December Monday, about as quiet as it can get at this time of the year.

Tess spots Maeve over in one corner, a garish Christmas tree at her shoulder.

Maeve waves when she sees Tess, a gesture that feels out of place. She puts her hand down quickly, as if she's just realised it. Tess notices the glass of wine on the table.

'I need one of those,' she says, pointing.

The first few minutes are awkward; neither feels able to ask how the other's family is.

'Let's just leave all that to one side, okay?' Maeve's voice sounds confident, as though she were convening some kind of official meeting.

Tess looks at her in surprise. 'You've changed.' Then: 'I'm sorry, what a stupid thing to say. Of course you've changed. Haven't we all.'

The waiter arrives, takes her order, disappears back into the murk of tinny Christmas music. Good thing it's muted.

'I'm glad you decided to meet me again,' Maeve says, with that tilt of the head that's becoming familiar.

Tess hesitates. 'I'm not at all sure what I'm doing here, to be honest. My husband would have a fit if he knew. This can only be between us. I mean, not just now, today. I mean always.' She looks at Maeve. 'You can't ever use these meetings against me, against my family.'

'You have my word.'

'Then what are we doing here?'

'There's a lot of things I need to tell you – no, no, it's not like that.'

Tess's face has begun to fall at 'a lot of things'. She is sitting forward already on high alert. She can't help it: the instinct to flee has taken over.

'It's just . . . there are coincidences, strange connections between us that neither of us could ever have imagined,' Maeve says. 'Not bad things. I just can't *not* tell you.'

Tess's drink arrives and she sips at the wine, forcing herself to sit still. 'Okay,' she says. 'I'm as ready now as I'll ever be.'

56

Aengus, Summer 2019

I couldn't wait to see Emily. I was outside her front door that evening at seven on the dot. She answered so quickly I wondered whether she'd been watching out for me.

'I missed you,' I said, and hugged her close.

Her face was pressed into my chest and for a moment she didn't move. Then she looked up and I saw how red-rimmed her eyes were. Before she could say anything, Dave, the guy from the flat above, came thundering down the stairs.

'Get a room!' he said and laughed uproariously at his own joke. Emily took me by the hand and turned away. We stepped inside her flat and closed the door. Seconds later, the door to the street slammed shut and the whole house seemed to tremble.

'Are you all right?' I said. 'How did you get on? Is Aimée okay?' I stopped. Because looking at her, it wouldn't take a genius to figure out that nothing was okay.

We sat on the sofa, and she didn't let go of my hand. 'No,' she said. 'Things aren't okay at all.'

'Tell me what happened.'

I know what shock can do. I'd seen it on the night of Luke's escapade in Howth. Or the day my mother discovered Granda Jack's metal box. Or the look on her face when she turned the corner to see the Garda car outside our house.

Emily's face was like that now: white, strained.

'Aimée wasn't home when I got there; she didn't wait for me.'

I could see the hurt in her eyes. I thought that if I never saw Aimée Killeen again it would be much too soon.

'Maeve – her gran – made me tea and we talked. She doesn't know what's going on, either. She's as worried as I am. Maeve says she's been talking to her through a closed door for the past week. She refuses to come out when anybody else is in the house.'

'Jesus.' I couldn't think of anything else to say.

'And she keeps going out on these massive runs. That's not like her, either.'

'So you didn't see her, then?'

She shook her head. 'No. Maeve said she'd try to bring Aimée around, and she'd call me if she had any luck. So I just went to my parents' house instead.'

I could see she was getting upset again, by the way she bit one side of her lower lip.

'I told my mum about it, but she said that Aimée had always been a bit of a drama queen. Then I got mad at her for saying that and we had a huge argument.'

I put both my arms around her and held her tight. 'You'll work it out, don't worry.'

She sat up straight again and blew her nose. 'Yeah. Well. Mum apologised this morning, and so did I. We're fine.'

'So, how did you leave things with Maeve?'

'She texted me late last night. Aimée knows I've been to see her; she knows where I am. There's not much more I can do for now.'

'What about the others that she hangs around with?'

'That was the other thing – she said I wasn't to talk to anyone about her. If I did, our friendship was over.'

'Wow.' I began to wonder whether Emily's mother might be right, about Aimée being a drama queen. But I didn't say that.

'I'm glad you're back,' was what I did say. 'You'll hear what's going on in a couple of days – your Maeve seems like a sound woman.'

She smiled. 'She is. She's the best.'

Emily dabbed underneath her eyes with a soggy tissue. I tried not to be too pissed off with Aimée.

I needed us to change the channel. I stood up and pulled her to her feet. 'Let's go out for a bit. It's still warm – we can sit and talk and have a change of scene, just for a few hours.'

She didn't let go of my hands. 'Will you come back and stay with me tonight? Chloe is staying over at Rob's again and I don't want to be on my own.'

I didn't need to be asked twice.

We walked through Rathmines together, feeling the warmth around us, smelling the way the air changes when summer arrives to the city streets. I opened the pub door for Emily and followed her through the dimness, outside to the green and bright and lively space of the beer garden.

I loved having Emily by my side, her hand in mine. I was happy that night.

57

Maeve, Summer 2019

'Aimée, I need you to open the door, now.'
I keep my voice as low as I can. Belle is in the back garden with Eileen, but I'm not taking any chances. If Belle suddenly decides she wants to come back inside the house, Eileen will not be able to stop her. She is just too strong, too quick. And when her instinct is aroused, when she feels that something might threaten her daughter, there is no stopping her.

There is no reply from the bedroom, but I know Aimée is in there. I'd heard her come back from another run. It had to have been around five in the morning. Her key in the front door woke me up. But I wasn't quick enough. By the time I'd made my way out onto the landing, she was back in her room again.

It's Sunday: usually a lovely, slow day in our house. I wait for the opportunity and take Eileen to one side. 'Distract Belle for me,' I say. 'This has gone on long enough. I have to find out what's going on.'

Eileen answers quietly. 'I rang Carmel again this morning. Just to let her know Aimée wouldn't be back tonight, either.'

'Has she remembered anything?'

'No. Says she's racked her brains, but Aimée seemed fine the last time she saw her – which would have been last week, Friday evening, before she went out.'

'Does she know where Aimée was planning to go, or who she was meeting?'

Eileen lowers her voice even further. 'She said she was going out to some party. Carmel said she was excited, and all done up.'

Carmel is an old friend of Eileen's. She has a big house close to the university campus, and Aimée is in digs there, along with another couple of students. We wanted to make sure that she was properly fed and looked after. Eileen and I both felt that Aimée wasn't sensible enough to be in a flat and looking after herself – although she kicked up a huge fuss about that.

'I'm perfectly capable of being on my own,' she said, eyes flashing. She was furious. 'And anyway, why can't I share with Em?'

'Because Emily and Chloe are already sharing. We can talk about it again, when you're going into your final year.'

Emily and I had already had this conversation. She's always looked out for Aimée. I didn't want her to feel any more responsible than she already did. I think she might have been relieved.

I press my face even closer to the bedroom door now.

'Aimée, please. I know something has happened, and I just want to talk to you.'

'I don't want to.' The words are muffled.

'Look, you can hibernate all over again, once we've spoken. I just need to see you're all right.'

'I am all right. Leave me alone.'

'I'll leave you alone as soon as I make sure you're all right. Aimée, don't make this into a scene.'

I hate doing this, but she leaves me no choice. 'You know your mother will figure out something is up. And you know how upset she gets. Just talk to me for five minutes.'

I reserve emotional blackmail for only the direst of circumstances.

I hear the key turn in the lock. Aimée opens the door and I'm so shocked at her appearance I take a step back. Her beautiful hair has been shorn; she looks thinner, almost brittle. I say nothing – this is not the time. She turns away at once and flings herself back onto the bed, face down. The room is stifling. The curtains are closed. Summer sunshine beats against the windowpanes. I sit on the edge of her bed.

'Something's happened, Aimée. This isn't like you. Talk to me.' I risk reaching out one hand, placing it in the centre of her back. Her tee-shirt feels hot, sweaty. She shakes me off.

'I don't want to,' she says again.

'Aimée, it's my job to make sure you're okay. Please. Don't shut me out. Whatever it is, I'll help you with it.'

'You can't,' she says, and her voice catches. 'Nobody can.'

Then she sobs. The despair in her voice is so raw I am suddenly terrified. I stand up quickly, make sure the bedroom door is shut to, and sit down beside her again. I stroke her spiky hair. 'Sssshh,' I say, over and over again and I wait. Until the storm passes.

She half-turns her head on the pillow so that I catch a glimpse of her flushed, tear-stained cheek.

'Something happened at that party,' I say. 'Tell me what it was, and we'll figure it out together.'

I feel this enormous weariness descend. Somehow I already know what she's going to say: know it as clearly as if I'd written the script myself.

She half-turns towards me. 'You can't make it better,' she whispers. 'Nobody can.'

'Come here to me,' I say. I pull her, gently, into sitting.

She rests her head against me, in that sweet space between my shoulder and my cheek, just where she used to rest as a baby. I fill with a fierce need to soothe her, protect her, make it all better.

I can't, of course, she's an adult. But I am not without resources, and I love her the way I love her mother. I need to find out whatever has happened. I have to help my granddaughter recover her balance.

'What is it?' I ask again.

'I shouldn't have gone upstairs with him,' she whispers at last. 'I shouldn't have had that much to drink. I shouldn't have had a smoke. Everyone will say it's my own fault.' She stops, her breath coming fast. 'What did I expect?'

And then she cries into my shoulder, a sound I never want to hear again. It reminds me of me.

Something falls inside me. 'Tell me,' I say. 'You know I'll understand. Just tell me what happened.'

When she finishes, I take her face in both my hands. 'This is not your fault,' I say. 'Do you hear me? It's not your fault. Nobody "deserves" what's happened to you. We'll get through this. You'll get through this.'

'Don't tell Belle,' she begs. 'It will destroy her. Please don't tell her.'

'One thing at a time,' I say. 'First things first.'

*

One look at my face is enough.

Eileen nods her head, just the once, and steps out from the kitchen into the back garden. Belle is hanging clothes on the line. Watching her, something sickly inside me slides up to the base of my throat. And I remember it all, as though it were yesterday.

Eileen, hanging out my pyjamas to dry in the summer sunshine. The poppies, the way they staggered drunkenly down the fabric until I could no longer see, no longer hear, no longer feel the ground beneath my feet. The same garden, the same bright laundry basket, the same riotous medley of pegs.

Jesus Christ. Does it never end?

For something to do, I put on the kettle while I hear Eileen excitedly telling Belle about a special afternoon tea on offer in Carlingford, and why don't they go together now, just the two of them?

Belle's face lights up. She gives Eileen a huge hug and then comes tearing into the kitchen, sees me, and stops. 'We're going out for our tea!' she exclaims. 'Mama Leen has invited me!'

'Wonderful,' I say. 'What a lovely treat for you both.'

Her face falls then, and she looks at me anxiously. 'But what about you?'

'I have a lot of work to do this afternoon, sweetheart. But thank you for thinking of me.'

I kiss her forehead. I can smell the sunshine off her skin. I hold onto her for a moment, feeling all the warmth of her innocent, trusting presence. 'Now, go and get ready and make the most of this gorgeous day.'

Twenty minutes later, I stand at the front door as Eileen drives away and Belle waves frantically back at me from the passenger seat.

Then I go back upstairs to my granddaughter.

58

Tess, December 2019

Two hours later, Tess feels as if she's coming up for air. 'I can't believe it,' she says, and then again, 'I just can't believe it.'

She shakes her head, keeps looking at Maeve as though there are yet more astonishments to be revealed. Secrets that this grown woman has hidden away somewhere, maybe in her pockets.

As she looks across the table, Maeve seems to get younger and younger so that she is once again the teenager that Tess spent her summers with; listened to *Saturday Night Fever* with; painted her nails with, for God's sake. She can see her, all over again, standing in the middle of Betty's kitchen, waiting for the popcorn to be done; standing on the cusp of that one moment: a little boy's accident that was about to change their friendship forever. All because of a red football and Tess's taking her eye off her youngest brother for five seconds.

'So Betty, my mother, and your aunt, Eileen, knew each other in Kilburn? She minded me when I was a *baby*?'

'Only from time to time,' Maeve says.

As if that makes a difference.

'But they were good friends,' she adds. 'And Eileen was very fond of Jack.'

'I don't have a problem with her minding me,' Tess says, 'I just have a problem – a big one – taking all of this in.'

Her mind is racing. She's thinking how, in other circumstances, at another time, a reunion would give such joy to both women: grandmothers, mothers, daughters, all together in one room. She feels almost light-headed as she thinks about it. But it's not going to happen: it can't happen, because of Luke and what he has done to all of them. Eileen, Maeve, Belle, Aimée – lives that will never be the same again.

Degrees of separation mean nothing here – aunt, mother, step-aunt, step-grandmother. Their ties are ties of love. They've all been stitched together in ways that have been designed never to come apart, not ever.

Tess drains her glass. 'I need another one of these.' She signals to the waiter. She needs to bring the conversation back to Luke, but she doesn't know how to ask, what to ask.

'And you're sure she and Betty didn't keep in touch?' she says instead.

'Yes, I'm certain. Eileen found it too hard, when she'd had to give up her own little boy.'

Tess can feel the sharp edges of what that must have been like. Time could not, would not, make a difference to that kind of losing.

Maeve pauses. 'Her son's name was Cillian. That's why I changed my name to Killeen. They sound similar. And I didn't want my own surname anymore. I wanted nothing to do with my so-called family.'

Tess remembers the day she'd called to the house, looking for her friend. The way her mother's face was hard, closed. *Something's on the stove.*

'So you still live in Dundalk, all of you together?' she asks.

'Yes. Eileen is just coming up to eighty. More or less the same age as your mum? And she still loves to sew. Betty taught her how to make quilts. I have the bug, too. So does Belle.' And she smiles suddenly.

'I don't know what to say to you,' Tess says. 'I just don't know what to say.' She wipes her eyes. Tears, maddeningly, have begun to escape. 'And we can't even talk about the elephant in the room.'

Maeve hesitates.

'What?' Tess asks.

'Will you meet me again?'

'I—'

'This isn't your fault. None of this is your fault.'

A sob catches in Tess's throat. 'That's a very generous thing to say. It feels like my fault. At least partly. I'm his mother.'

'But,' Maeve smiles faintly, 'this is not your sin. I listened for too much of my young life about all the "sin" – whatever that was – belonging to me, and none of it to anyone else. Let's put the responsibility where it lies.'

'Can I even ask you if Aimée is doing okay? I mean . . .' and she trails off. She's afraid to say anything else.

Maeve stands up, puts one hand on Tess's shoulder. 'Let's meet, just once more. After that,' and she shrugs, 'we won't, if that's what you want.'

'When?'

'Let me text you.' And just like that, she's gone.

She moves so swiftly and silently across the lobby to the street door that she looks like a ghost. Tess has an instinct to call after her, but she doesn't. She watches her, instead, as she makes her way past the hotel window, out of Temple Bar and away into the busyness of the city streets.

If she had called after her, what else could she have said?

59

Aengus, Summer 2019

Emily and I are in the middle of a WhatsApp call when there's a knock at my bedroom door. It can only be Luke.

'What?' I say.

He opens the door. 'Got a minute?'

I'm grudging. 'What is it?'

He comes in – uninvited – and sits on the edge of my bed. I swivel around to face him. 'I'm busy right now, Luke. What do you want?'

'Can I talk to you for a bit?'

There's no point in saying no, or that I'm on a call, or can it wait. I know by the set of him that he's not going to go away.

'Em? I'll call you back in a bit.' I end the call and turn to face my brother. 'What is it?' I ask again.

As I listen to him, I feel my future fall away from me. I see my whole family disintegrating. I see myself losing Emily. Losing any chance of a focus on anything other than Luke.

*

I shoot up in my seat. 'What? Wait. What the fuck? What are you saying?'

He sits forward, elbows resting on his thighs, just looking at me.

'Why didn't you tell me this before?' I say. 'What else have you been lying about?'

'Nothin'.'

'Are you really telling me that *two* of you had sex with her?'

'Well, yeah, kind of. But she agreed. And now she's saying we . . . assaulted her.'

I can't help myself. 'Kind of? How can you "kind of" have sex? You both either did or you didn't – which is it?'

He ignores my question. 'The cops have already interviewed Hunter, but he's in the clear.'

He says this almost casually. No big deal. But the only thing I hear is the name. I focus on that. All the rest of it is just too much to take in.

'That entitled creep?'

He looks startled. 'Hunter's not a creep . . . he's—'

I don't let him finish. 'So is that what you're telling me? That the girl said yes to both of you? That she actually said the words, Luke? For fuck's sake, what do you take me for?'

He lifts his head and looks at me again. 'She didn't say no. I swear, I thought it was okay. I really did.' His eyes fill.

'Jesus Christ, Luke.' I put my head in my hands. 'Where have you been? What the fuck? What part of "consent" do you not get? Tell me exactly what happened.'

I listen as he tells his story. With each new detail, I feel as though all of my nerve ends are flaring.

'Hunter told me we could use his bedroom and that he'd follow us up in a while. He had some dope that he wasn't sharing with everyone, just with us.' He stops for a minute. 'I was going upstairs with her when he said that.'

'So what happened when you got there?'

He shifts uncomfortably. 'We lay down on the bed.' He stops. He looks down at his hands. 'We kinda started getting together, you know, and after a while, Hunter came in.'

The room grows colder. The back of my neck begins to prickle as though some unknown attacker is hiding behind me somewhere, maybe under the bed. That he's getting closer and closer. Ready to pounce.

'So,' I say, taking my time with every word, 'two of you and one of her.'

He looks at me. He begins to shake his head, but slowly. As though he has to explain something to me that I'm still too thick to get. As though he just has to be patient until I do. 'It wasn't like that.'

Then I explode. 'That's *exactly* what it was like. Two of you and one of her. What the *fuck* were you thinking?'

His face is suddenly chalk white. I feel a savage sense of satisfaction. But my heart is about to leap out of my chest.

'We were all a bit out of it.' He looks down at the floor. Then, an instant later, he looks back up at me. He's on the defensive again.

'Why is it all *my* fault? Why? She had as much to drink as I did. Why didn't she say no?' But his last question falls lamely into the room around us. I think it sounds hollow even to him.

'Can't you hear how you're contradicting yourself?' I say. 'A minute ago you said that the girl said yes, that she agreed. Now you're telling me she didn't say no. Because she was out of it. You said so yourself. *Did* she even say a word? Before you decided to fuck her?'

I can't see straight. The room has turned bright red. The only thing I can make out is my brother's shape. He fills the space between us. He has sucked all of the oxygen out of the atmosphere. I have never been so angry in my life.

He doesn't answer.

'So – her being in the room was enough for you, was it? From a girl whose name you don't even know? Is that really what you're telling me?'

'She was fine . . .' he begins.

I stand up. 'Enough,' I say. I raise both hands, warding off his lies. 'Don't tell me any more. I really don't want to know any more.'

And now I'm able to hear all of my own contradictions. Tell me everything. Tell me nothing. I need to know everything. I don't want to know anything.

'She cried,' he says, suddenly. 'And then I kinda came to. I dunno, I . . . I just saw what I was doing and then I stopped.' His lower lip begins to tremble.

'That's rape, Luke,' I say. My voice is startlingly quiet. The words fall like stones into the room. 'You do realise that?'

He shakes his head. 'It wasn't . . . that wasn't what it felt like, not then.'

'How about now? What does it feel like now?'

'Help me, Aengus, please.' His eyes, his face, his whole body fill with pleading. 'And don't tell anyone.'

I look at him in disbelief. 'Seriously? Are you for real? If the cops are going to interview you again, everyone's going to know sooner or later, don't you think?'

'I mean, don't tell Mum and Dad any of the details. Please. Just wait. Please. You have to promise me.'

I promise. Against my better judgement. But I promise. 'You'll have to tell them. Eventually. And if you don't, and this goes any further, then I will. You can't keep them in the dark, Luke. You won't be *able* to keep them in the dark.'

'I'm over eighteen,' he says then, the old defiance in full-throttle flight once more.

'For fuck's sake, what difference do you think that makes?' Now I'm shouting at him. 'If anything, it makes it worse. You're an adult. You're supposed to know better.'

'Any interviews will be confidential. I've already looked it up.' He glances at his watch.

Something about that shocks me. I don't realise why until a couple of days later. It keeps bugging me until I get it. The way he looks at his watch. The way there is something so *ordinary* about it. Calculated. It's out of place with all the tears and the pleading and the drama of a few minutes earlier.

That is the moment that afterwards makes me sure that my brother had been pulling my strings all along. The way he always did.

'And if goes further than a formal interview?' I ask.

'I'll tell them then, but only if I have to. It's my life, not yours.' There is a snap in the last line.

'Ain't that the truth,' I say, furious all over again. 'So why the fuck are you putting me in the middle?'

He doesn't answer for a minute. When he does, I almost cry with rage and frustration. I feel an anguish I've never felt before, not even when Granda Jack died.

'Because you're my brother.'

'Sometimes, Luke . . .' but I can't finish because finally, finally, the static in my head begins to clear.

I know what I need to ask. At the same time, I don't want the answer. I don't want to hear it. I don't want him to say it.

'Stop pretending you don't know the girl's name,' I say. 'I'm not going to lift a finger to help you until you stop pretending. Tell me her name.'

He shrugs. I swear. He shrugs and looks back at me over one shoulder as he's leaving my bedroom.

'Her name is Amy. Amy Killeen.'

60

Maeve, Summer 2019

'Here's what we're going to do,' I say. 'I've looked it up online, and we need to go to the Rotunda Hospital.' I pause, waiting for the explosion. 'There is a sexual assault unit there and—'

Aimée's hands are in the air at once. 'No,' she says quietly. 'I'm not going there. They'll tell the guards. I don't want anything to do with the guards.'

Her mood has shifted again. She must be exhausted, but she has finally stopped crying. Now she looks hollowed out; dark circles under her eyes; shoulders hunched as she sits at the kitchen table, her hands wrapped around a mug of coffee. She's biting her fingernails again, a habit she'd worked so hard to conquer, years back.

'They won't tell the guards. I promise. That's not why I'm taking you there. Aimée, look at me.'

Slowly, she lifts her head. Her eyes are unrecognisable. Their green depths are unfathomable. I can't find her in there. In the last hour she has moved so swiftly from rage to passivity to hostility that I can no longer keep up.

'I'm taking you to the clinic to make sure you won't become pregnant.' I speak very quietly and then I wait for a moment, struggling to find the right words. 'And to have you properly checked out.'

I can't bear to name the horrible possibility of infection. I just can't.

She looks at me in surprise. 'What do you mean, they won't tell?'

'Your visit to the unit will be confidential. It's nothing to do with the guards, unless *you* give permission. This is about your health. Telling the guards is up to you, and that's a whole other day's discussion.'

'I won't do it. Don't even *ask* me to do it.'

I wait. Allow the silence between us to settle. I'm not yet sure what she's refusing to do: tell the guards or come with me to the Rotunda.

'I'm not going to make a statement. Have you any idea what appearing before a jury would do to me? The questions I'd have to answer? My entire *life* would be dragged through the dirt.'

I almost welcome the flash of anger in Aimée's eyes. At least she's back.

'Have you forgotten Belfast?' she says.

'No, Aimée. I have not forgotten Belfast.'

I wait for a minute, to get my voice under control. 'I'm not going to force you to do anything. I promise. But please, just let me look after you today.'

Despite myself, my best efforts, my voice cracks. 'Not you as well, Aimée. Not another generation,' I say. 'Please, just not again.'

Her outline begins to fill in. It's as though she's coming back into her body, little by little. It makes enough of a difference for me to know she's listening. Slowly, she nods. 'You mean, no more babies in this house.'

'Not like this,' I say, shaking my head. 'As many babies as you choose, my love, just not like this.'

'Okay.' Her smile is false, brittle. 'We'd better get going, then, before Belle comes home.' She stands up.

I'm baffled, at the way her mood shifts again, like light on water. But it doesn't matter. Right now, she trusts me; she's with me.

'And we're not telling my mother.' She looks me right in the eye. It's not a question.

'No,' I say. 'Belle doesn't need to know. But you have to keep talking to me, Aimée. You have to. For all our sakes.'

'Let's go,' she says and starts walking out of the kitchen.

I don't hesitate. I grab my keys and my bag and follow her out to the car.

*

I used to marvel how, when she was a child, Aimée would chat to me so easily, swinging her legs as she sat on the kitchen counter, while I got things ready for whatever cake she wanted to bake next.

As long as I was busy and kept my head down, Aimée shared all sorts of things with me. Her candour used to take me by surprise. It comforted me, that level of trust. Once it was there, I felt nothing would ever go as badly wrong for her as it had for me, back when I was Fiona.

Once, when my head and shoulders were in the attic, as I stowed away the Christmas decorations for another year, Aimée told me about being bullied at school. She would have been about fourteen at the time, in second year. She was matter of fact, almost blasé, as she told me of the daily torture inflicted on her by some little madam called Briony.

'I don't want to go back to school,' she said. 'I hate it there.'

When I came back down the ladder, I saw her face was streaked with tears. Her Christmas mascara had run, making her look like the vulnerable child she was, rather than the sophisticated teenager she was trying to be.

We had a hug and baked a cake together afterwards. We weighed and measured, creamed and folded, working together in our usual rhythm at the kitchen table. We talked about things until she didn't want to anymore.

I've learned over the years that there is something about direct eye contact that makes my granddaughter shy away from offering confidences.

So now, as I drive along the motorway to Dublin, my eyes on the road ahead, I don't even glance in Aimée's direction. Not once. She sits to my left, quietly at first, and then less quietly as the kilometres speed by.

I don't even need to ask her any questions. She tells me every sordid thing there is to know about that horrifying night, and I keep my face neutral and I breathe as slowly as I can and I keep my heartbeat under control and I listen and I listen and I listen.

*

I remember another car journey, decades earlier, when I sat where she's sitting now. I can see the grim set of my father's face. The grim outline of my future. I fight to stay in the present now, but it's as though I am filling up with decades and decades of past lives.

I pay attention to all that Aimée says, I do, to each and every last detail. I cover her hand with mine from time to time. I let her know I'm here, that I'm still listening.

I remember the day she was born. The day her mother was born. I think of Eileen's story, of my own story, of all those other stories that we don't yet know or don't want to know, the ones we pretend not to hear, the ones that we like to believe have nothing to do with us and for the first time in my life I thirst, madly, for revenge.

Somebody needs to pay for this. Somebody *has* to pay for this.

61

Aengus, Summer 2019

When Emily half-opens the door to me, her eyes are blazing. 'Did you *know*? Tell me the truth, Aengus! *Did you know?*'

Her question makes me furious. 'No!' I shout. 'Of course I didn't fucking know! I've only found out half an hour ago!'

'Come in,' Emily says. She slams the door to the street, and I follow her down the hall and into the flat.

As soon as she closes the door, she crumples. There is no other word for it. I catch her and half-carry her to the sofa. I'm almost afraid to touch her, but the alternative is letting her fall and that's not happening. I sit at the other end of the sofa from her. I wait for her to say something.

'Maeve rang,' she says.

'Tell me.'

'She took Aimée to the sexual assault unit at the Rotunda. Everyone was very kind, she said, and Aimée talked to them. And she told Maeve in the car about everything that happened with Luke.'

Tears are streaming down Emily's face now and she makes no effort to wipe them away. 'She's not pregnant. But they said there's no longer any DNA evidence present. There's nothing that can be collected – it's been too many days.'

I hate myself for this, but my heart lifts.

If there's no hard evidence like that, then maybe me and my family won't have to be dragged through the court with my brother. This flash of hope is instantly brushed aside by the guilty memory of Aimée, the last time I saw her. Full of light and mischief, laughing with Emily as they plotted some kind of birthday surprise for one of their mates.

'Maeve says that Aimée keeps on changing her mind about her statement to the guards. Maeve encouraged her to make it. Well, she admitted to me that she pushed her to do it, because she's so angry. But she's not sure if Aimée will see it through. She keeps talking about withdrawing it.'

I am a mass of emotion. I feel guilty by association. Then remorseful for the hope I'd just felt that Luke – that all of us – would be off the hook. I'm sorry for Aimée and for Emily, too, still distraught beside me on the sofa. And I'm terrified of what this will do to the two of us.

And then I think about Grandma Betty, my parents, my mother in particular. The future is suddenly bleak. Cold and empty. But I have to be honest with Emily. I have to.

At that instant, she reaches over and takes my hand. 'I know you're not your brother,' she says. 'I know it, but this is hard. I don't ever want to be in his company. Don't ever ask me to be in the same room as him.'

Hope nudges again. 'Of course I won't. And I swear to you I had no idea about him and Aimée,' I said. 'It never even occurred to me.' I swallowed. Then I could barely get the words out.

'He had an informal conversation with the guards ten days ago – that's all I know. He said nothing after it. He only told me the truth this afternoon.'

She looks at me then. She says nothing for the longest time. 'You never said.' Her voice is very quiet. 'You never said that he'd been questioned. Why would you keep something like that from me?'

Something dangerous hovers in the air between us.

'Because I never even imagined it could have anything to do with *us*. Besides, I haven't wanted anything to do with my brother since I was *six*.' The moment I say it, I know how true it is. I remember the weekend of my sixth birthday. Everything ruined because of him. The first of so many times I've lost count.

'I know nothing about his life. I don't *want* to know anything about his life. He destroys everything he touches.' And then I break. The sense of relief is huge. I just let go. I sob in a way I haven't done since I was a child. Emily sits beside me, saying nothing, just waiting until I finish.

'I'm sorry,' I say, angry that this is happening. I wipe my eyes roughly.

'I have to go to her,' she says at last. 'Aimée has said she'll see me. Maeve thinks she's doing a little better. I'm going to Dundalk tonight.'

I feel any earlier hope drain away. I don't want to ask her if this is the end for us. If it is, I don't want to know. I'm not ready for that yet.

'Can I do anything?' I ask instead.

'You can come with me to the station.'

'Really?'

'Yeah. I honestly don't know how, or if, we'll get through this, but let's keep talking.' She reaches up and kisses me, gently. 'You're a good person. You're not to blame.'

'No,' I say. 'I know I'm not to blame. But this will change how you see me. It already has.' I stop. 'It changes everything.'

She doesn't argue with that.

We leave the flat and make our way to the bus. We don't say a whole lot, but Emily takes my hand when we sit down. I remember the Polish movie we saw together, a couple of weeks ago. On *that* Friday. *Cold War.* The way she took my hands then, telling me without words that she loved me.

I wish I had somewhere to go, somewhere other than home. I can't bear the thought of being under the same roof as Luke.

I walk Emily to the platform.

'I'll text you,' is the last thing she says as she boards the train. 'And we'll talk when I get back.'

'Yeah,' I say. And then I don't know what else I *can* say – I can hardly send my best wishes to Aimée, can I? Or my apologies to her mother, her grandmother, and whoever else in that house who've just had their lives blown apart by my brother?

I cross the echoing concourse and make my way to the Dart platform. I don't really care how long I have to wait for the next train.

I don't really care about anything.

62

Tess, December 2019

It's five in the morning. Another sleepless night.
Tess gets up and dresses in the dark. She makes her way quietly down the stairs, avoiding the last creaky step. She checks the porch door and the front door and puts the two sets of house keys into her pocket.

On her way to the kitchen, she sees that Luke's backpack is in the hall, his coat thrown over the newel post. He can't have left, because all the doors, back and front, are locked. She'd made sure of it last night, once Luke was home and in his bedroom.

Aengus is staying with Betty. She hasn't been well, and Aengus has offered to keep her company. Yesterday evening, he wasn't able to hide how glad he was to get away. Mike isn't due home until the weekend.

This is Tess's chance to get Luke on his own.

She puts on the kettle and sits down at the kitchen table to wait.

*

At seven-thirty, she hears Luke's footstep in the hall.

A few minutes later, he appears at the kitchen door. He's irritated. 'I can't find the house keys,' he says. 'They're not on the hall table. And the front door is locked.'

'I know. I locked it.'

He looks puzzled. 'Well, can you open it, please? I've an exam this morning and I can't be late.'

'I know. I'll open the door when I'm good and ready.'

He is taken aback. He starts to say something and then thinks better of it.

'I'll open the door once you've listened to what I have to say to you.' Tess takes a sip of tea, replaces her mug on the table. 'Sit down. You've become very good at avoiding me recently.'

'What?' He shifts from one foot to the other. He glances over Tess's shoulder.

'The back door is locked, too. Oh, and by the way, so is your bedroom window. I made sure of that last night. Sit down, Luke.'

'What is this?' he says. 'Another interrogation?' He pulls out a chair, angrily, and sits down across the table from his mother.

'I don't need to interrogate you, Luke. I already know the truth. I know what happened with Aimée. I know what you did. Think of this as your last opportunity to stop lying.'

*

Tess tells him, calmly, about her recent meetings with Maeve, about their old friendship. She tells him about Belle and Eileen. About Betty. About the threads of connection that tie them all together. And she tells him something about Aimée, about how she's struggling to pick up the pieces of her life again.

When she finishes, his face is still closed, but she has seen shock register there.

'We'll hammer out the details with you later, Luke, but your father and I have agreed. While you're under our roof, you keep to our rules.' She leans forward. 'Look at me, Luke. This is how it has to be.'

'What?' he says. 'What do you want from me? What am I supposed to do?'

Something in his tone makes her feel a nudge of optimism. She has Betty's voice inside her head: *Never cut them loose.*

'At a minimum, you attend counselling. You have a lot of attitudes that need to change. That's not negotiable.' She takes another sip of her tea. 'Oh and telling the truth from now on would be good.'

He looks over at her. She notices that his hands have begun to shake. He shoves them into the pockets of his coat as he stands up.

'Can I go now?'

'Yes.'

She reaches into the pocket of her dressing gown and hands him a set of keys. Before he takes them, she says: 'Those are the rules, Luke. Court case, or no court case, that's how it has to be. There are consequences to what you did.'

He takes the keys from her.

'And this is the first of many conversations, by the way. You need to do better. We all need to do better.'

He starts to say something. 'I didn't mean . . .' and then changes his mind. 'Forget it.'

She watches as he leaves the kitchen and closes the door quietly behind him.

Then she refills the teapot and sits back down at the table again until the dawn, a dirty orange glow in the east, begins to appear at the edges of darkness.

63

Tess, February 2020

Tess sees Maeve as soon as the train pulls into Dundalk station. She's waiting on the platform, just as she's promised. They've decided to meet outside Dublin this time. Tess knows nobody in Dundalk, apart from Maeve. It feels safer that way.

As they step outside onto the street, the February winds are biting.

'We don't have far to go,' Maeve is saying. 'The Imperial Hotel is very close.'

They don't say much until they are inside. Maeve has reserved a table for them in the corner of the lobby, away from even casual eyes.

She orders tea and they take off their coats and sit, facing each other across the small, polished table.

'I wanted to tell you this, face to face,' Maeve says. There is that bluntness again, that taking control of the situation. It's hard to get used to. Tess has a familiar, sinking feeling. Is even more bad news about to be shared?

'Aimée has withdrawn the accusation against Luke.'

'What?' Shock ripples through Tess. An electrical charge.

'We've fought about it, she and I. A lot. We've taken legal advice. Sometimes, the DPP will proceed anyway, if the guards feel there is enough evidence. Apparently, in this case, there is not.' Her tone is even, factual.

Tess can't take it in. The words sound all wrong.

Maeve is watching her, and Tess is ashamed of the sudden leap of hope that now makes her sit even further forward. Does this mean . . .?

'There isn't enough evidence to charge Luke,' Maeve goes on. 'That doesn't mean your son isn't guilty, though, not by a long shot. I need you to know that.'

'I do know that – I've never doubted what you told me. I've believed Aimée for months. But I'm confused. Why, after all this time, has she changed her mind?'

'She has not "changed her mind".' Maeve's tone is sharp, now; angry. 'Don't think that for a moment.'

'I'm sorry,' Tess says. 'I didn't mean that the way it came out. I'm just trying to understand what's happening.'

'Aimée won't go ahead because she says the stress of it all is crippling her. She can't face being pulled apart in court, her whole life exposed. And we've more than enough examples in this country to prove she's right.'

'I know. I know we do.'

Tess can see herself as she was a couple of mornings ago, standing in the kitchen, making coffee. Mike is putting cups and plates and cutlery onto the kitchen table. The radio is on in the background.

In one of those strange conversational lulls that sometimes happen, Tess hears the newsreader's words and stops what she's doing. She and Mike both stop. They look at one another, horrified.

An ex-soldier has just been jailed for ten years for twelve rapes on eleven occasions. 'His victim,' the newsreader continues, 'endured five days of cross-examination'.

'Jesus Christ,' Mike says. His face is white.

Five days.

Remembering this, Tess is afraid even to move. She waits for Maeve to continue.

'It would be like being on trial herself. It's too traumatic and she's just not doing it.' Maeve looks over at Tess, her eyes still alight with anger. 'Aimée has done nothing wrong. She's already suffered enough. Why should she be punished again?'

'She shouldn't.'

Maeve clasps both hands together. It feels as if she's waiting for something more.

'I'm not sure what you want me to say.' Tess speaks quietly. She's already ashamed of what she's feeling. A guilty wave of relief for herself, for Mike. For Luke. There's compassion for Aimée, too, but she knows better than to say that. Maeve is much too angry to hear it.

Maeve doesn't answer for a moment. 'I don't expect you to say anything, really. You're Luke's mother, so of course you're hugely relieved. I get that. But my granddaughter hasn't even begun to recover. She's also angry at me.'

'Why?' Tess is surprised.

'Because I was the one who insisted she go to the guards. But by the time she did, there was no forensic evidence left. She'd been running for days, showering, trying to wash the whole experience off herself.' She shrugs. 'She says I shouldn't have forced her to report it. That it's her life, not mine. And I can't argue with that.'

'I'm so sorry,' Tess says. 'For all of it. For all of you.'

'I'm tired,' Maeve says, and the edge of her earlier anger is just underneath her words. 'I'm so tired of the real sinners getting away with things.'

'You mean Luke.'

'Among others.' She pauses for a moment. Her face fills with emotion.

'Several months back, a woman contacted me. She'd seen my photo on Facebook, or Instagram – one of the promotions I ran recently about the shop. Ironically, Aimée took the photos and wrote the text.' She doesn't seem able to continue.

'Who was it?' Tess asks, softly.

'Her name was Joanie – or at least, I knew her as Joanie. Her real name is Elizabeth. But I'll never be able to think of her as anything but wee Joanie. She was with me at St Brigid's.'

Tess wonders what she's going to say next.

'Joanie was only fourteen when her son was born. She's been living in Nottingham for donkeys'. Hasn't set foot in this country since the eighties. Her son has finally traced her, after almost forty years.'

Maeve stops and her face softens. 'She's coming back for another visit next month, with Charlie, for St Patrick's Day. I'll see her again then. We still have a lot to say to each other.'

Tess stays silent.

'Have you any idea how many thousands of us there have been, over the years?' Maeve's tone is abrupt.

'No,' Tess says, softly. 'I don't. And I don't think many of us do.' She hesitates, not sure if she should bring it up. 'Isn't the Commission of Investigation report due soon?'

'I have no expectation that that will heal anything,' Maeve says. 'Our stories have never been listened to, not really.' She shrugs. 'The people in power don't care about us, don't really want to know what happened. I try not to be bitter. But it's hard.'

Tess reaches across the table. She places one hand on Maeve's. Sees again the teenage bedroom, hears *Saturday Night Fever* on the record player. Posters on the wall. She can almost smell the nail varnish.

'I truly don't know what to say to you,' she says. 'I can't make this better. But we're dealing with Luke as best we can. Please, tell me if there's something, anything at all I can do.'

Suddenly, Maeve lowers her head. Tess stands up and moves over to the chair beside her.

'I'll do anything,' she says. 'I'll meet with Aimée, if you think it would help. I'll support her in any way I can. I'll do anything you ask.'

Maeve sits back. 'There is something,' she says. 'There is something that I think would help.'

They sit, as the day darkens around them. Tess listens carefully to everything she says. When they leave, hours later, Maeve is calm.

As they reach the hotel door, she places both hands on Tess's shoulders. 'Thank you,' she says. 'Talking to you has helped. And thank you for agreeing to do what I've asked.'

'I'll make it happen,' Tess says. 'And I want to keep in touch with you, properly. To support you. I won't let you down again, I promise.'

Maeve smiles. In the fading light, her face is almost ghostly. 'We'll keep talking. There is nothing that is ever made better by silence,' she says. 'Nothing. Particularly in this country.'

She walks Tess to the train station.

The last sight Tess has of her is of a slight, greying figure receding into the distance as she lifts one arm and waves to the departing train.

Afterwards, Tess will remember how she looked both fragile and enduring. She had no idea what was approaching; neither of them did.

64

Betty, 2020

Aengus arrived here a couple of weeks back with what he said was an old laptop.

A couple of weeks.

Really? Is that all it has taken to catapult us from one world into another?

The laptop didn't look old to me, but he told me you'd never know by the outside. Its motherboard was slow, he said, and it didn't have all the functions of a newer one.

'A bit like your Gran,' I said softly, just to make him smile. 'My motherboard is a little on the slow side these days.'

He sat on the kitchen chair, still keeping his distance. 'Will you not come and stay with us, Gran? We can all be locked down together, and we can look after you.'

'It's very kind of you all, but I'm better off in my own house, where everything is slow and familiar.'

The truth is that our daughter's whole family is holding on by its fingernails. That poor girl – I don't know her name or anything about her: Tess said it was better that way. I didn't insist. But I still can't stop thinking about what happened. She withdrew her complaint against Luke recently, but Tess and Mike are taking a very hard line with him.

She is still not herself. It's as if something that is essentially Tess has disappeared, leaving her sadder, quieter, less substantial than before. When she comes to see me, she asks the same questions over and over again and always ends up at the same place. On that particular circle of motherhood where she blames herself. Asks 'Where did I go wrong?' That's where I come in. Where I can be comforting, and a little bit wiser. Maybe. But mostly, I just listen. To all of them.

Luke has been here a few times, bringing groceries. I wasn't sure what I was supposed to know. Sometimes these knots of secrecy, of who knows what and when and from whom, can be exhausting. Once, when he was leaving, he looked me in the eye and said: 'It'll be all right, Gran.' His blue eyes were so earnest, his face so open, I truly wanted to believe him.

But I've had too many years of children looking me in the eye and telling me one thing, when the opposite was the truth. I no longer believe in the sincerity of the direct blue gaze.

*

And now I'm living through the strangest days of my life, Jack. Not a soul on the streets, day or night. An astonishing silence while the world is too terrified to exhale. Even the birds stopped singing for a while. And those awful pictures from all over the world: from Italy, from Brazil, from the US. I worry about MylesandConor. I worry about all of us.

And I am tired. Hidden away like this, I no longer get any energy from the neighbours I used to chat with on the street or over the occasional coffee, or a talk at the local library. There's no news from Lithuania from Konstantin in the vegetable shop down the road, no banter with Jarek in the butcher's, no stories about Poland and Latvia. There's no Sunday lunch around Tess's generous table, no hugs, no kisses goodbye.

But I'm staying put. It's easier for everyone, that way – including me.

'I'll see you a few times a week, one or the other of you,' I said to Aengus as he finished setting up the laptop, 'even if it's only on my doorstep, and now I'll be able to see you every day with this when we Skype.' I nodded towards the laptop on the kitchen table. 'I count myself very lucky to have you all so close by. I'll be grand.'

I saw him bite his lip and I almost got up from the table and crossed the careful distance between us, to put my arms around him until I remembered that I couldn't. Because I might be dangerous to him. Because he might be dangerous to me.

My heart has been broken many times over the years, Jack, but that was painful. Not being able to touch my own grandson.

'Is your Kindle charged, and full of stuff?' Aengus said, and we both ignored the waver in his voice.

'It is, and look, I've got a big pile of photograph albums ready and waiting. I'm finally going to put some order on all those boxes of snaps. Granda Jack is dancing a jig in heaven at the thought.'

He laughed then. 'And your sewing machine is okay?'

'Yep, I got Tess to take it in for a service.'

'What are you going to make?'

'I have bags of remnants under the stairs. Your gran is going to indulge her creative side.' I made a wicked face. 'I might even subject you to one of my designs. Something like, oh I don't know, maybe a pink sequinned waistcoat?'

'Cool,' he said, and we both laughed.

'You really don't need to worry, Aengus. I'm happier in my own place, knowing that you're only a phone call away. This is truly my own choice.'

'Well, you're all set up now. Let me show you how this works.'

After he'd shown me, I asked the question that I'd been wanting to ask for weeks. 'Now that things with Luke are being . . . resolved,' I said. What was the right word? I had no idea. I don't think there is one. 'That lovely young girl you told me about – Emily, isn't that her name? Are you two okay again?'

He looked at me in surprise. 'How did . . .' he began, and then he grinned.

I tapped the side of my nose. 'I'm a gran,' I said. 'I know things.'

He laughed outright then. 'Yeah,' he said. 'We're working things out. Emily's great,' he said. 'She reminds me of you.'

65

Christmas Day 2021

B etty was with them on Christmas Day. 'I'm so delighted to be with you all again, like this,' she said. She clapped her hands together like a child. 'I missed you all so much last year.'

She looked over at Luke. 'And you were so sick; you had us really worried.' She shook her head. 'I'm so grateful none of the rest of us were stricken.'

'We're not out of the woods yet, Betty,' Mike warned her. 'Omicron is raging out there. We still want you to continue to be careful.'

'Oh, I am. Sure, I hardly leave the house. But I've been busy.' Her face filled with sudden mischief. She bent down and reached into the bag at her feet. 'I can't wait any longer,' she said. 'I've been so looking forward to this.'

She handed each of them a parcel, beautifully wrapped, tied with bows of tinsel and ribbon.

Aengus's waistcoat was multi-coloured, flamboyant. Betty had stitched together diamond-shaped panels of silk and wool and cotton and lined the whole thing in shocking pink satin. The waistcoat was a perfect fit.

'Just what I've always wanted!' Aengus said, grinning.

Luke's sweater was a cashmere colourblock. 'I looked up the latest fashions online,' Betty said, proudly. 'And I copied the fanciest design. Do you like it?'

'Yeah, I really do, Gran.' Luke held it up, and the shades of blue made the colour of his eyes even more startling. 'I love it. Thank you.'

For Mike, there was a selection of Jack's books. For Tess, several albums of photographs.

One was filled with black and white prints. Betty turned the first page. 'And here is Granda Jack and his pal, Jimmy, in 1970. Imagine,' she said. 'More than fifty years ago.'

'Thanks, Betty,' Tess laughed. 'Thanks for that timely reminder of my advancing age.'

Aengus and Luke stood behind their grandmother, one at each shoulder, as she pointed to the grainy images. 'Look at the pair of them, would you, grinning from ear to ear,' she said. 'Those smelly green waders used to drive me mad.'

'Never mind the waders,' said Aengus. 'Would you look at the size of that fish!'

'It's a pike. They grow really big. Your Granda used to say they were predators. They hide in the weeds, and then attack – fast and furious. Always unexpected. He showed me their teeth once,' she shivered. 'Wouldn't want to meet any of *them* in the water.'

'Did they eat the fish they caught?' asked Luke.

'No – they'd have someone take a photo of the catch before they put it back into the river.'

'Why?' asked Luke. 'I mean, why didn't they eat it?'

'Pike isn't all that tasty,' Betty said. 'At least, not to us. And back in those days, nobody in this country would've thought about eating it.'

'Did you ever go fishing with him?' Aengus asked.

'God, no. I never really "got" the whole fishing thing. Maybe I could never sit still for long enough. And I've never liked the cold. Besides,' and she dug Aengus in the ribs with her elbow, 'takin' six kids along with me would have scared the daylights out of the fish, don't you think?'

Betty turned another page. 'And here's your Aunt Eleanor, sitting on Sheila's knee. Her glasses are crooked, as usual. I'm not sure when that one was taken, but I can see the bit of Elastoplast that's holding her specs together.'

Tess remembered. 'I know when that was! Think, Betty,' she said. 'Remember the Chawke brothers? The bullies? Sheila and I went after them one day, down the back lane. We taught them a lesson they'd never forget.'

Her mother's eyes cleared with the memory. 'Oh my God. How could I forget. I was so worried about what the neighbours would think, with the pair of you scrapping on the street.'

They looked at the photo together. Eleanor's eyes were looking down at a book and her thumb had been caught in the act of sneaking its way towards her mouth.

On the facing page, Eoghan was pictured on the day of his Confirmation. Tess looked at her twelve-year-old brother, all gangly legs and embarrassed smile. She didn't know until years later what that boy had been going through.

The final photo was of MylesandConor. They were sitting close together, their arms folded on the wooden school desk, each of them smiling for the camera, gap-toothed.

When Tess looked up, her mother's eyes had filled. Betty drew one hand across the glossy surface that held the photographs in place. 'And as for these two,' she said, and shook her head.

*

Afterwards, Aengus observed that Betty had been on a roll. They heard story after story, about Granda Jack; about Kilburn and all the people they used to know there; about the thrill of coming home at last to Dublin when Tess was a one-year-old. She had everyone's full attention.

There was so much Tess was tempted to tell her then, but she stopped herself. Those wounds had only just started to heal, for everyone. She would not open them up again.

But that day, around the Christmas table, Tess felt that her mother was trying to tell her something. Even her stories about MylesandConor were full of humour. Full of forgiveness.

66

Epilogue, *January 2022*

Maeve

Belle comes to the shop with me now every morning. I welcome this apparent return to normal life with a huge sense of relief. I hope that it will continue. That we are finally out of the woods. The last two years have been particularly difficult for Belle.

Her carefully honed routine was thrown into chaos. She couldn't understand why her life had been turned upside down. Couldn't understand why she had to be so cautious, why we had to sanitise everything, why we couldn't go out like we used to.

We tried our best to explain. But Belle picked up on our anxiety and became fearful and fretful. It took the three of us several weeks to calm her into a different kind of daily routine. We moved from hour-long blocks of sewing, to baking bread, to colouring pictures.

Eventually, she settled and became contented again. But we continued to shield her from the news. In a way, we all welcomed this pressing need to shut out the world. There was little out there that we wanted to see.

Aimée was wonderful with Belle. In the way these things sometimes happen, the restrictions of lockdown allowed her to have another focus. She devoted herself to Belle, and what she needed. Aimée told me that managing her mother through each day helped her get out of her own head.

'I don't miss the campus,' she told me when I asked her how she was doing. 'I don't miss anything about it. Besides, Emily is just a few streets away. She's the only one I care about.'

She abandoned her studies for that year. We agreed we'd discuss that again, at some future date.

Day by day, little by little.

*

I'd heard Belle and Aimée talking together, early one morning, sometime in April of that first horrific year. I'd come downstairs for breakfast, and I heard Belle's voice, verging on the shrill. I paused in the hall and took longer than usual to pick up the post off the floor.

'I know something was wrong,' Belle was saying, 'but nobody ever tells me. I want *you* to tell me. You're *my* Aimée, not theirs.'

I turned and climbed the stairs again. I knocked on Eileen's door and put my head around it. 'Morning,' I said. 'I'll bring you up tea and toast in a bit. Belle and Aimée are talking, and I don't want to interrupt.'

Eileen sat up. 'Does Belle know?'

'I think Aimée is just now giving her a version she can handle. We'll know in a bit.'

Eileen smiled over at me. 'I think that will be very good for both of them.' She reached over and took a book off her bedside table. 'I think it's high time I had a duvet day. You can let me know when it's safe.'

*

Afterwards, Aimée let me know that, halfway through telling her mother a very simple story, Belle had said suddenly: 'Is there flour? Can we bake this morning?'

'So I knew she'd heard enough. She knows somebody hurt me last year. I told her that I'm okay now, and there's nothing for her to worry about.'

Aimée ran both hands through her hair: an old gesture. She used to pull it back from her face like that, and tame it into a ponytail, or a messy bun, often secured with a pencil.

When she cut her long hair so bluntly after Luke, I couldn't get used to her new appearance. It hurt me every time I looked at her. All of her softness was taken away, although I'd never have said that. I was glad to see she was letting her lovely hair grow again.

'And how okay are you?' I asked, softly.

She half-smiled at me. 'The sessions with the Crisis Centre help. Having Emily to go for walks with helps. And being here' – she spread both hands wide – 'with all of you helps most of all.'

I didn't want to ask about Luke. She'd tell me in her own good time.

Right then, things were good enough.

One foot in front of the other.

Tess

Tess opens the front door and steps into the hallway. She bends down and picks up the post off the floor. Junk mail, mostly. The odd bill. What looks like a few delayed Christmas cards.

The air is cold and unnaturally still. Betty's energy has already leached away, and the wintry chill of absence has taken her place.

Tess makes her way quickly to the kitchen. If her mother's ghost is anywhere, it will be at her own kitchen table, drinking tea. Or at the sink, filling the kettle. Tess smiles to herself, remembering her teenage battles about women and kitchens and the endless unfairness of housework.

She switches on the heating and sits down at the small table, looking out at her father's garden. For the first time, it looks winter-sad, neglected. She'll go out later and sweep up the leaves.

But the kitchen is as neat as ever. It's as though Betty has chosen her moment, her own time of readiness. She'd folded her tent and stolen off into the night, a few days after Christmas.

Tess is grateful that they'd all managed to paper over the family cracks on Christmas Day. They'd made Betty the centre of attention; it was good to see her look so happy. Tess had convinced Aengus to put his anger to one side, just for those few hours.

'You really want me to pretend?' he'd demanded. 'You want me to play happy families with Luke?'

'Yes,' said Tess. 'Yes, I do.'

He'd glared at her then. Before he spoke again, she'd reached out and placed one hand on top of his. 'Listen to me, Aengus. It's not for me,' she said. 'I don't think Betty will be with us for very much longer. Let's all do this one last thing for her.'

Finally, Aengus had nodded his head curtly, just the once. 'For her, then.' And he'd walked away.

It was Aengus who found Betty on the following Tuesday morning, her eyes closed, peaceful. The duvet was tucked under her chin, the hot-water bottle cold at her feet.

*

Tess pulls the envelopes towards her and opens up the first. A Christmas card to her mother, signed in a shaky hand, but one that still has echoes of old-fashioned copperplate elegance.

'Dear Betty, These have been difficult years, in more ways than one. Despite it all – or perhaps because of it all – I'd love the two of us to meet, quietly, whenever it's possible for us to do so. In the meantime, stay safe and well. I think of you and Jack often, with great affection. Eileen Garvey.'

Tess's eyes fill. She'll write to Eileen and let her know.

The shadow of Luke still lingers over everything, although Tess has begun to feel that she's finally learning to live with what has happened, rather than being overwhelmed by it.

Mike is a different story, though. He's told Tess that he feels adrift, rudderless. All of his certainties have been taken away. His work, his family, his daily life: he says he no longer recognises himself. They're both trying, little by little, to put all the pieces back together again. Things can't be the same as they were. They know their family will have a different shape, but they'll mould it together, as best they can.

*

Luke had been very ill last Christmas. He'd tested positive on Christmas Eve. The next several days were filled with his wracking cough, a high temperature, sporadic fits of delirium that had terrified Tess.

She'd nursed him as best she could, kitted out in home-made PPE, barely able to breathe, herself. Once, as she was leaving his bedroom, he called out to her, shakily.

'Mum.'

She turned. 'Don't try to talk, Luke. I'll be back to you in half an hour.'

But he shook his head and tried to raise his arm. 'I'm sorry,' he croaked. 'For all of it.'

'We'll talk when you're better. Try and rest, now.'

Later, as she discarded the PPE, put her clothes in the washing machine, stepped into the shower to scrub herself until her skin hurt, she wondered.

Had that been real, or was it fever talk?

*

Eileen's card reminds Tess that it's time to get in touch with Maeve again. The day they'd met in Dundalk, Maeve had asked her to make one thing happen. She wanted an opportunity for Aimée to confront Luke, face to face. The girl had said that was what she needed, and Tess had promised to set it up.

She admired the girl's courage, and said so, but the prospect alarmed her. 'Is Aimée sure she's ready? I mean, of course I'll do it, but is it wise?'

'I don't know,' Maeve said, simply. 'But it's not going to happen immediately, so I've time to try and make sure it's the right decision. What Aimée needs right now is to know that she's listened to.' She paused for a second. 'And that you believe her.'

'I do believe her,' Tess said, at once.

Her conversations with Aengus had left her in no doubt that Luke was guilty. And that he had lied. The day she and Mike told Luke what Aimée needed from him, he looked shocked.

'Do I have to?'

'Yes, you do. It's the very least you can do. You can talk to your counsellor about it, and we'll figure out the best way forward, but yes. This is about Aimée, Luke. Not about you.'

*

After he'd recovered from Covid, Luke said he was ready to meet Aimée. On Zoom, to start. Or FaceTime, or whatever she wanted. He'd told Tess this one morning last January, leaning against the kitchen counter in the same way Aengus had done, on *that* Friday last summer.

'Okay,' she said. 'I'll get in touch with Maeve and ask if that's still what Aimée wants.'

Tess knows a conversation happened, perhaps even more than one. But it doesn't feel right to ask. And she's not sure if she can ever forgive Luke.

But it's one of the last things her mother had said to her, shortly before she died. They'd been sitting across from each other at this same table in Betty's kitchen.

'I know it's hard,' she'd said. 'But he's your son. And he needs you.'

'I'm tired,' Tess said. 'We're worn out by it all, Mike as well as me.'

'One foot in front of the other,' Betty said. 'And you'll get through this. Whatever you do, don't cut him loose.'

*

Tess stands up now and goes in search of the key for Betty's back door. She'll go out and sweep the leaves away from the shore before the light goes completely. Her father would never forgive her if she let the yard flood. But at the last minute, something makes her change her mind.

Instead of stepping out into the garden, she goes down the hall to her mother's bedroom. The sight of Betty's empty bed makes a well of grief open up inside her, and she stops at the threshold, waiting for steadiness.

When she finally steps inside, the room feels warmer than the kitchen, as though it has only recently been abandoned. Something draws her towards the dressing table. Like everything else in her mother's domestic life, this old-fashioned dressing table is tidy, orderly. Except for the out-of-place presence of an Afternoon Tea biscuit tin.

'Can't survive in chaos,' Betty used to say, shaking her head. 'It takes you over. Makes everything else blur at the edges.'

Perhaps that's why the biscuit tin is such a surprise. The way it sits there, brazenly, as though it has the right. Now that its owner is no longer in charge, waiting to tidy it away.

Curious, Tess lifts the lid. There is a sealed white envelope resting on the top of other bits and pieces: a faded child's painting; a cheap brass key ring: B for Betty; a bracelet made out of what might be silver. Tess prises open the envelope, carefully. It is addressed to her.

She pulls out a green ribbon. Instantly, she remembers the dress her mother made for her – in apology or forgiveness, Tess was never sure which. But how she loved that shift dress: and the luxury of the satin ribbon for her hair.

'I hear you, Betty,' she says.

She puts the ribbon back into the envelope. She returns to the kitchen and switches off the heating and the lights, pulling the door to behind her.

On her way out to the car, she goes back into her mother's bedroom once more and lifts up the biscuit tin. She steps out into the freezing January air and locks up the house.

Then, filled with the light of memory, she makes her way home to her family.

Afterword

Mother and Baby institutions in Ireland were part of the architecture of containment, created and maintained by Church-State collusion, that kept 56,000 women and girls, between 1922 and 1998, in conditions of coercive confinement.

Their 'crime' had been to become pregnant outside of marriage. It is probable that the proportion of Irish women in mother and baby institutions was the highest in the world. Conditions within the grim walls of these institutions were harsh.

Babies were routinely stolen from their mothers and trafficked around the world.
Infant mortality rates were high. A total of about 9,000 children died – approximately 15% of all the children in those institutions. In 2017, the shocking discovery was made at the Tuam (County Galway) mother and baby home of the bodies of almost 800 babies, buried in an underground tank.

The Irish government's recent report from the Commission of Investigation (2021) into mother and baby homes has been condemned by survivors as 'incomplete, a cop-out, and worse'.

*'The nature of these findings and the treatment of victim-survivors and their testimony leads to the conclusion that neither the Commission nor the Irish government have been interested in believing victim-survivors or treating them with respect and as rights holders'.

(James Gallon: Institutions and Ireland: Mother and Baby Homes and Irish Transitional Justice. Irish University Review. Spring/Summer 2022)

Acknowledgements

The author gratefully acknowledges the financial support received from An Chomhairle Ealaíon (The Arts Council). The award of a Literature Bursary in 2019 was central to the creation of this work.

Thanks also to the Bogliasco Foundation, New York, for a Fellowship in Liguria in 2019, during which an early draft of this novel was written.

*

Writing is a mostly solitary occupation. There is no substitute for the hours at the desk, the seemingly endless drafts written and revised, the sometimes terrifying stops and starts of the writing process. But novels only come to life when they have readers. That's where a writing group, such as WEB, becomes invaluable.

My membership of this writing workshop continues to play an important part in my life. It is a constant source of support and friendship. My thanks to all who have listened and responded and given such constructive criticism over the years. May we live long and prosper!

Particular thanks to Lia Mills and Celia de Fréine, who have read more drafts than I – or they – care to remember. And to early readers of the penultimate draft, for cheering me on: Joan Abernethy, Linda Weale, Marian McCaffrey and Enrica Ferrara, along with Nicola Barr of The Bent Agency.

Grateful thanks to Robert Purcell of M.E.Hanahoe Solicitors, who talked me through the challenges and complexities of the legislation around rape in Ireland. He gave very generously of his time. Any mistakes arising from our conversation are, of course, my own.

Sincere thanks, too, to all of those who read advance copies of A GOOD ENOUGH MOTHER and responded with such generosity.

And to my son, Eamonn. You know why.

Finally, I have nothing but praise for the dynamic trio behind Betimes Books who have taken such care with all aspects of the production of A GOOD ENOUGH MOTHER: from editing and cover design, to printing and promotion. You have all been a joy to work with, and I thank you.

About the Author

Catherine Dunne is the author of twelve published novels, several essays and one work of non-fiction. *An Unconsidered People* documents the lived experience of some half a million Irish immigrants to Britain in the dismal years of the 1950s.

Catherine's novels have been shortlisted for a number of prizes, including Novel of the Year at the Irish Book Awards and the International Strega Prize.

The Things We Know Now won the Giovanni Boccaccio International Prize for Fiction in 2013 and *The Years That Followed*, published in 2016, was longlisted for the International Dublin Literary Award.

Her latest novel, *A Good Enough Mother*, won the European Rapallo Prize for fiction in November 2023.

Her work has been translated into several languages.

She was the recipient of the 2018 Irish PEN Award for Outstanding Contribution to Irish Literature and is a member of Aosdána.